POTTERS' RUN

By
Charles Sage

CHAPTER 1

The sign waned in the increasingly rocky terrain, now he was following the trend and soon, he knew, all he'd have left was a feeling. He stopped the machine with the hand brake and set it. Turning off its ignition, he sat quietly a moment just listening and looking at the scene.

The brush had opened where the rocks grew. The trail diminished among the tops of what seemed to be granite bubbling up and a few giant boulders that had stopped their tumble a millennium ago or so. There was a slight rise in the terrain to what might have been a precipice ahead where a lone tamarack had somehow taken root.

It had started with a single boot print. It was complete and correct in size and tread pattern. Then another and many incomplete prints which created the track of a man panicked in isolation and afraid at what might be the end of his life.

As the rocks grew out of the packed dirt, the track was less clear and marked by sign like synthetic fiber snagged on alder branches and a single white hair that dangled from pine bark, glistening only when looked at from just the right angle.

The hunter had strayed so very far from where it was sensible to expect him. Maybe that was why Jeff Potter would always find them. Jeff knew a thing or two about straying from the sensible path.

He inhaled deeply and failed to detect the smell of a fire, or cook stove fumes. Or decaying flesh, but it would be too early for that.

Looking at the tamarack, he was drawn to it. It was short as such trees go, but it didn't really belong in this terrain, and it grew as best it could.

The track had led generally downhill, like it would at this stage, but this rise in the rocky ground wasn't significant. The tree and the view beyond would give the hunter hope of a new view, an important perspective, perhaps, to help orient him.

Jeff knew the hunter would be disappointed.

Dismounting the four-wheeler, his knees cracked and ground with crepitus, and he winced at pain in his lower back. Unstrapping his pack from the front rack, he slid his crippled left shoulder in first, then the right arm. He fastened the waist belt and chest strap like they girded him against the old injuries, and he stood tall against whatever it was he was about to find.

Jeff scanned the rocky surface for anything it would reveal, but he knew he was into the realm of his intuition now. It would have made more sense to continue in the direction of travel of the four-wheeler, where he had been following the trend of the original track.

But the hunter would be drawn to that out of place tree and the view he hoped would unfold beyond. Rather than finding orientation at this point, Jeff knew that the hunter would see nothing that would help him from the precipice. In exasperation or panic, the old man would be nearby, in one condition or another.

Walking to the lone tree, he looked carefully for more sign. There was nothing but bare rock. Over the edge he saw on one side was a near vertical drop ending in a scree slope that showed no sign of what would have to be a body. To the left, however, was a slope that may have been navigable, to a younger man, thinking rationally, without the burden of a pack or a rifle. It was close to vertical enough that Jeff, despite his level of training and experience, wouldn't try without a rope.

About 100 feet down was a clump of thick shrubs.

"Mr. Harries, Aubery Harries... Are you there?" Jeff yelled and just as his echo began to return, a groaning sound emerged from the shrubs, and it built in strength and culminated in a single word.

"Help."

"Are you hurt?"

"Leg... Leg's broke."

Jeff could see motion; the hunter was waving a towel or something from under the shrubs.

"Hold on, I've got to rope up. I'll be there in a minute, and I'll get the cavalry started."

Slinking out of his back pack, Jeff pulled the Satphone from one of its pockets, oriented the antenna and powered it up.

As soon as he had signal, he hit send on the dispatch number.

"Hey, Jeff Potter here, I've found Mr. Harries here north of Galiuro Peak with grid to follow. He's conscious and alert, reporting that he's broken his leg. I'm going to have to rappel down to assess him. This will require at least a technical rescue or helicopter so may want to start getting Two Bear or the Air Force guys in the loop. Ready for grid?"

Jeff read off the coordinates from the GPS on his wrist as he walked back to the four-wheeler. The dispatcher gave a good read back, and he started unstrapping the rope bag from the rack.

"I'll call you as soon as I'm with him and have an assessment of his injuries, out here."

Folding the phone antenna, he hefted the rope bag and returned to his pack at the edge. There was a decent boulder and a couple of cracks he could jam cams in for anchors. He thought about the tree for a moment but was afraid he'd pull the shallow rooted thing down with him if he incorporated it in his anchor system.

"Mr. Harries," he yelled over the edge. "I'm setting my anchor here, and I'm going to rappel down to you. I've called the Sheriff's dispatch and given them our location. I'll be down to you in a minute and get that leg looked at and make sure everything else is OK."

"Alright," the man groaned in response.

Taking webbing from the rope bag, Jeff fashioned a Swiss Seat. Making sure all the important components of his manhood were properly adjusted and out of the way, he clipped a carabiner through the front loops then clipped into the 8-ring wrapped onto the rope.

The rappel was less than dramatic, just a steep walk down the slope with the assistance of the rope, but Jeff was glad he'd taken the time to set up the rappel rather than try to down climb.

He found the old man huddled half in a sleeping bag under the brush.

"I can't believe you found me, I can't believe anyone was even looking for me." The old man spoke quickly.

"I'm Jeff Potter, Mr. Harries. Your neighbor reported you missing. Your truck was found at the trail head. Rest of the team is searching the trail. You've been gone a while now." Jeff slipped out of his back pack. He handed the hunter a bottle of water.

"Just sip at it right now. Did you run out of water?"

"A few days ago. In the morning there's this trickle down the rocks there that I gather with my towel and squeeze into my mouth... not enough, but better than nothing."

Jeff dug into his trauma kit.

"Tell me what happened, Mr. Harries."

"I got lost. Fifty some years of hunting... never been lost like that. It was terrifying."

The old man's eyes welled up.

"It's OK, Sir. You're not lost anymore."

"I hate to be a bother."

"No bother at all. We all need a little help from time to time." Jeff was crouched next to the man. "How did you wind up here, with your leg like that?"

"Thought I saw a stream down there, figured I'd climb down, follow it. I slipped."

"Did you hit your head or lose consciousness at all, do you know?"

"Naw, just kinda slid down into it, snagged that leg on the way down and heard and felt it go."

Jeff was checking the man's pupils.

"Any abdominal pain as a result of the fall?"

"Naw."

"Alright, now the tough part. We gotta look at that leg. It's gonna hurt a little."

"It already hurts, you got anything you can give me for that? Emptied my flask the first night here."

Jeff smiled, as he pulled out his shears.

"No, sorry, gotta be careful what we give you before the pros get here. They might decide you need surgery. Let's see what we got."

As carefully as he could, Jeff cut the pantleg. The foot was at an unnatural angle, and he hoped it was just a simple fracture of the lower leg, but it was clearly fractured somewhere. Cutting the pants above the knee, that joint looked intact and properly oriented to the rest of the upper leg. As Jeff gently palpated the lower leg, the old man grimaced against the pain and tried not to cry out.

"Bad news or good news first, Mr. Harries?"

"Bad."

"It's broke, closed classic Tib/Fib fracture. Good news is that they're pretty good at fixing those these days. I am going to get a Sam splint on there for you. It's going to hurt more as I set it and get it into the splint, but you'll be a lot more comfortable afterward."

"OK." Jeff exuded a certain contagious confidence, and the older man was quickly comfortable with him.

Jeff pulled the padded aluminum splint from his kit and unrolled it, forming it to the shape and size he needed. He pulled out the bandages that would hold the splint in place and staged them within easy reach.

"Look, I don't have any drugs to give you, but I can give you a bandage to squeeze or something."

"Naw, it's OK. Just keep talkin' to me, Jeff."

"What would you like to talk about?"

"What's happening with the war, they let any more nukes off?"

"No," Jeff grasped the man's foot. "Just those one's they set off in-theatre. The world is still kind of stunned and not sure what to do next."

Without further warning, Jeff pulled on the foot until it felt as if the bony obstruction was clear, then turned the foot into position, and the old man howled as the leg was set.

The old man's breath was heaving and sweat formed on his brow, but the flash of severe pain subsided, and Jeff had slid the splint into place.

"Well, there's lots of folks worse off than me right now, and maybe there's no one that loves me in this world, but at least there's no one that hates me. It's a world full of hate right now."

"No family, Mr. Harries?"

"None that keep in touch. Wife is gone for years now, and the boys have their own families to keep'em busy."

"Do you ever call them?"

"Oh, I don't want to bother them."

"Well, do me a favor, when you get back from this, call them."

"Oh, I can't do that, I feel foolish enough with a stranger, bein' lost and all."

"No shame in it, Mr. Harries. Everyone gets lost a little from time to time."

The old man managed a smile.

"What are you, a paramedic or psychologist?"

"Neither," Jeff smiled back

"Well, you're right, I should call. I'm worried for my Grandkids. Did they push that draft through? That was supposed to get passed, or did they put a stop to it?"

"No, it's started. The President signed it as soon as it was approved by Congress, the whole War Powers Act."

"Buncha' damned foolishness if you ask me. Bad enough to be drafting boys for this nonsense, but now they're drafting the girls too? What a crazy world, like they never learn."

Jeff nodded as he finished wrapping the splint.

"Male and female, 18 to 45."

"And they have no choice, huh, Jeff?"

"There's always a choice, Mr. Aubrey."

"Well they'll send 'em to jail if they don't go to war."

"It's a time of difficult choices, Mr. Aubrey."

The old man looked closely at Jeff.

"Jeff, I think you musta' cut your cheek somewhere, you're bleeding on the left side there."

Jeff touched his cheek and saw the fingers came back bloody, and he felt the area a little more firmly and realized it was another one ready to come out. Without hesitation he squeezed at the area until the offending bone fragment came out.

He looked at it with disdain and wiped it in the dirt at his feet.

"Old injury, comes back to haunt me once in a while." Jeff didn't say anymore, especially the part about the bone fragment not being his.

*   *   *

"Sheriff, you got your radio on?"

Taylor paused with the heavy saddle in his gloved hands.

"Ah, I left it in the trailer," He said as he slung the saddle up on the mellow chestnut mare. "What ya' got, Craig?"

Deputy Craig Markdale sat astride his four-wheeler, pressing his earpiece into his ear.

"They got him, Sheriff. Sounds like Jeff Potter got'im. Potter said he's assessing the guy to have a broken leg in rough terrain, requesting air evac. A little dehydration and broken leg, and Potter said he had to rappel down to him."

The Sheriff nodded.

"Tell them I've given a verbal for air, I'll make it official when I get back to the office." The Sheriff slipped the saddle back off the horse as a second four-wheeler rolled up behind Markdale, it was Deputy Ted Zites, fresh off field training.

"Sorry, Betsy, guess we don't get to play today." Heaving the saddle back to the trailer he yelled over his shoulder. "That's the trouble with being the boss, guys. Never have time to do the fun stuff. Have to leave it to all you young guys to be the heroes."

"Well, Potter anyway. Somehow he always seems to find these guys."

"He kind of seems to live for this stuff, Craig."

"I think he feels like he's making up for something."

The Sheriff shrugged.

"I'm just glad he's on our side. You may be right, I don't know him well, seems to like to keep to himself mostly. And I'm glad the old guy's alive, that's what matters most." The Sheriff walked up the ramp to stow the saddle then came back out addressing Zites.

"Getting the hang of it?"

Zites had set the brake and shut off the machine.

"Yessir."

The Sheriff sank his thumbs behind his Sam Browne and looked at the snow dusted towers of granite beyond.

"Big difference from San Francisco I imagine, Ted, getting to experience some of the differences with rural policing. It can be really rewarding and less headaches."

"Yessir." The new deputy smiled and nodded, but something about it seemed artificial to Sheriff Taylor.

"Well, this is about as good as it gets, a good call with a good outcome. We get to get out here in this great wilderness, interact as a team with the community volunteers that make up the SAR team and get to bring a missing man home." The Sheriff chuckled and grinned widely. "Relax, Ted. You're here now, leave all that big city stress behind, you were just part of a team that helped save a man's life."

Zites smiled and seemed to soften a bit. Maybe it was just new guy nerves, the Sheriff thought.

*   *   *

The boy half squatted on the log, kind of folded over the cold, blued steel of the rifle.

"I'm sorry, Son, I never meant to pressure you to take the shot. I just wanted you to know how to, and to know you could if you ever needed to."

Jeff fought the frustration welling up inside as the boy slumped, unresponsive.

"This is going to be one of those times isn't it?" The father leaned against the tree and shook his head with a sad grin. He wanted to finish the animal quickly, but this was going to be complicated. "Like that time when we were all trying to get ready to go to the museum in Washington... Or the time during the pandemic in January when you wanted to go for a walk barefoot... Or that time you were overwhelmed at school and wouldn't even get out of bed.

"I handled those times poorly and I'm sorry. You're just locked up on me again. Won't talk, won't move." He looked back from the little gully and down at his feet.

"I was gone too much, I think. It was what I had to do... or I always told myself that. That if I fought them over there, we wouldn't need to worry about them over here. And that I was helping other American Dads and Moms come home to their kids, that was what I always told you... and told myself.

"Ya' know, I'd be home for a few months, and I might do some really stellar things as a father... but you'd have one of these spells, and I'd handle it poorly. I'd go away again, and I wouldn't think at all about all the things I'd done right as a father. I went away, and I was always haunted by the thing's I'd done wrong. Maybe you didn't even remember, maybe they weren't that significant to you.

"It wasn't really about me, was it, Son? I mean, I know I'm probably kind of intense... But really, it was just something in you that needed space. It was just your way of handling things that made you uncomfortable, and it wasn't something I could fix. Maybe it wasn't even something I was supposed to fix. I shoulda' just given you space... But that was always hard for me because I was already worried there was too much space between us. That and that I'd spent a career violently fixing problems others created.

"I'm sorry I've spent the last eighteen years trying to *make* you happy when I should have just *let* you be happy."

Jeff looked down the hill at the thrashing buck.

"I'll finish him, Son, if you want me to... it was a good shot for the distance and angle. You spined him, he's done for and not going anywhere, and you didn't waste any meat with that shot.

The boy looked up at his father and tried to force a smile, and the father's heart sank because there had been so much wasted time figuring such things out.

"They won't take me, Dad, right?"

"No, Son, they won't."

"I'm OK, I can finish him, Dad."

"Good, let's make it quick, he's a fine animal, and he shouldn't suffer."

* * *

This was the kind of call the Sheriff always had to consciously steel himself to ahead of time. He couldn't rely on the surge of adrenalin-charged judgement that never failed him. The outcome of this was not in question. Nothing good would come of it, and he couldn't kid himself otherwise.

Zites was out ahead of the Sheriff, behind the SAR team leader who was blazing the path with the younger son. The new Deputy called quietly over his shoulder.

"Second hunting accident in as many weeks, is that normal, Sheriff?"

Taylor sped up a few steps and caught the young deputy by the sleeve.

"Keep going, Breske." he called out to the Team Leader. "I need to rest a spell."

The boy and the SAR volunteer continued their arduous climb through rocks and brush. The Sheriff looked at the new Deputy and took a moment before he began.

"Sheep hunting is a dangerous thing, but this one is unusual. We don't get these often. Now, this community is small enough that it pays to be very sensitive to any loss like this. This family is good people, they own the bakery on 3rd. Good kids, darn shame this has happened to them. And it would be a tragedy to any family and any folks in our County. I expect my Deputies to handle things like this with the utmost compassion and sensitivity. I'll ask you to hold any extraneous talk and questions until debrief out of respect to the people we serve."

"Yes, Sir. Sorry," Zites sighed.

The Sheriff nodded and smiled reassuringly.

"Alright, let's catch back up with them. This terrain doesn't get any easier."

They caught up with Breske and the boy at a rocky outcropping that grew clear of the alders and devil's club. The Sheriff was feeling winded and achy already, and they hadn't even really started yet. He hated himself for it and looked up the hill a few paces to where Breske stood fit and square shouldered, even under the burden of his heavy pack and two halves of a Stokes litter he carried strapped to it. Breske was almost always smiling, even the one time the Sheriff had to wrestle the logger into cuffs after a late-night drunken brawl in town. Today Breske's smile was noticeably diminished.

"We were here, Sheriff," the young Whitaker boy stated meekly. "We were glassing the rocks above, trying to find that big full curl ram Dad saw last year. We'd been out for a few days and we saw one about 250 yards upslope. Preston had gone around the trail over there to check the back side of the peak. He'd been gone a while when we saw the ram."

The boy bit his lip and looked down. The Sheriff didn't like interviewing him alone like this, but there was no other way. He looked at Breske who was surveying the route ahead, and then to Zites who was looking over the scene for evidence.

"I'm real sorry for all this, Tim. You're a wonderful family. Your father's a good man, and I've always admired how he raised you boys. And you're a good kid, and I know you'll be a good man. Sometimes bad things happen to the very best of people… Look, nothin' I say can make any of this better. Just know that I feel for you, the whole town is praying for you…. I have to ask some questions that I need to record, and I need to collect some evidence along the way. Some of the questions will be difficult for you to hear and, frankly, they'll be difficult for me to ask."

Timmy nodded.

"What happened, Tim?"

"After we shot there was this weird sound that almost seemed to be Preston… Not a scream… I don't know what it was, but Dad and I, we rushed up the hill to the sound. But it was quiet by then."

"You said 'we', who took the shot, Tim?"

"Dad, Dad fired the shot." Timmy was looking down, shuffling his feet amid the wet leaves.

"Did your Dad mistake Preston for a ram?"

"No, Sir. You'll see. We got a piece of that ram, there's a blood trail 'bout a quarter of the way between here and… between here and Preston."

"I got a shell casing here, Sheriff." Ted was holding it on a pen and placing it in an evidence bag like it would be rushed out to the FBI Lab tomorrow. "7mm".

"You got a photo?"

"Yessir."

"Mark it on the GPS and flag it with the marking tape so maybe we can see it from uphill."

The low sun angle that had glinted just right off the expended 7mm brass reminded the Sheriff they were rapidly running out of daylight. He zipped his jacket up against the chill he felt as they had been standing still for a while. Looking up to the crest of the rocks over a thousand yards above, he could see a puff of smoke forming.

"Tim, this is where I have to ask one of those questions. Don't tell me what you think I want to hear, just tell me the truth. Were there any bad feelings between you and your brother?"

"No, Sir, none, Sir." Tim was looking hard and fast into the Sheriff's eyes.

"Tim, did you shoot your brother?"

"No, Sir." Tim looked down. "My father made the shot."

The Sheriff nodded and patted Tim on the shoulder.

"We need to get to your father, and get Preston out of there, OK?"

"Yes, Sir."

*   *   *

"What if I want to go, Dad? Everything you've taught me... I could put it to good use."

"Do you want to?" He ran the operating rod for her.

"I'm not sure."

"That's as good as a no. If you choose to go of your own accord I could respect that, but this isn't your fight. I won't just let anyone take you or your brother."

The hammer dropped with a click, and the muzzle of the ten-pound rifle was perfectly still through her trigger pull and follow through.

"Whose fight is it then, Dad?"

"The Europeans and I guess now, the allied Asian nations.   America isn't in a place to help Americans right now, we sure as hell can't help anyone else." He ran the operating rod again to reset the action for her.

She ran her hand through her short hair, then settled back in behind the big rifle.

"Whose fight was Afghanistan, or Iraq?"

Another perfect trigger pull ended in a sharp click.

"We were attacked, and the world was different then... and for the record I was against the Iraq invasion."

"But you still went."

"I had my orders, my duty."

"Maybe it's my duty now."

"I was already in when we went into Iraq. And what I did there was very specific in its nature."

"Dad, I know you did a lot of stuff in the Army, I know you saw a lot of things. Do you ever think you're a little biased, that maybe it's the PTSD doing the talking?"

He grinned for a moment and said nothing. Taking a second, he sat up and crossed his legs. She was prone behind the rifle.

"Your trigger pulls are great, your natural point of aim looks good, but you need to keep that right heel down, it always creeps up on you."

"Or was it when Mom died? Is that why things changed for you?"

He sighed and leaned his elbows on his knees. Was it all daughters who knew just the thing to say so it felt like a knife blade through the ribs sometimes? Like they were so skilled in subtle, venomous use of language to cut the heart, or was it just Jane?

"I've done a lot of things wrong in the raising of you two, I know that. The worst being that I was never there. And I always told myself the same thing then, too, duty and orders. And it was the way to provide for you all. But your Mom was able to be there for you always, and she was better for you. I figured that balanced all the things I did wrong."

He smiled and looked at her holding the M-1.

"I memorized manuals they gave us for everything from the M-4 carbine to ANVIS-9 Night Vision Goggles to the Pandur Light Armored Vehicle. But, I never got the manual on how to be a good father."

"You once told me I was the son you always wanted."

"Yeah, there were a lot of things I should have said and done differently, Jane. You were always the stronger one. Tom was always a good spirit, but he was always a little soft around the middle and that's OK. But I didn't know how to handle it at the time."

"And now you don't know how to handle me."

She was digging the knife deeper, and he didn't know why.

"I know you don't approve of the way I am," She pressed.

"In my day you just would have been what we called a tomboy." He shrugged, not wanting to go any further.

"No, Dad, in your day I would have been the same. I just couldn't be open about it."

"Enough dry fire today. We'll load up the four-wheelers and work out at 600 yards tomorrow."

"My ex said you were intolerant once, Dad. At the time I just told her you were old fashioned, but it's more complicated than that. I'm not Daddy's little girl any more. I haven't been for a long time."

"You'll always be my daughter, and I'll always do what I can to protect you."

"Is that why you brought us out here? Do you think it's more *defensible*? Is that what the Ruby Ridge guy thought too? There are options, we won't necessarily go to the front lines, we might serve other ways. Hell, Tom might not even be selected. He might not make it through the psych exam or whatever they do. We can't win against the government."

"You don't always walk away from fights you can't win. Sometimes those are the ones you have to stand up for the most."

"Then why not just join up and fight the Russians and the Chinese and get this over with just like your grandfather did with this." She spun into a sitting position facing him and presenting the M-1 Garand as if it was evidence of her moral certainty.

Jeff looked down at the dirt and thought a moment before continuing.

"This is a rich man's war. I don't want my kids dying for it. If the rich want to prosecute yet another war, let them send their kids. But they won't, they never do. They're the ones who always find a way out."

"Like bone spurs," Jane said.

"Or like going to Oxford… Really, there are a lot of good reasons for an individual not to go to war. Even more good reasons a nation shouldn't."

"There are a lot of innocent people caught in the middle of all this, dying over there. And they have no choice, it's happening around them, Dad."

"That's true, that's really the saddest truth of war. But this time our country is in really bad shape, and we have our own concerns that need to be addressed right now. Our politicians want a distraction. They have decimated and diverted our military over the past decades to the extent that we can't begin to handle what is now a two-front war. And this is shaping up to be total war. We lack the national will to fight that. So, the politicians bang on the drums of war because it will make them money, or keep the public from noticing the sting of failed policies. And they can blame all their failures on this war they say they didn't start.

"I don't want my children to be any part of it. If it's a fight you want, I'm sure you'll have one in your life time, but not this one."

"I'm 19 years old, Dad. I can make my own choices."

"You haven't listened to me. I've said as much. If you want to go fight this war for your reasons, because you believe in it, because you feel it's your duty... Go. But if you want to fight this war because you want to rebel against me, because you want to hurt me... Don't bother, you've done enough already."

*   *   *

Sixteen-year old Preston Whitaker lay cold beside the fire his father had built. The sleeping bag was pulled up to his chin and his eyes were closed peacefully. His head was propped up on his father's jacket. Preston was bled out and dead from the gunshot wound that penetrated the center of his chest at a high angle.

The fire split the dark, overcast, mountain night with the popping and sparking of the green saplings with which his father had hastily built it. Preston's pale young face was illuminated by the struggling fire. The father forced himself to look at the boy's face as he fed the fire with the spindly wood he had hacked down in a rage with his sheath knife.

His boy would be warm.

Sheriff Grant Taylor and his party had raced the setting sun up the rocky slope and lost. The father stood and looked up at his surviving son with fresh tears welling in his eyes, his face smudged by old ones. Sheriff Taylor felt very much like he was intruding and gave the moment the solemn silence it needed. As if it could get any worse, it began to sleet, rain and snow.

Tall and lean, the elder Whitaker's smudged face was sculpted by a lifetime of honest, hard work. The father extended his hand to the Sheriff. The Sheriff took the father's hand in a firm grip; the father would have been shattered by anything less.

The Sheriff studied the man's face in the dancing yellow light. He looked less than himself. Diminished by circumstance and vacant of the spirit of the man with the smile stocking the shelves of the bakery he had owned and run with his family for the last seventeen years.

The Sheriff shook his head.

"Bob...," the Sheriff wiped his face. "Bob, I don't know what to say. I admire your family. You've raised fine boys. Saying sorry just doesn't seem enough."

The father said nothing.

"There are things we need to do."

"I know, Sheriff. Whatever I need to do..."

"First I'll need your rifle, Bob."

"Right." The father leaned over and picked up the rifle. He opened the bolt, and handed the empty rifle to the Sheriff.

In the light of the headlamp the Sheriff examined the hunting rifle. Its stock had seen a lot of time in the field with chips and creases here and there in the grain of the walnut. The bluing was well oiled. The snow melted into beads on the barrel and the receiver where the Sheriff read "REMINGTON MODEL 700 30-06 CALIBER. Ted was picking up Tim's rifle and in the light of his headlamp came to the same conclusion at the same time. Ted was about to say something, but the Sheriff looked at him and shook his head.

"You know I have to ask you some questions." He slung the rifle and pulled out his notebook and pen.

"I know."

"What happened, Bob?"

"I was down the hill, you came up that way. There was a ram up the hill. I turned around and took the shot… Preston had gone around the hill to scout the north side, I didn't think about him comin' up over."

"You're sure there was a ram?"

"Yessir, I caught a piece of it. There's a blood trail couple hundred yards down the hill. I didn't just shoot Preston thinkin' he was a sheep. I shot a sheep and it carried through. We didn't know he was up here…"

"Did anyone else shoot?"

The father paused, looked at the fire, then looked back at the Sheriff almost suddenly, his eyes a little wider.

"You know, Sheriff, I was usin' Timmy's rifle there."

"Oh… You guys exchanged rifles."

"Yes, Sir."

The Sheriff looked at Timmy who nodded. The Sheriff looked at Ted who gave him a disapproving smirk.

"What time did this happen?"

"Bout five hours ago I guess."

"How did you find him?"

"There were sounds. Two impacts. The bullet smacking the ram and then... Preston. And he gave a short yell kind of. It didn't register at first for some reason. I found the blood trail and then I thought about it and called out to Preston. We ran up and found him. It was easier in the light."

"Was he..."

"He was dead before we got to him."

Ted was taking pictures of the scene and the body, getting GPS coordinates and making his own notes. The sound and flash of the camera caught Bob's attention, and he appeared unsettled.

"Bob, we're gonna need to examine the body and put him in the bag."

"I know." Bob looked over his shoulder at the body. "Just treat him right, OK, Sheriff."

"You know we will."

"I know... It's just, he's my boy." The father turned and looked quickly away, shoulders shuddering. He embraced Tim as the boy walked up to him.

The Sheriff and his Deputy removed the sleeping bag and found the entry wound square in the center of the chest. Rigor had already set in, or maybe it was the cold, but the body was a little stiff as they rolled it over. The exit wound was low in the back. It was not a particularly large exit wound but there was a lot of partially congealed blood.

They carefully lowered the body onto its back, and the Sheriff was suddenly aware of how cold the night was.

Ted pulled the body bag out of his pack. They unfolded it together and set its length beside the body. The Sheriff unzipped the bag and opened it up as much as he could. Looking back over his shoulder, he saw that the father and brother were looking away into the darkness. The Sheriff lifted from the shoulders and Ted lifted from the feet. For a 16 year old he seemed particularly tall and heavy. The stiffness of the rigor and the stiffness of the bag made it awkward as much as it was solemn, and it almost seemed like a struggle to get the shell of a life so young into a lifeless yellow bag.

When it was done, the Sheriff let Ted zip the bag. He wasn't sure he could do it. Instead he busied himself with assembling the Stokes and arranging the straps to accept the body.

They hefted the body bag by the handles and settled it gently into the Stokes. They strapped the body securely but gently as if there was still life to it. The father and Tim were watching.

Preston's rifle was a few yards down the hill. Ted recovered it and slung both boys' rifles.

The Sheriff looked at the father.

"We're all ready, Tom."

The father looked at Timmy who nodded, and the two led the way.

The lifelessness of the boy's body lay heavy in the Stokes, and the steepness of the terrain and the rapidly enveloping undergrowth conspired to make a miserable task even more unbearable.

The headlamps they wore etched through the darkness of the wet mountain night; the light jagged against the relentless grabbing branches and prick of the occasional devil's club.

The Sheriff held on to the Stokes with one hand and braced himself on trees and branches with the other. Young Ted bore most of the load and did so without complaint. The treacherousness of the mountain took its toll quickly on the Sheriff, and he cursed.

He cursed not at the weight of the boy, not at the father or whoever had shot the boy, but at himself for not being stronger to carry the boy's body over such terrain. The boy deserved better, the father and the brother deserved better, and all they got was a burned out former big city cop with a bum knee.

He cursed himself when he told Ted he needed to rest. Cursed that he couldn't just keep going and get it done with and be off this damn mountain and be done with this damned call.

His knee ached, and he knew he couldn't put the surgery off any longer. He cursed himself for thinking of his own suffering right now when the suffering of the man and boy in front of him were more than he would ever want to imagine.

"OK, let's go. I'm good."

"You want me to spell ya, Sheriff?"

"No, Bob, you guys lead the way and find us the best route, I'm fine."

They slogged on, headlamps flashing through what was rain again. The Sheriff fought for his balance with every step. When he could see Breske, the Sheriff firmed his resolve. They were close now, the SAR guys were there, and they were eager for it, the work of it anyway. They could turn the body over to them, and it would be easier the rest of the way.

The SAR team turned on their flashlights and headlamps at the sound of the party's approach.

Tony Breske walked up to Bob and reached out his hand only to pull him into a big, wordless hug. Tony patted Bob on the back, then turned to Tim and hugged him. He walked over to the Sheriff.

"Well, you guys did the hard part. We got it from here."

"Thanks, Tony." The Sheriff hobbled over to the four-wheeler. "Bob, you guys wanna ride down with us?"

"Naw, thanks Sheriff, we're gonna walk with Preston."

The Sheriff nodded and turned the key starting the machine. Ted took the lead down the trail, and the Sheriff took the tail end. It seemed a long ride. The closer they got to the trailhead, the more people joined the party. Hand over hand they shared and relieved the burden of the Stokes. The support of presence and a share in the tragedy was felt by all.

At the trailhead, the ambulance was surrounded by a crowd that respectfully parted as the body was carried through. The Sheriff and his deputy faded into the background as they loaded the four-wheelers onto the trailer. The flashing red lights of the ambulance lit the night, and they heard the backdoor slam with finality as the crowd dispersed to their cars for the slow procession back to town. The Sheriff and Ted were cinching down the straps on the trailer and were alone at the far end of the trailhead.

"You know the other boy did it."

"Suspect so…"

"Well?"

"It was an accident. We investigate. We submit our report and all the evidence to the County Prosecutor, he decides where it goes from there. We deliver them to the justice system if the Prosecutor decides to take it that direction. We're not the judge and jury, that comes later if it needs to and not from us."

Ted stammered a bit.

"That's all I'm gonna hear about it. Go home to your wife and hug your kids tonight, Ted."

Ted nodded and walked to his truck.

The Sheriff unlocked his truck, opened the door and swung his sore knee in. He reached across to the glove box for his cigarettes and lighter. He lit one and took a long drag. Taking the cell phone from his pocket he hit the speed dial for Will.

It had been a while since he'd talked to his son.

*   *   *

He sat down in the rocker on the porch with the handful of mail he had just brought in. As he lowered himself to the rocker he tried not to make the old man sounds his body tried to make. He suppressed the groan of knees, contained the cry from the lower back and absolutely rejected the whimper that tried to come out from moving the shoulder just the wrong way at just the wrong time opening the letter.

There were two of them, actually, and he found that particularly unkind. Maybe it was meant to be. The paranoid part of him thought it was deliberate, but maybe it wasn't meant to be hostile. It was rumored in selection that there was something beyond the Long Walk, beyond the board, beyond the psych exam. Some said there was something in the blood. Maybe they wanted his kids because whatever it was, it was in their genes.

There was a time when he had planned for and even encouraged Tom to go in. Slicing the envelopes open with his pocket knife, he stowed the knife and stared at the page without reading.

Jeff had known it was coming.

He knew it was coming when training exercises went hot, when rumors of war suddenly became actions of war and then declarations of war. When the economy slid from a questionable stability to an obviously artificially maintained fantasy. As fuel and food became rationed. As nations aligned. As flying a blue and yellow flag became the latest way of showing you cared without really having to do anything. As throwing colossal sums of funding into the war machine went unchecked and without oversight.

Soon they were going to need more.

Soon they would need bodies.

The letters were addressed to each of the kids.

He read the large bold letters.

ORDER TO REPORT FOR ARMED FORCES PHYSICAL EXAMINATION

A sick feeling washed over him as he wondered if a part of him wasn't in some way responsible. Having played along with it all, he had participated to the degree that he had been the striking surface of the hammer of the machine itself.

The knees ached their protest, and the back seemed to stab itself and the shoulder burned, and now the head began to swim the way it sometimes did these days...

Looking out to the lush green valley, instead, he only saw the dusty backroad behind the compound that early morning so long ago.

He felt the bandaged sore on his cheek where the latest bone fragment had emerged and fought to bury it deep before he lived that day again.

*   *   *

The bureaucrat on the other side of the desk laughed vacuously, and Jeff inhaled as he forced himself to listen to her as she continued.

"You don't understand how the system works, Mr. Potter. At this stage your son and daughter are merely required to report to the MEPS station for physical, mental and moral evaluation. Once that evaluation is complete, the registrants will have ten days to file for deferment or exemption. At that stage the system will catch the fact that we have two siblings who are registrants."

"First of all, Ma'am, you are going on the assumption that anyone but you and your fellow drones believes the system works at all," Jeff inhaled again and tried to calm himself. "Secondly, Jane is the only one who registered. She did it as soon as they made it a requirement for females."

"Oh, well that would have done it right there, Mr. Potter. Your son was required to register with Selective Service within thirty days of his 18th birthday. They cross reference it with state driver's license records now, and they are cracking down on failure to register." She punctuated her sentence with a curt smirk.

"You can take your system and systemically shove it. I'm done participating, I'm out and so are my kids." Jeff spoke calmly, and the woman sat back, unsure what to make of him. He stood up and left the office knowing how the rest would go.

*   *   *

After deliberately taking a break, Jeff walked out onto the porch and sat in the rocker. He had worked on it for days. It was his fourth revision, and it was meticulously hand written. He removed it from his pocket, pulled it from the envelope and held it out at just the right distance to read it one last time.

To Whom It May Concern,

I proudly served in the United States Army for over fifteen years before being wounded in action in Afghanistan when I was medically retired from the military. I spent an additional five years working as a contractor in Iraq and Afghanistan. I have supported our country and military beyond words.

Now, our country and our military are racing toward deeper involvement in a global war that we cannot afford. This war is being fueled by corruption, and now they want to further stoke the fire with bodies of the institution of enslavement known as conscription.

My children are not slaves to you or to any system. Conscription is not good for the military, and slavery is not good for our country. Now we have people willing to sacrifice their daughters on the altar of 'progress,' and we are throwing them into the draft as well. Children who are unsuitable will be selected, they will be sent, and they will die in a war that benefits no one but the rich and the elitists.

This cycle continues because people are afraid to use one simple word.

But I'll say it;

No.

It is the most powerful word in the English language because it gives the ultimate power to the user, and it is the word that we are so afraid to use. It's a word they're afraid we'll learn, so they make it difficult for us to use. So, most of us just go along. We submit. We just fill out the forms. We just pay our taxes. We just take the injection. We just surrender our children.

Maybe we are afraid to be powerful.

Maybe we'll learn. Maybe we'll learn more than just saying no, maybe we'll learn that we aren't the only ones with children, and we aren't the only ones with homes and addresses. Maybe we'll learn that when we have paid our dues, it is time for someone else to pay theirs.

Sincerely,
Jeff Potter

Concise, he thought. He folded up the letter and placed it back in his pocket. Standing up, he descended the stairs and walked to the truck. This would accelerate things. Tom didn't want to register, and the man Jeff was twenty years earlier would have been aghast. Now Jeff saw so many things differently.

The drive to town took about forty minutes. Traffic was worse now. People moving from places where they had already voted for bad policy, or had allowed it to happen. When he had moved here ten years earlier, that was different too. It had much more of the small town feel, and now it seemed to be more touristy. He had come to this place to escape many things and one of those things was people. But they had followed him here. And that was part of why they'd sold the house closer to town and moved to the cabin on the mining claim.

All he wanted since he had been forced into retirement was to be left alone, and that was all he wanted for his kids. He had done enough, bled enough. Just like his father and grandfather.

The Potter family was going to sit this one out.

Jeff Potter wanted nothing more to do with war, but he was still prepared for it.

Parking in the lot of the Federal Building, he thought a moment of the Glock holstered inside his waistband.

It wouldn't be coming off today.

Walking up the sidewalk to the glass doors, he smiled warmly at the woman trimming the shrubs.

As he saw his reflection in the glass door, he thought for a moment without pausing. So much had changed, and he was glad of it. He was resolute in what the path was now.

Inside he stopped short of the metal detector and pulled the letter out of his pocket. He had left it unsealed so it could be easily inspected, and he had been sure to print his name and return address in clear letters on the envelope.

He spoke to the security guard who seemed to be in charge.

"Could you just make sure the Local Draft Board gets this."

"Uh, we don't really…"

"Please, I'm a disabled veteran. I don't want to walk that far."

"You could mail it."

"Well, I'm already here, and besides, I want them to know I'm serious."

With that Jeff laid the envelope on the table.

"Thank you." He turned and left.

He knew the guard would read it, he knew the guard would get it to the draft board and probably other places.

Walking back to the truck he pulled out his note book and added to his list. The Northmost cache needed to be completed in the next week. They would be coming soon, and he needed to have everything ready.

CHAPTER 2

"Sheriff." The secretary's voice came over the intercom and he hit a button on the phone.

"Yes, Mary?"

"There is a Federal Agent here to see you."

The Sheriff laid down the report and looked up at the Deputy.

"Expecting someone?" the Deputy asked.

The Sheriff just frowned and shook his head.

The Deputy grinned a little.

"That's never good."

The Sheriff hit the button again.

"Send him in, Mary."

The Sheriff leaned back in his chair and stroked his beard.

"Should I stay?"

The Sheriff nodded, and the door opened as a man in a suit let himself in.

He was slight of build but the well-tailored suit hid a lot of that. His hair was well kempt and he had a mustache that was thin and failing.

"Sheriff Taylor." He spoke urgently and presented his hand over the desk as the Sheriff rose slowly from his chair. The man looked sideways at the Deputy and didn't bother to introduce himself. "We need to speak alone."

The Sheriff sat back down and hit the button on his phone.

"Mary, who did this gentleman say he was, and who did he say he was working with?"

"Uhh... He didn't, Sheriff, he flashed his badge and just said he was a Federal Agent, I'm sorry..."

"No, no, it's ok. Thank you, Mary." He looked up from the phone to the man hiding behind the suit and the bad mustache.

"Who the hell are you, and what are you doing in my office?"

The man looked sideways at the Deputy again, and he suddenly appeared aggravated.

Reaching into his inner breast pocket he produced a badge wallet and laid it on the desk.

"Your eyes only, and really, just a courtesy."

Sheriff Taylor laughed, unimpressed with the man's smugness.

It was an FBI badge and ID. The Sheriff had seen enough of them to know it was real, and the attitude, the suit, the hair cut confirmed it. The mustache was a curiosity.

"Everything about you says FBI, Special Agent..." The Sheriff squinted at the ID to get the name as he handed it back. "Special Agent Prather. Except the pornstache, that kinda threw me. What's the deal with that? Thought you guys couldn't do facial hair except for undercover work or something."

"No, it's permitted. Just not many guys do, more a cultural thing."

"Yeah, I suppose everyone's standards are dropping."

The Deputy stifled a laugh.

"Sheriff, I'm not here to discuss FBI grooming standards. I would like to speak with you alone."

"This is Deputy Craig Markdale. One of my senior Deputies, one-hundred percent a trusted agent."

"Alone, please, Sheriff."

"Well, I suppose. Since you suddenly found your manners." The Sheriff gave the Deputy a nod, and he left with a smile.

The man in the suit produced a portfolio he had tucked under his arm. From it he pulled a glossy photograph of a vaguely familiar face.

The Sheriff took the 8x10. It was obviously blown up from a service ID. The face looked familiar, but the hair was high and tight.

"Jeffery Potter, Sheriff. I believe he is on your SAR team."

Taylor laughed.

"OK, yeah. Fairly long hair and beard now though."

"Good to know. So, you know the man, Sheriff?"

"Yes."

"How well?"

The older man paused, and the Special Agent sensed the defenses going up, so he smiled.

"I mean. are we talking professionally? He has no record."

"Is that just because you never had enough to bust him? Do you know him personally? Like you hang out at his place and have a few beers every Friday night."

The Sheriff leaned back in his chair and sighed.

"Jeff Potter *is* a volunteer on our Search And Rescue team. He goes out by himself on his old four-wheeler when we get calls. He knows his way around the woods, and he knows how to find people. He's single handedly found five people in the ten years he's been here, saving the lives of at least two of them. One was hypothermic, the other suffering from a gunshot wound. Jeff is a good man, and if I ever needed to call out a posse, he would be among the first I'd call."

"Well, that's ironic. Why would you call him out, Sheriff, is it because of his military back ground? Or is it because you know him so well?"

"I wouldn't say I know him well, he keeps to himself. He's a quiet man. When there's a search, he just goes out and does what needs doing. Which drives our SAR team lead crazy, but it seems to work. As far as his military background I just remember his application said something about being retired Army."

"How do you get in contact with him?"

"We generally don't, he contacts us."

"So, this guy is like Batman?"

"No, Batman requires the Bat Signal. This guy is more like Billy Jack, he just shows up when we need him."

"Who is Billy Jack? Is that another DC comic thing, 'cause I only follow Marvel since the Dark Knight. They've really gone downhill."

The Sheriff squinted a little.

"Yeah, I don't follow… That."

"So, this guy just shows up when you need him, and you've seen him on the Search And Rescue team… but, there's more to him than that, isn't there?"

"I suspect so."

"You never asked him about it? Nothing about his back ground or politics ever came up?"

"He didn't seem to care to talk about it." The Sheriff leaned forward on his desk, his fingers clasped in a low steeple. "I spent some time in the service myself, not a career and not anything too exciting, but I worked around certain communities enough to recognize that some considered impolite to ask too many questions. If they could, or wanted to talk about where they'd been or what they'd done, they would. Some men are just glad to let the past be the past, and I respect that. He has no criminal record, not even a speeding ticket for the last ten years."

The Special Agent tossed one of the files from the portfolio on the desk in front of the Sheriff.

"His DD214, Sheriff. What are your thoughts?"

The Sheriff held it at just the right distance and still had to squint a little as he gave his observations.

"Tabbed Ranger, with the 75th for a few years. Then the rest, some ambiguous stuff at Fort Bragg. Afghan and Iraq service medals. GWOT medal. Bronze Star with V. Three Purple Hearts. It's about what I would expect for a man of his caliber."

"You have a lot of respect for him."

"You don't?"

"He's breaking the law, and so are his children."

"How so?"

"Neither of his children have responded to the initial Order To Report from the draft board. His son didn't even register. And then there is this." Special Agent Vince Prather then pulled a copy of Jeff's letter to the Local Draft Board from the portfolio and handed it to Taylor.

The Sheriff read over the copy of the letter.

"Jeff Potter is a man of conviction, it appears."

"It's the last part that gave us our terrorism nexus."

"Terrorism nexus?"

"18 USC 2332b... subsection two, whoever threatens..."

"Threat?" Taylor read aloud directly from the letter. *"Maybe we'll learn. Maybe we'll learn more than just saying no, maybe we'll learn that we aren't the only ones with children and we aren't the only ones with homes and addresses. Maybe we'll learn that when we have paid our dues, it is time for someone else to pay theirs."*

"Clearly threatening government officials."

Taylor laughed.

"A threat or just a reality, Prather? Surely you study the Constitution in your academy, right?" Taylor looked down and pulled a drawer out of his desk. Shuffling around for a moment he pulled out a small, palm-sized black book. "Here, you can keep it. I make all my Deputies read and carry it... pocket constitution. Page 50 you'll find the amendments, you'll find the first amendment of interest here."

The Sheriff held it out to the Special Agent over the desk.

"I don't need that." Prather waved it off.

"Au contraire, I think you do..."

"Our warrant was vigorously reviewed and approved by counsel."

Taylor shook his head and put the little book back in the drawer.

"Of course, it was. What are you going after him for?"

"The terroristic threatening and draft law violation. And I'm sure we'll find more, probably Assault Weapon violation."

"The new draft? The conscription of women?"

"Yes."

"Some people question whether it's a legitimate law, with that stuff that happened in Congress."

"It passed, it's law..."

"And you need to make an example... And Jeff Potter is the perfect example given his service."

"I would think, as a military man, he'd be glad to have his kids participate in this. It's pretty clear cut."

"Yeah, just like the Gulf of Tonkin was clear cut? Or the dastardly Iraqis throwing Kuwaiti babies out of incubators was clear cut? You do know what the first casualty of war is, don't you?"

The FBI Special Agent either didn't know the quote or didn't care, and he ignored the remark.

"They're breaking the law, and I'm tasked with dealing with this case."

"I thought this would be Marshals."

"Everyone's shorthanded with the riots, I'm lead on this. One of their junior guys will be working on it. We may need some bodies from you."

"Well, we'll see, like you said, everyone is shorthanded these days."

"I don't see many riots in your area here, Sheriff."

"Exactly. Seems I might have all my people properly deployed, wouldn't want to interrupt that delicate balance between enforcement and compliance, would we? You guys understand that balance, right? The whole social contract?"

The young agent looked at the Sheriff, trying to get a better read on the older man.

It was quiet for a moment as each man hesitated to say what he wanted to.

The Sheriff sighed then finally spoke.

"About two years ago, Jeff Potter lost his job as a federal contractor because he wouldn't take the vaccination. About a year later, he lost his wife in a car accident. He sold his house close to town and moved with the two kids out to a cabin on his old mining claim. If I had a DO NOT MESS WITH list, he'd be near the top of it."

The agent's lips cracked that smug grin beneath the emasculate mustache.

"So, you're afraid of him, Sheriff?"

"No, you misunderstand me. He's a good man who has been handed a lot of bad things in life, and he always takes them in stride. He doesn't feel pity or seek sympathy. He moves eagerly from one challenge to the next. He's a good man who's been handed a lot of bad things in his life, and he doesn't deserve what you're about to bring down on him. And most importantly, if you take his kids, he has nothing left to lose. With his background, you should understand that makes him *very* dangerous."

Prather stood up straight and looked down his nose at the Sheriff.

"Will you provide assistance and personnel or not, Sheriff Taylor?"

"I will, personally. I can't spare any Deputies, but I'll avail myself to you for whatever you need."

The Special Agent reached in the portfolio and produced a handful of papers.

"I'll need you to sign this Non Disclosure Agreement."

"What? We've never done NDAs. Besides, you'd need to NDA me prior to giving me the info. You just screwed up."

"Part of the new War Powers Act. And maybe I did give you the NDA first…"

The Sheriff opened the top drawer to his desk.

"That's not what this digital recorder will show. Look, I'll tell you what, Vince. You run an ethical, legal investigation, and my lips are sealed. You step outside those bounds I go to your supervisors, I go to my senator, and I go to the press. That should be easy, right?"

"Fine, and let's keep this professional, Sheriff Taylor. I prefer to be addressed as Special Agent Prather and my preferred pronouns are he, him."

The Sheriff laughed.

"Ya' know, you can call me whatever you want. I don't much care and suspect I've been called worse than what you could come up with. You can show yourself out and give me a call when you need me… Vince."

*   *   *

At the precipice of the rocky vista, he levered himself painfully to one knee with the aid of his rifle. Both knees burned him, ground with audible cracks of bone on bone where it shouldn't be. On days like this his back didn't bend without a stabbing pain, low and deep that made only movement more painful than stillness.

It was the price he'd paid for too many parachute jumps with a heavy load and a few helicopter crashes. And then there were the bone fragments that still emerged and threatened infection.

But this was the only place he allowed himself the luxury of self-pity, and these were the only eyes he would allow to see his own perceived weaknesses.

Wrapping his arms around the rifle in a kind of embrace, he clasped his hands and began.

"Lord, I'm sorry." He kept his eyes open when he prayed here, taking in all the beauty and majesty. "I'm sorry I'm not more for you, please forgive me. I am trying, now. I'm trying to be better, I'm trying to understand. I'm trying to be the man you want me to be. I'm trying to finally be the father the kids deserve, the one they need me to be.

"God, please give me the wisdom to see what is right and the strength to do it. I feel like you've given me the foresight, and I'm trying hard not to be blind to that blessing. It's so hard, God. I know what's coming. I know what they're going to do. I know what I'm going to have to do, and I'm afraid my tired, crippled old body may not be up to the task.

"Help me guide the kids to you, so they can find the strength and wisdom for what is about to come. I'm sorry I didn't understand sooner. I thought I was supposed to teach them, I bore that impossible burden for too long and, it was foolish and arrogant of me. The most important thing I should have done was lead them to you, and all the rest I have done was really just filling in the blanks.

"Please, God, let me continue to be there for them, now that I'm at least figuring out that piece. But if I can't be, please let my preparation be adequate for them, please, God. They deserve more than I've given them and I see that now, and I'm trying to get caught up.

He inhaled deeply, consciously filling his lungs with the cool alpine air. At this elevation there were patches of snow, and on the breeze there was carried just enough chill to make him feel alive and let him know he was being listened to.

"Thank you, Lord. You've given me so much more than I deserve, and I feel bad asking for any more. But I just want it for the kids at this point... Amen."

Leaning heavily on the rifle, he struggled against the old injuries and waivered a moment. Through the pain and consternation, he allowed a smile to break through. An eagle circled below, and for a moment, he sought some greater meaning in that, then he let it go.

*   *   *

"Hey, Josh."

"Mr. Potter." The UPS driver looked anxiously up and down the remote gravel road.

"So, ah…" Something was clearly amiss, and Jeff didn't see the young man reaching for a package. "Is there a package for me or something?"

"No, sorry, Mr. Potter. I had to make that up." He continued to look about nervously.

"What is it, Josh?"

"I had some FBI guys talk to us back at the hub. They were asking about you."

"What were they asking?"

"The things I remember most were, if I delivered right to your door and if you were armed when you picked up packages."

Jeff looked down at the butt of the Glock 19 sticking out of the appendix carry holster in the waistband of his pants. He looked back up with a reassuring smile.

"What did you tell them, Josh?"

"I told them sometimes your driveway was bad up here, and I'd give you a call and you'd meet me down here. That's why I had to tell you that you had a package today." He looked around nervously again. "I didn't want to say any of this over the phone in case they were listening… and as far as the gun thing goes I just told them that half the people up here have guns on them when I see them, and that's the God's honest truth anyway. Did I do OK, Mr. Potter?"

Jeff nodded with a smile.

"Of course, Josh. I'd ask no man to lie for me."

"What kind of trouble are you in, Mr. Potter?"

"We're all in trouble right now, Josh. And we all have to watch out for each other. You did well. Thank you."

"They told me not to tell you, of course."

"Tell me what, Josh? I think I must have forgot already." Jeff's smile broadened, and the young man managed a smile in return.

"I've got to get going, Mr. Potter." He started to step back into the truck and turned back to Jeff. "Thanks again for finding my Grampa. He always says you saved his life."

"Naw, your Grampa's a tough old coot, you can tell him I said so. He'd a lasted a while out there. Probably would've crawled his way out eventually."

"Well, anyway, he said you made him promise he'd call when he got out, and he did. And we talk pretty regularly now. There was some little stuff between him and my Dad, but that didn't really seem to matter anymore. You kind of helped everybody see that."

Jeff shook his head.

"You're giving me way too much credit there, Josh. Thanks for the heads up today. Good people just have to keep being good to each other, and we all have to watch out for each other to get through all this."

The young man nodded with a smile as he sat in the driver's seat and hit the ignition.

"Have a blessed day, Mr. Potter."

"You too, Josh."

*   *   *

"Sheriff."

This time the older man didn't bother getting up. He leaned back in his chair and crossed his arms.

"Vince, twice in less than a week. To what do I owe this pleasure?"

"Well, I just wanted you to know I've started conducting interviews in the area, in case you start getting some phone calls."

"Already have."

"Who called?"

"Concerned citizens."

"What did you tell them?"

46

"Not to be concerned. They just wanted to make sure you weren't a con artist and it wasn't some kind of scam more than anything."

The FBI agent pursed his lips but didn't say anything for a moment.

After a long pause, the Special Agent looked at the floor, then looked up as he spoke.

"I just wanted you to know that I've got three DHS Predator Unmanned Aerial Vehicles allocated to this investigation. They'll be providing us twenty-four hour overhead coverage."

The FBI man paused again, and the Sheriff got the distinct impression that he was supposed to be impressed.

Instead, he just raised his eyebrows inquiringly.

Special Agent Prather inhaled, then spoke.

"In case anyone notices them, the cover story is they are looking for forest fires."

"Fire season is about over, and we've had a particularly wet year."

Prather leaned a little to the right, then back to the left facing the Sheriff.

"Then we need to tell people they are conducting environmental studies."

"Will they show up on ADS-B flight trackers?   People around here look out for that sort of thing."

"Well, uh… I'm not sure."

"If they show up as DHS birds, you might need another cover story."

The Sheriff couldn't suppress his grin as the FBI man crossed his arms and looked down at the floor.

"You could just tell folks they're monitoring the border." The Sheriff offered this up almost out of pity.

"Yes, that's perfect." Prather rubbed his chin. "Sherriff, I have myself and another Agent coming in from Salt Lake, he's a regional SWAT guy, and two Marshals who will be coming into town in the next few weeks who will assist in the surveillance and the raid. How many men will you commit"

"I'll be there. That's the best I can do right now."

Special Agent Prather crossed his arms and looked down at his feet.

"I'll have access to two up-armored Suburbans. We could use that MRAP I saw sitting on your back lot."

"The old Maxx Pro? That thing hasn't moved in years. And it would eat the rest of my patrol fuel budget for the year just getting up Potter's driveway."

"You would, of course, be reimbursed for fuel and maintenance."

The Sheriff laughed.

"You'd have to pay up front and, no, we have a policy in place of only using that for barricaded suspects and rescue under fire. I'm sure you can scrounge your own armor if this is that important. Besides, the Suburbans are lower profile. If that old MRAP moved off my lot, it would be all over the internet and anyone with so much as a guilty conscience around here would be on alert. And hell, you don't have enough people for it anyway, is everyone getting their own vehicle for this raid?"

Prather thought about it a moment.

"It would be worth it to intimidate him, help him know we're serious."

"Well, I suspect no matter what, he'll know you're serious. And really that MRAP won't intimidate him. He's the type who would know every weakness of that thing and know how to exploit it. As hard as you hit him, he'll hit back. Ever think about just calling him in to talk with him first?"

"Can't risk it, with the threatening tone of that letter he wrote to the Draft Board."

The Sheriff grimaced and looked down at his desk.

*   *   *

She looked back from inside the well-concealed hole with the headlamp blinding him enough, Jeff had to hold his hand up in front of his eyes.

Jane reached up and turned it off as she lowered the brush covered hatch.

"Dad, I'm not sure if I should be impressed or freaked out. How long did this take you?"

"Most of this year, since the thaw." Potter calculated in his head. "and a good bit of last year before winter."

"You've spent like a year constructing a hidden bunker?"

"Not a bunker, that would be a fixed fighting position. This is a cache."

She turned the headlamp on again, lifted the hatch and crept down the cinderblock steps. It was about ten by twenty, and the walls were lined with rudimentary shelves filled with vacuum sealed packages. MREs, spam cans of 30-06 and heavy plastic-bagged battle packs of 5.56mm ammo. Heavy mountain sleeping bags, more food, spare water filters, everything double-sealed against moisture.

He followed in behind her.

"Drainage is one of the big things, keeping out as much moisture as you can. That and concealment. Doesn't do you any good if someone finds it."

She ran her hands down the shelves, then lowered the headlamp to wear it necklace style as she turned to speak to him.

"What is this for, Dad? Is this for if the Russians invade, and we have to go all *WOLVERINES!*"

"It won't be the Russians. It'll be the Chinese, and it won't be an invasion, they'll be invited." He tried to laugh a little at the end, but it didn't help. "Fixed fortifications like bunkers are a bad idea. Staying agile will be important. This would be good for a night or two if you needed to, it is ventilated. You wouldn't want to do it if you knew you were being tracked, though. You'd want to come here during a heavy snow, for example, rather than after a fresh snow fall."

"Dad," she sounded exasperated. "Who is going to be here? We are in the middle of nowhere at the center of a National Forest miles from anything resembling a road."

"Actually, we just crossed the border into Forest Service Land five miles back, didn't you see that on the map?"

"Dad, does it make a difference?"

"Could you find this again? After that last GPS waypoint, with the landmarks and pacing I showed you?"

"Yes." She deflated and slumped her shoulders. "Does Tom know about any of this?"

"No, just you. I know you can handle it. It might be more of a burden for him right now."

"Can we go now, Dad?"

He just nodded and backed out. When she came out and lowered the hatch, he made sure the camouflage was set.

Jane started walking back toward the four-wheelers.

"Look at your landmarks, remember your pacing. You need to be able to find this during any season, day or night."

She said nothing and continued walking.

He shook his head and adjusted the AR on its sling. Hobbling behind her, Jeff finally caught up with her as she reached the four-wheelers a quarter mile away.

"What?" he asked as she straddled her machine.

"I think I'm really worried about you, Dad."

"Why?"

"Why? Are you being serious?" She motioned up the hill toward the hidden cache, then toward the carbine slung across his chest. "That, and that for starters. You don't need to carry an AR all the time out here."

"I've spent more of my life strapped with one of these than not. It's comfortable for me."

"Maybe you need to re-evaluate that, Dad."

"Things are bad, Jane. They are continuing to get worse."

"And really, Dad, what will any of this do?"

"Help us survive."

She just shook her head, looking suddenly exhausted. She turned the key and hit the starter.

"Let's just go, Dad. I can find it if I need to."

He painfully mounted his machine and hit the ignition. It turned and turned but didn't fire. He stopped and let the starter cool a minute before trying again. Then the undeniable smell of fuel hit him.

Jane looked at the machine then hesitantly up to his eyes, like she had been looking forward to the long ride back without having to interact with him.

"Probably the fuel pump gasket, just like the other one. I should have laid in more non-ethanol fuel. Never occurred to me that they'd up the ethanol, and that they'd run out of everything else. Looks like we're down to one four-wheeler now. The parts for the other one are already on back order, and they said it would be six months to a year."

He swung down off the machine and started untying the tow strap. Jane repositioned her four-wheeler without saying a word.

*   *   *

Deputy Craig Markdale waited a while after seeing the FBI agent leave, then got the nod from Mary, and she buzzed him in.

The Sheriff looked up and smiled.

"What this time, Sheriff?"

"Well, Craig. They've got themselves some steady stare aerial surveillance, and they want our Maxx Pro."

"What did you tell them?"

"No."

"How many guys they got now?"

"Four or five, not nearly enough."

"How many did they want from us."

"Don't care, all they are getting is me."

Deputy Markdale furrowed his brow, and the Sheriff leaned back in his chair and continued.

"I'm not going to subject any of my people to this impending mess, but at the same time, Potter deserves to have someone there to serve as an honest witness to whatever goes down."

"Do they have a plan yet?"

"Yeah, seems like they want to drive a convoy of vehicles up to his front door, they want our MRAP to *intimidate* Potter."

"Intimidate Potter? Do they not get that he's a pretty serious dude?"

The Sheriff shrugged.

"I tried to give them the idea, but I'm not going to do their investigation for them, besides, one of the guys they got coming in is Regional SWAT. Prather made sure to let me know about that."

"Regional SWAT, not even HRT?"

"Nope. I imagine most of those teams are tied up with the riots on the coasts."

The Deputy laughed.

"Prather sounds like an absolute wedge."

"A what?" The Sheriff shook his head a little.

"A wedge, a divisive tool."

The Sheriff laughed.

"Yeah, I'd say that's pretty accurate."

"So, what do you think about all this, Sheriff? I mean they *are* draft dodgers."

The Sheriff paused. He inhaled loudly and leaned forward on his desk as the Deputy sat down and crossed his legs in the chair across from him. Markdale knew when the Sheriff did this, he was about to speak at length about something which he had given much thought.

"I served a while in the post-Vietnam Army. I went in with a pretty dim view of draft dodgers, honestly, because I was volunteering. A lot of the career guys I served with or under, who had been to war with conscripts didn't have a lot of good to say about them. Can you blame them? Not everyone's a warrior. In a perfect world, if the war is noble enough, everyone will do their part."

"It's not a perfect world though, is it Sheriff? I mean, they had to draft people into World War II."

The Sheriff nodded.

"Conscription has been around all the way back to the Revolutionary War. The Civil War. World War I. Obviously, it's not a perfect world. And there *are* cowards. But do you really want them in your military? Do you want anyone unmotivated there? Are we beyond that as a culture?"

The Sheriff shook his head then continued.

"I don't know. I do know that Jeff Potter has done his part. He has fought against evil where he could, how he could, when he could. He hasn't done as much as some, but he's done a hell of a lot more than most, and he's paid a price for it. The man lost his wife in that car accident a year ago or so now. And maybe he's lost part of his sanity to the things he's seen and had to do. I know that's how they are going to try to play it. Now, they want to come and take his kids away? He's a man with not much left to lose. All I do know for sure, is that, here, in the time he's lived in this area, his presence has been a net positive and I trust him and his judgement over some FBI dweeb."

*　　*　　*

It should have been a running day.

But really even on a good day, that was a gross exaggeration at this point. At best all it ever was, was a slow, painful shuffle with his knees and back cursing him the entire way.

Today it would just be a long walk down the driveway, up the road and back. There was much to consider and even more to let go of, to unload. He carried, tucked under his left arm, a leather-bound Bible that had been a gift from a team mate. He was almost through his second read of it.

He remembered a conversation he'd had with an interpreter in Iraq. The man was a Syrian Christian, and he found him reading his Bible one day under the camo netting of a smoke pit on the compound. It was before Jeff had received his own gift from his friend. Before he'd given the Bible a whole lot of thought. Before a lot of things. Jeff had always been intrigued by that particular interpreter. He was an older man, quiet in a kind way, not sinister. Jeff had often noted that when the man did speak, he usually reserved it for something that was probably worth listening to.

That day, the thing the man said that stuck most with Jeff was that the Bible needed to be read at least three times. He said the first time through wouldn't make a lot of sense. The second time through, things would start to come together, but that true understanding wouldn't begin to happen until the third time through.

Jeff was an avid recreational reader, and he liked the occasional challenge. That was what had brought him to Solzhenitsyn, and Rand and then after the conversation, to the Bible. Of course, when he was younger he'd tried reading it, but was discouraged when it didn't speak to him in ways he thought it would.

The day after the conversation with the interpreter, he stopped by the Chaplain's quarters. He was given one of the little digiflage cover Bibles they handed out, a New International Version with very fine print.

Now, he was reading Revelations again. While he didn't necessarily see this as the End Times, he definitely took away the certainty that things wouldn't be getting any better until they got much, much worse.

And he thought about all his preparations and tried to suppress all the failings there. He had calculated out the best he could their needs for both gasoline and diesel. He never imagined the diesel would run out first and the trips to build the caches, especially the distant north cache, took twice as much gasoline as he had calculated. He couldn't afford to pay for fuel that went bad before he could use it, and it turned out the three hundred gallons he had treated and laid in, wasn't enough. All they were selling these days was high ethanol, and it had played havoc on the fuel systems of his Hondas.

He was down to one four-wheeler, and it would have to do, but really wasn't enough, especially with his crippled legs. Jane could pack a load, but Tom had been slow to learn to test himself. Timid in the face of adversity, the young man had not yet learned to challenge himself despite, or perhaps because of, Jeff's attempts to push him.

Jeff shook his head.

He had to deal with what he had, not lament which he lacked or long for that which he couldn't get.

At the bottom of the drive, a large pasture unfolded at the road, and the valley spilled out into the lake. No matter the weather, it was always a beautiful and inspiring view. Today that was particularly the case. Cool fall air, but a beautiful summer sky swept with high wisps of cirrus clouds.

He liked reading the Bible here, with a view of the water and the valley and now the snow dusting the mountain tops. His real hope in reading it and in prayer was that he would come to a greater understanding of the world and his place in it. That it would guide him in his true path.

Some days it all seemed so clear, others, it got a little fuzzy.

Lately things seemed to be getting fuzzy for Jeff, and he desperately wanted some clarity.

Crossing the road, he was headed toward the bank of the stream.

An eagle calling somewhere above made him stop and look.

It circled low and cast a shadow over him as he looked up and smiled, but something else really caught his eye.

Below a white swirl of cirrus, something grey and angular orbited. The right angle of where the wing joined the fuselage caught a shadow, and his eyes locked onto it.

An old MQ-9 Predator.

Jeff looked down at the leather-bound book, then back to the Pred. He nodded in silent thanks for the sudden clarity in purpose, and he turned and began jogging back the mile long driveway up to the cabin.

The pain and crepitus of his old injuries were pushed aside, and he burned like a rekindled fire with resolve as he thought through what exactly would come next.

He was winded when he got to the cabin, but not as much as he might have been. Grabbing his carbine from the rack just inside the cabin door and the keys from the kitchen table, he trotted out to the shed.

There, he put the keys in the ignition and fired up the four-wheeler. The suppressed muffler put-putted at idle as he grabbed a can of two cycle mix fuel and his chain saw and ratchet strapped them to the front rack of the machine.

CHAPTER 3

Prather didn't even acknowledge Mary's attempt to stop him as he reached for the door handle of the Sheriff's door. The steel door was firmly latched and he piled into it as he looked sideways, awkwardly at the middle-aged woman behind the desk.

"I have to buzz you in," she said.

The door opened unexpectedly from the inside, and the FBI agent stepped away from it with a start.

"Vince," the Sheriff sighed. "Again, you have to work on your manners. I don't care who you are, you just don't go barging in on people unexpectedly."

"It's urgent."

The Sheriff shook his head.

"We're gonna try this again." He shut the door.

The Special Agent motioned to the door.

"Please?"

Mary responded with a cordial smile, pressing a button on her desk.

"OK, Mary go ahead," the Sheriff called from the other side of the door.

The electronic latch on the door clicked open, and the Special Agent tentatively grabbed the door knob, opening it slowly.

"We really don't have time for games, Sheriff."

"We don't really consider good manners to be games in these parts, Vince."

The FBI man inhaled deeply and pulled the portfolio from under his arm. He spilled a couple of pieces of paper onto the Sheriff's desk as the Sheriff rounded it to take a seat.

The Sheriff could just make out that it was aerial photographs in GRG format, but he had to don his reading glasses to make out anything specific. When he did, he saw a chevron of overlapped trees felled across a road.

"That's Jeff Potter's driveway."

The Sheriff laughed.

"What the hell is he doing, Sheriff?"

"That's an abatis."

"A what?"

"An abatis. If someone knows what they're doing, and Potter does, you're not getting tanks through that without clearing it first. By the time you clear it, he'll be long gone."

"Well, I imagine you can find some charges to stack on for this, and give me more assistance."

"Charges? That's his land. He doesn't need to make it easy for you."

"You mean us, don't you, Sheriff?"

"Oh, of course, Vince."

*　　*　　*

He was unbuckling the chainsaw chaps as he heard the motor approaching. Jeff looked up to see the grill of Jane's little Jeep Cherokee stop abruptly in a cloud of dust just short of him and his well-planned obstacle.

"What are you doing, Dad?" Jane yelled as she exited the Jeep and slammed the driver's door behind her."

"Denying avenues of approach."

She held her hands up and was about to speak, but she realized she hadn't quite put the words together. For a moment she just stood there staring at the tangle of trees and branches and inhaled the smell of the fresh cut ponderosa pines and the two-cycle chain saw exhaust that hung in the still air.

She looked at Jeff. He was grinning, and he moved stiffly as he laid the chaps across the seat of the four-wheeler. Hefting the hot chainsaw to the front rack, he took off his gloves and Jane found her words.

"What the hell, Dad? I have to get to work."

"No need for the language, Jane. Some things have changed."

"Bullshit."

"Jane."

"Dad, you have lost your mind, and you're worried about my language?"

"I'd like you to drive back to the cabin and get Tom. We need to all have a talk. Life is going to be a little different for the time being."

"Dad, what am I going to tell work?"

"I appreciate your work ethic, Jane. I have always admired that about you. You won't be going to work for a while. And you don't need to."

"What are you talking about, Dad?"

"Go back to the cabin and get Tom, we'll all talk about it together. Cool off a little bit, you seem emotional."

"*Emotional?* Are you keeping us here against our will?"

"We are hunkering down for a while, Jane. I'd rather just talk about this with you and Tom together."

"And I'd rather just go about my daily life, but I guess we can't all get what we want now can we, Dad? Tell me what is happening."

Jeff sighed. He stepped up and sat side saddle on the four-wheeler as he spoke.

"We have enough of everything stored up to stay here on the claim for at least a year. A lot more if we stretch it and supplement with deer and elk."

"Why, Dad? What's happened... What have you done?"

"It's not about what I've done." He looked up. It was still there, orbiting. "We are under surveillance by federal authorities."

He pointed to the unmanned aircraft.

She followed his finger and squinted a bit until she saw it.

"You're serious... I mean... That's a Predator drone, isn't it?"

Jeff nodded.

"Who are they, and why are they here, Dad?"

Jeff sighed and crossed his arms. He would have to go through this all again later with Tom.

"Most likely FBI, I think this would fall under their authority, or really a joint task force headed up by FBI. DHS is still running the old Preds, so there are probably other agencies involved."

"Why, Dad?"

"Because I promised Tom I wouldn't let them take him... or you."

"Dad?"

"Some letters came in the mail for you guys a few weeks ago now. From the Local Draft Board. It was the initial report notification, ordering you two to report for preliminary screening."

"Why didn't you give those to us, Dad?"

"Because I handled it."

"*You what?*"

"I took care of it."

"How?"

"I went to the Local Board, then sent them something in writing."

"What did you tell them, Dad?"

"I told them... *no.*"

"You can't tell the government *no*, Dad."

"You absolutely can, Jane. In fact, there are times when it is your moral obligation to do so."

"No, that was for us to do if we chose. How can you think this is right, Dad?"

"Tom doesn't want to have anything to do with this. He's not fit for the fight."

"Then I'll go, they don't send siblings."

"You both got the same notice, and that is apparently not a hard, fast rule, especially since Tom hadn't registered. I think they were going to make an example of him, of us."

"So, what, I'm a prisoner here?"

"No, Jane. You can leave anytime you want."

She gestured down the tangle of pines with silent frustration.

"Well, you can't leave that way. Not in the Jeep anyway."

"How do you see this ending, Dad?"

"Hopefully they have bigger fish to fry. Hopefully the Feds are tied up with the food riots on the coasts. Hopefully they leave us alone until all this blows over…"

"You always told us hope wasn't a strategy."

Jeff looked down at his feet.

"It's not. I have a plan."

*   *   *

"Good morning, Mary."

"Good morning, Special Agent Prather." She forced a cordial smile and looked at the man with him.

"This is Special Agent Booth. We need to speak to the Sheriff, please."

She picked up the phone, dialed in, advised the Sheriff and buzzed them in.

As they entered, the Sheriff was leaned back in his chair with his fingers laced behind his head.

"Hey, Vince.   What can I do for you today?"

"Sheriff Taylor, I would like to introduce you to Special Agent Booth. He's on loan from Salt Lake Field Office. He's one of our Regional SWAT guys."

The Sheriff stood up to shake hands and raised his eyebrows feigning deference.

Booth gave a firm handshake and a curt smile.

"Thanks to Special Agent Booth's contacts, we've got a new solution to this Jeff Potter problem."

The Sheriff sat back down, leaned back and resumed his position.

"Oh?"

"He's got us set up with a DHS Aerostar helicopter out of Spokane."

Booth smiled and slipped his thumbs behind his riggers belt on his 5.11 pants, then spoke.

"Classic infil to the X." He said.

"Oooh." The Sheriff said.

"It means we go right to the target," Booth clarified with great seriousness.

"Oh, I know what it means, Booth. What branch were you in?"

Booth gave a cocky laugh.

"Well, all my service has been with the Bureau. Did a couple of tours in Afghanistan."

"Booth...," the Sheriff leaned forward on his desk. "I have to tell you... yer not infil'n to the X. You're landing a helicopter on this guys' front yard. And he's going to be ready, because he's done this hundreds of times in places like Afghanistan and worse. He knows how this goes, he knows the weaknesses and how to exploit them. Do you understand this guy's background?"

"Unit guy out of Bragg, yeah, I know the type."

The Sheriff nestled his bearded chin on his steepled fingers and looked down at his desk.

"They aren't super men, Sheriff," Booth said. "Nothing to be afraid of, they put their pants on one leg at a time just like everyone else. They're also subject to break down like anyone else. This guy has lost it."

Prather picked up the narrative from there.

"PTSD, right wing religious extremist. It's a bad mix, Sheriff."

"Where are you getting this from, Vince?"

"Our analysts watching the Pred feed see this guy walking around his property with a Bible..."

"I guess that's not on the approved reading list, Vince? What do you walk around your place with, a copy of Tiger Beat?"

Booth smirked, and that seemed to make Prather even more discomfited.

"We're establishing his pattern of life," Booth picked up before Prather embarrassed himself further. "Once we've developed the intel we need, we'll execute the raid."

"You guys couldn't just go in and talk to him… You tell me he puts his pants on one leg at a time, and you have to go in the middle of the night with a helicopter, overwhelming force and drone overwatch. But you were too afraid to go talk to a guy who was just exercising his first amendment right. That letter was only a threat to the bureaucracy because it has no idea how to handle people who stand up for themselves and expect the constitutional protection they deserve. The bureaucracy shouldn't be protecting the government, it should be protecting the people it's supposed to serve."

Any notion of joviality had disappeared from the Sheriff's face.

Booth looked at Prather who was looking at the floor then to the Sheriff. He smiled and spoke.

"We need to get this guy in custody, Sheriff. You tell us we should go talk to him, but you tell us he already has us outclassed. We're going to take every precaution necessary. What if we cut power and jam SAT and cell coms to his cabin. Do you think that would draw him out?"

Booth handed the Sheriff a drone image of the cabin and the immediate surroundings.

"No, he's pretty self-sufficient up there. These big propane tanks, they could probably run a generator there for a year. And he probably has at least enough food to last twice that long. That's not uncommon in these parts. Potter is probably set up to be as nearly self-sufficient as possible."

"We find ourselves short staffed. We need personnel because we don't have overwhelming force beyond our technological advantages. Can we count on your assistance, or do we need to quit communicating our intentions to you?"

The Sheriff inhaled and leaned back in his chair, trying not to let his smile look too forced.

"I'm with you, but just me. I won't subject any of my people to this. Your mismanagement of staffing isn't my problem."

"These are extraordinary times, Sheriff."

"For certain."

Booth eyed the Sheriff suspiciously.

"I'll be frank, Sheriff. There is concern you may be compromised here."

"My loyalty is to the people of my county and the people of this country, not the bureaucracy. If that makes me compromised, so be it."

"Sheriff, I think you are well aware that there are rumors of Congress pushing federalizing all law enforcement as part of this developing second War Powers Act. It might be time to get on board."

The Sheriff just laughed.

*　　*　　*

The Deputy called out to the barn, so as not to startle the Sheriff during his morning ritual.

"Markdale comin' in."

"Yeah, Craig."

The Deputy slid the barn door open and walked to the far stall where the Sheriff tended to his favorite mare.

"Hey, Sheriff." The Deputy was holding an apple up. "May I?"

"Sure, Betsy loves that." The Sheriff was just finishing up with the dandy brush.

"Sorry I didn't catch up with you yesterday after the feds showed up again. I was helping out with that domestic up Round Top." Craig walked over and reached out to let Betsy eat the apple from his hand.

"Ah, how'd that go?"

"The usual. She said she's leavin' for good this time."

"Ah."

"Zites was on it, he's just off Field School, and I don't think he'd been to the Watkins place yet so I thought I'd help him out."

"Good call. How'd he do?"

"He's fine with it, just needed some help with the paper afterward, is all." Craig leaned against one of the stalls. "I heard that Feeb brought a partner. How's that whole thing developing?"

The Sheriff ran the body brush over the mare's flank.

"Not well, Craig. They're gonna roll heavy on him. Worse yet, they're underestimating his abilities and overestimating their own. I gotta bad feeling they're gonna get people killed with this. Prather is an idiot lookin' to promote out of here and get to a big city field office. Working this area and the Res is beneath him, you can hear it in his voice. This other Agent, Booth, I think it was, well, he seems mildly competent, but he's got something to prove"

"What is their plan?"

"Well, Potter's formed an abatis with fallen trees on his driveway." The Sheriff laughed.

Markdale looked at him quizzically as he fed the mare the apple.

"It's a defensive obstruction with interlocking logs. Of course, Potter's consists of over a dozen 120 foot Ponderosas or so. There's no driving anything up that driveway now. No SUVs, no MRAPs. You can't get tanks through something like that without clearing it."

Craig raised his eyebrows.

"Potter knows something's up?"

The Sheriff nodded.

"The guy is surveillance savvy. He knows what's up. He knows what to look for. Heck, I bet he can just feel it. Anyway, now they are planning an air assault. Helicopter, *infil to the X* they said." The Sheriff shook his head. "Potter will be waiting for us."

"*Us?* You're still gonna do this?"

The Sheriff just nodded grimly and brushed the mare without much thought.

"I'm taking a body cam and documenting everything. Somebody has to."

"There has to be another way, though, Sheriff."

"There is, but the feds won't do it." The Sheriff continued combing, but his mind was elsewhere and even the horse knew it. Taylor snickered a little then went on.

"Ya know what I'd like to do, Craig? I'd like to assemble a posse and ride up there with thirty or so armed, deputized locals and get between Potter and the Feds. I know I could get a hundred volunteers at least if I got the word out, probably get 20-30 suitable guys out of that. Yeah, ride up there like a real Western Sheriff."

"You'd never lose an election if you did that."

"You know this is my last run. No more elections for me."

"Really think the Feds could let a Sheriff get away with that? I don't think they could even let you survive something like that."

"I could get a hundred volunteers. Most of them wouldn't be up for it physically. They'd still mount up and ride. I could have twenty, truly dangerous men that could stop the initial federal attempt. They couldn't leave it there though, could they? So, when I really think about it, I know I can't go John Wayne on this, it will just get more good men killed. Or is that me just rationalizing away my own cowardice?"

"That ain't it for sure, Sheriff. Seems like there's no good resolution to this. Maybe Potter will just give it up."

"That will never happen, and that's why they're really scared to death of a man like Potter. And I don't mean Booth and Prather, not at that level. They aren't smart enough to understand how dangerous Potter really is. But I mean institutionally, the Government is scared to death of a man who says no. Heck, if he gets away with it, what if others start doing it? They can't have that now. So, I feel like I'm caught between these two massive tides, and all I can do is watch as they come crashing together."

Deputy Markdale just winced a little as he thought of what was to come.

"I guess I'm just gonna build a little dike between those two forces of nature and see how it holds up… best I can do, I reckon."

The Sheriff smiled and put more thought into brushing the mare.

*   *   *

"So, this was what you were getting ready for, Dad?"

"I got us ready for a lot of different things, Tom."

"They want to arrest us? What did we do wrong? I just want to be left alone."

"It's ok, Tom. We can sit here a long time. We have food for over a year without gardening or hunting, we've got enough propane to last about that too. Maybe two years even."

"But they won't just let us sit here for two years will they, Dad? Otherwise you would have just locked the gate." Jane sat with her arms and legs crossed in the chair next to the wood stove. She was pouting, and he hadn't seen her do that in years.

"Yeah, Dad, why cut down all those trees to block the driveway? What do you think they'll do?"

"It's just to be ready, Tom. It keeps it from being easy for them is all."

"The real kicker in all this, Dad, is that I hadn't told you yet, but I was going to move out this weekend. Already put my part of the security deposit down. Guess I can kiss that good bye. I guess I should have seen this coming sooner. You've lost your mind."

"Why don't we just turn ourselves in, Dad?"

"Do you want to go to war or to prison, Tom? Because that's what happens if we just go turn ourselves in."

"We might as well be in prison if we're trapped up here."

"This is a great life here, Jane. You've loved coming up here for years."

"I've always tolerated it because I didn't really have a choice, did I? Now I'm 19 years old, and I feel like I'm being held hostage. I was so close to being out on my own. I stayed longer than I wanted to because I worried about you after Mom died. I didn't think you'd do something like this though."

"The world out there is really bad right now, Jane. Here, it's not bad. Here we are living in nature, and the deer don't care about the war. The elk don't worry about the draft. The bears just go about their day, and so will we."

"They are going to come for us, and you know that, Dad. What do we do then?" Jane was looking at him with her arms crossed. "Is that when it goes full on Ruby Ridge, or Waco where they burn us out?"

"Patton said *fixed fortifications are monuments to the stupidity of man*. If they come here for us we go mobile. I've taught you everything you need to know to survive for long periods of time in the wilderness. That knowledge and the caches will keep us alive a good long time. And there are plenty of people in this area who are sympathetic to our beliefs who will help us when we need it..."

"Your beliefs, Dad," she corrected.

Jeff sighed and leaned against the log wall. He looked down next to the door beside him and the rack of three carbines sitting in it. He had tried so long to gently ease them into being prepared. To never push it far enough they would worry excessively, but enough to teach them everything they needed to know. He tried to do it on a nearly subconscious level, so it would be tucked away in case they needed it.

"I have tried to impart on you two all the things you needed to live in a dangerous world without alarming you. I've tried to pass on my values. I've tried to do all this despite being gone so much."

His lip quivered a little as a notion of some kind of failure flashed through his mind. He buried it. Pushed it to the back little dark place in his mind where other such worthless thoughts could live without doing damage.

"We will get through this." He looked at the leather-bound Bible on the arm of his recliner on the other side of the room. He wanted to bring up God's part in all of this, but he knew it wasn't a good time. It would just make Jane push back even harder and that in itself brought that sense of failure close to the surface again.

"How, Dad? How do we get through this?"

That brought him back to the plan, shook him loose from the binding, heavy thought of having failed to teach the kids right. The plan could correct a lot of that, with God's help.

"We are presently under aerial surveillance. They'll spend weeks assessing our defenses and pattern of life. They'll surround us, probe our perimeters, then try to cut us off. Initially by siege. Eventually they'll grow impatient, and they'll move on us. When they do, we won't be here.

"I've already got the four-wheeler loaded up. We've only got the one, but it will carry everything we need so one or two people can walk without having to schlep a big pack. Jane knows where all the caches are. We'll have all the resupply we need to last a year out there. Eventually, we make contact with a sympathetic party and go from there."

"You already said we're under aerial surveillance, Dad. How do we even leave the cabin? I've seen all that drone footage, they can see in the dark. It doesn't matter what we do."

"These are early model Preds handed down to Department of Homeland Security from DoD a few years ago. All they've got is FLIR. It's sensitive to heat. They can see in the dark, but they can't see through walls or even dense tree cover. That's why I never cut the trees back at Tom's window. Remember when we did all that clearing a few years ago for fire mitigation? Well, I figured I could get those trees in a hurry if I needed to but they provide ample overhead cover back to the old mining trail which also has plenty of overhead cover. The Four-wheeler is in the mouth of the mine, ready to go. We can stay under tree cover to the old logging roads, they're just as over grown now. We'll be outside their coverage area before they even know we're gone. Then we have thousands of square miles of wilderness that they'll have to search."

"They'll bring dogs too, Dad."

"There's a lot of things we'll talk about in the next few days, Jane. We'll get through this."

She wouldn't look at him.

The chime for one of the solar powered motion sensors on the west trail went off.

Jeff grabbed his carbine and binoculars and headed for the outside stairs to the roof.

"It's probably just deer, Dad."

"I know, Tom, just gonna check."

He was out the door quickly, and once he got to the steps, he charged the AR and slung it so it hung ready across his chest. At the roof, he rested his elbows on the big log parapet and glassed downhill to the Western approach to the cabin.

A lone rider on a chestnut-colored mare. A man whose face was concealed by the brim of a tired Stetson. The rifle scabbard strapped to the saddle was conspicuously empty, but the man wore a six-gun low in a cowboy rig on his thigh. The man rode light and easy in the saddle, he wasn't out for anything but a quick trip. As he drew near, Potter made out the star clipped to the left breast of his Carhart. When the man lifted his head, Jeff saw the bearded face of Sheriff Grant Taylor.

Jeff lowered and shook his head, sighing to himself. After taking a moment, he scurried down the stairs.

As the Sheriff reigned the horse over to the gravel driveway, he saw Jeff waiting for him and smiled. Jeff kept his hands clear of the carbine across his chest, but he didn't think about taking it off.

"Sheriff," Jeff said coolly.

"Hey, Jeff." The older man raised his hands. "Just the old six gun for the mountain lions, basically unarmed in your book."

"I know. Saw you comin' a ways out."

"I figured."

"You're not here to take me in?"

"Federal warrant. I'm not interested."

"But the people who are interested are here now." Jeff pointed up and watched. He waited until the Sheriff saw the long slender wings set against the high overcast. "They've tried all kinds of paint schemes but under the right conditions, most airplanes still show up as a little black dot with wings. Kind of surprised I warrant my own Pred coverage, with the war on and the riots and everything. Been parked at about twelve thousand feet all day.

"How do you know?"

"Geometry, relative size. Clouds are at fifteen… you know this is all B.S., Sheriff."

The Sheriff nodded.

"I know, but the Feds… you know how they get. That letter you sent… Well, they couldn't have let that go now, what would others do? They'll make an example out of you, Jeff, and there's only so much I can do to slow them down. I've tried to tell them they're making a mistake."

"I appreciate that, Sheriff. I really do."

"People are going to die over this, Jeff."

"People are dying right now, Sheriff. Just not my kids. Shouldn't be any of ours dying over this. This is a war of *their* making, send *their* kids."

"You know what I mean, Jeff. Here, now."

"If we don't stand up to them here, now… Then where and when?"

The Sheriff nodded and leaned on the saddle horn as the horse jostled a bit.

"It's real easy, Sheriff. They leave me alone here, no one gets hurt. They come here after my kids… That's a different story. They send you to try to talk me down?"

The Sheriff smiled a moment and shook his head.

"Nope, they didn't know I was coming out here, guess they do now." He looked up to the Predator. "Imagine I'll catch hell for it when I get back."

"Why did you come, Sheriff?"

"Somebody had to try to talk to you. *I* had to try to talk to you. This has a high likelihood of going badly, Jeff. I don't want that for anyone, not even the FBI dweebs, but most of all I don't want it to go badly for you or your kids. How old are they now?"

"Tom's 18, Jane's 19."

"Always so fast. Seems like just last year I got called to the middle school for that incident with Jane."

Jeff winced and shrugged a little.

"Well, that little bastard had it coming," the Sheriff laughed. "She choked him out cold. I think he liked her... of course, his family had just moved up from California and wanted to make some kind of federal case of it. They were screaming lawyers and news media and funding my competition in the next election. I can't believe they are considering drafting her, Jeff. I swear sending her into battle against the Russians or the Chinese would have to be against the Geneva Convention or something."

Jeff laughed with the Sheriff.

"There's no talkin' you down off this mountain is there, Jeff?"

"No, Sir. Appreciate your comin' up though."

"And the kids won't come out?"

Jeff shook his head.

"It has to stop, Sheriff. The insanity of this war. The policies that led to it. There is no way we are ready for what's coming as a nation."

"I imagine we weren't ready before Pearl Harbor either, Jeff."

"We don't have the industrial base to spool up we had then, it's been shipped off to China. Our military has been emasculated in every way, and they think that's a good thing. They promote diversity over competence for the sake of politics, and they have developed risk aversion to the level of institutional cowardice."

"What's that they say, Jeff? You go to war with the army you have, not the one you want, or something like that. Maybe some harsh reality will do us some good."

"At what cost, Sheriff? It goes beyond the military. There was a time when initiative and a little daring meant a lot in America. Now they've domesticated us. They want dogs, not wolves."

The Sheriff sighed and shook his head.

"I can't argue with a thing you've said, Jeff. But others won't see it that way. They are going to make you out to be some shell-shocked vet, some guy who's gone unhinged out in the woods, or worse."

"It's war, there will be heroes made and villains revealed, lots of villains to go around. But truth… Truth is gonna be hard to come by, Sheriff."

"That's a fact, Jeff. We need men like you now more than ever."

Jeff smiled.

"For what, Sheriff?"

"I think the war that's comin' is bigger than they are planning on. If you and the kids come down with me now, I'll do everything I can to protect you all. Maybe you get some time in the federal pen, you can handle yourself there. Maybe the kids wind up doing service in Job Corps or something. They say they're not all going to combat, they just trying to put people to work."

"Listen to what you just said, Sheriff. You're a good man, I know that much about you, but listen to the talking points you just rattled off. I don't believe any of that. Do you? I know that's what they are telling people. But look at the realities that we know are true.

"Essential services are falling apart, the supply chain failing, power grid dropping off line, the social contract is broken. The gears that keep our civilization going are grinding to a halt. It's not the end of the world we're facing, it's the end of the western world. It's the end of the United States as we know it. If people think things are bad with America in charge, just wait until they see who rushes to fill the void. China? Some one-world government that the World Economic Forum types try to install? So, they've got themselves a world war, and they want my kids to go fight it? No."

The Sheriff sighed and slumped a little. He had done all he could, had done more than some would think he should, but it wasn't going to be enough.

"How much time do we have, Sheriff?"

"Not as much as you'd think. I'm not one to be easily impressed by Feds, but these guys are pretty far beneath even my low expectations. Your abatis really threw them."

"What agencies and how many?"

The Sheriff laughed.

"I've promised them if they stay within the boundaries of the law and reasonable ethics in this investigation, I'm not going to give anything away. And for your solace, I'm not going to give them anything I see or have heard here today beyond what they can see with their damn drone. I've got to let them think I've given them something, or they'll consider me compromised, and I won't be in a position to help later."

"Roger that."

"Godspeed, Jeff."

"God help us all, Sheriff."

The Sheriff gave a tip of his hat, pulled on the reins and wheeled the horse around to return the same route from which he came.

CHAPTER 4

Prather was waiting for Booth who was still a few minutes behind. He didn't have the fortitude to start without him. As he waited he looked around the Sheriff's office. There was a noticeable lack of an "I Love Me Wall." One wall was dominated by a map of the county and state. Another with photographs of horses. The wall behind the Sheriff's desk was a bookshelf filled with legal books and a cased revolver with a nickel finish that looked like an old Western cowboy gun, but Prather didn't know about such things. He didn't know what the certificate that was in the presentation case was about either, but he could read the letters "SASS" that stood out bold and in a larger font.

Finally, Booth was buzzed in behind him.

Prather had been disinterested in small talk, and now he was steeled by the presence of his partner.

"What the hell were you thinking, Sheriff?" It was almost a yell, and a vein was popping up in Prather's forehead.

"I'm sorry? What are we talking about here?"

Booth silently dropped a surveillance photo on the Sheriff's desk. Taylor was waiting for that.

It showed him on his horse talking to Potter.

"Oh, that."

"Explain yourself." Prather was working up a sweat.

"I just thought someone should try to talk him down before you guys go all Michael Bay on him."

"And?" Booth inquired.

"He said no."

"No, what?"

"He's not coming down, he's not letting anyone take his kids. He just wants to be left alone for a while is all."

"What can you tell us about his preparations, has he fortified his position?"

"Oh, heck, he doesn't need to fortify that place. It's over a hundred years old and built from huge old logs, you won't penetrate that place with anything less than a .50 cal. It's an old miner's cabin, built before the big fire here about a hundred ten years ago. It survived that, it's gonna take more than what you can pack in one helicopter to burn the place down."

"We don't intend to burn that place down," Booth said sternly.

"Oh, well that's good to know because that's how these things seem to end with you guys a lot of times."

Prather steamed but didn't say anything.

"Are we compromised, Sheriff?" Booth asked plainly.

"Would I go with you if we were?"

"I guess that would depend on the level of compromise, wouldn't it?"

"I suppose so." The Sheriff leaned forward, his elbows on his desk. "I told you, and I told Potter, I'm not giving away anything as long as you operate within the bounds of the law. Is this investigation going to be conducted within the bounds of the Constitution?"

"Of course," Booth said steadfastly.

The Sheriff held up his hands.

"Then no problem."

Prather stammered, and Booth spoke over him.

"There is a problem, Sheriff. You went cowboy on us, rode up there on your horse without a plan, you may have alerted him to our presence… put him on guard. You make a big noise about trying not to cost lives. This raid is dependent on speed and violence of action to preserve life."

"Bull." The Sheriff leaned forward, suddenly serious. "He's already aware of your presence. He's seen your drones. And he's spent the better part of his adult life on guard. No matter what you do, he'll be ready for us, and he's already three steps ahead of us."

"Alright, Sheriff Taylor. Here's your chance, you lay out a course of action. What would you have us do?"

The Sheriff didn't hesitate.

"Maintain aerial surveillance, leave it at that. Let him know you're watching. Then leave them the heck alone."

"That's it, Sheriff?" Booth was grinning. "It's that simple to you, really?"

"Yes."

"Well, the world is a complicated place now a days, Sheriff Taylor. There are pressures and influences that can't be ignored here."

"We allow the world to be complicated so that we have an excuse to not stand up for the simplicities that life is really based on. The law is the law and shouldn't be shaped by *pressures and influences.* The Constitution is designed to protect people like the Potters, whether you or I agree with them or not. It's not meant to be leveraged to protect you and I if we go up that mountain and kill them. The badge is not a shield to separate us from our moral obligations to protect our citizens from abuses of the law."

*   *   *

The large log parapet was an artifact of the original lean-to roof. It was over two feet in diameter and was still in excellent condition, compared to the rest of the original roof. When he lost his job, Jeff spent most of his time cleaning and restoring the old cabin. He had the roof replaced with a steeply sloped metal A-frame roof for better snow shedding and fire mitigation. The walls of the post and beam original construction were all still sound and solid.

The condition of the original roof had allowed for years of moisture and assorted rodent intrusion, and Jeff's initial efforts were on cleaning up the mess and making it a sanitary and livable space. He built a basic subfloor himself with a few hidden compartments. Then built walls to allow three small bedrooms at the back of the cabin. In the thick walls of each room he cut holes to allow for the installation of windows that would open to allow for summertime ventilation and emergency egress.

The last few years had all been in preparation for something. He hadn't really imagined this, but he was as ready for it as he could be, and now it just had to happen.

He had filled over 400 sandbags with the help of the bucket on the tractor. A ladder and some traffic cones allowed him to fill five at a time. And the kids had helped, and he had told them they were for landscaping and drainage purposes, and many were. Now, however, they stood properly flattened and stacked on a purpose-built rack in front of the front and side windows. Not all the way up, but enough.

Because the space behind the parapet was not enough to really be considered a balcony, he had only ever bothered to put a large round of unsplit pine there for a seat. Instead of his favored precipice, now he came here. He didn't want to leave the immediate area of the cabin because he figured they would come soon. If they were smart, they would try to come at night, but from what the Sheriff had said, there was no banking on the intellect of the ones he was dealing with. That could make them more unpredictable.

He cradled the now ever-present carbine and looked out down the valley across the pine covered slopes. The carbine was no different than the other two. An Eotech, sighted in to his eyes, a Streamlight with a simple butt cap switch mounted on the left, all on a dependable, quality Daniel Defense AR-15 with a 16-inch barrel.

He was accustomed to shorter barrels and suppressors, but that would mean federal paperwork and additional cost. The guns were an absolute last resort, and since suppressors weren't really silencers, if it came to it, he would just be loud.

All this time, Jeff had eschewed social media. Tried to spend as little time as possible on the internet, but now he was thinking that, like the carbines, being loud didn't really matter. In fact, it just occurred to him that being loud might be of service to him. Maybe he could exploit the internet to get the word out. People would support them, maybe help even.

Jeff shook his head. He wasn't trying to start a movement. He was just trying to protect his kids.

Instead, all electronics would have to go dark soon. All cell phones and internet were going to have to go down. He wasn't quite ready for that fight with them. Especially Jane. He'd educated them on the tracking and surveillance ramifications of personal electronic devices. Tom was better equipped to go without them. Except for games, and soon there would be other things to occupy his time.

Bowing his head, he clasped his hand.

"God help me, I'm trying to do right here. Trying to do right by the kids. Please help them see it." The only sound in reply was the wind washing through the pines and the flapping of the flags. The US flag that flew was one of a few he had left that had accompanied him on missions overseas. He had vowed not to take this one down until the current regime left office. So, its fabric was faded but not its meaning. Below it, now snapping in the increasing wind, a battered Gadsen. Its edges were well frayed but the coiled snake and the words; *Don't Tread On Me* still clear.

"God help our country, we are in real trouble here. For all our faults, for all we've done wrong in the past. A world without the real America is in trouble. I see that, God, a lot of us do. Maybe not enough. Maybe I didn't see it soon enough to do the right things. Forgive me Lord, for my greed those times when I thought chasing a paycheck mattered so much. Forgive me for my lust, those times when I wandered. God forgive me most for not bringing my kids to you and leaving them lost. I taught them everything I could to survive in this wilderness before me here, but in this wilderness of the world gone mad, I've failed…"

He was interrupted by the sound of footsteps on the stairs.

It was Tom, carbine slung over his back. Jeff was proud of the boy, finally starting to listen to him, but ultimately ashamed of himself in the realization that he had failed in the most important ways.

"Dad." The boy spoke quietly as he always did, and the only reason Jeff and his battle-damaged hearing could process what he had said was by catching the movement of his lips.

"Tom."

The boy said something else, but it was lost in the wind and was really more of a mumble anyway.

Jeff smiled.

"Speak up for me, Tommy... Tom." The boy had made it clear that he didn't like the Tommy moniker that he considered a holdover from childhood. Jeff pointed to his ears and shook his head a little. "They just don't work as well as they used to."

"Dad, why was the Sheriff here?"

Jeff paused. He tried to treat the boy like the young man that he really was, but it wasn't easy. To Jeff, Tommy would always be his boy. Any of the things he saw as Tom's shortcomings, Jeff blamed on himself. As he considered Jane to just be a tomboy in a world gone by, Tom would be considered just a little different. It wasn't a lack of intellect, the boy was very well read. It was merely a lack of application. What Jeff told him was always with this in mind.

"He came to talk about the way things are going, Tom."

"He wasn't here to arrest us?"

"No, Tom." Jeff was taken aback by this question. Tom didn't always openly address the realities of circumstance. Like when he shut down and wouldn't talk for a month when his mother died. Was this a break through, or at least progress?

"Jane said the FBI or somebody will come for us... But the Sheriff, he should too, right?"

Jeff was glad they had been talking together. He'd long given up that Tom should come to him for everything and was just glad when there was indication he was at least talking to *someone*.

"The Sheriff is a good man, he won't enforce bad laws. He came here to warn me of what's coming."

"What's coming, Dad?"

The wind sang stronger through the pines and tugged harder at the flags, and Jeff took his time formulating his answer.

"What's coming, Tom, are men who will enforce bad laws. Men who will blindly follow orders, men who will hide behind a badge. The Sheriff is none of those things. Understand that. Understand that if things go badly, and you don't know anyone you can trust, you can trust Sheriff Taylor."

Tom just nodded a little, absorbing what Jeff had said. He had his carbine slung across his chest and rested both hands on the buttstock as he looked out across the parapet down through the valley. He looked at ease with the AR, a testament to all the thousands upon thousands of rounds Jeff had supervised him putting through such firearms. The one thing Jeff had done right, he thought to himself.

Or was that right?

More time on the spiritual and less on the physical… Jeff pushed that back to one of those dark corners. He'd done what he had, what he thought was best at the time. Prepared as best he could with everything.

"The sandbags in the windows, Dad. They were never for landscaping, were they? You knew this was all coming, didn't you?"

"No, Tom. I never wanted this." Jeff leaned back against the log behind him. "Maybe, I did know, on some level this would come. I didn't invite this, and I would have been happier starting to use those sandbags to establish terraces for some wild flower gardens. In my mind, that was what I really wanted. But, maybe on another level I knew it couldn't really be the outcome. The world I've seen and the world I've wanted have never been the same, and I've always operated in the world I've seen."

Jeff was drifting off now and talking more to himself, and he felt the sting of a new sore on his left arm near the shoulder. He stopped talking and felt the emerging sore near his deltoid under his t-shirt. Another one, so soon. Another bone fragment coming to the surface so soon. He shook his head and waited a long while for Tom to say something.

He didn't. Wordlessly, and without any visible display of emotion, he simply turned and walked back down the stairs.

"God help us." Jeff bowed his head against the barrel of his AR.

*   *   *

"It's tonight, Sheriff."

Taylor was groggy, he'd awakened to the driveway alarm being tripped and had just enough time to throw on his robe and a shoulder holster with his Sig 220 and a flashlight as he watched the caravan of Suburbans pull up to his door. He had opened the door with a shake of his head as he realized it was the Feds.

Now his brain was catching up with what they said.

"Wait, what do you mean?"

"Grab your battle rattle, Sheriff," the voice he now recognized as Booth's said.

"I don't have *Battle Rattle,* Booth. Give me a couple of minutes, I'll grab my plate carrier and patrol rifle though."

"Whatever you want to call it, Sheriff. And if you don't mind, I'd like to come with you."

"What do you mean, come with me, Booth?"

"I'd just like to accompany you so there aren't any compromising phone calls made. Purely for OPSEC, Sheriff, I'm sure you understand."

"Oh, for goodness sake, Booth." The Sheriff realized he was squinting because they had stationed the Suburbans in front of his house with the headlights and probably a spotlight or two on the doorway.

"Why do you even want me to come?"

"I don't." Booth said flatly.

"Well, you're gonna need a warrant to come into my house, Booth."

Another voice took over that sounded distantly familiar and far less curt than Booth's. Taylor realized by the silhouettes they were all in full raid attire, to include helmets and mounted night vision goggles.

"Hey, Sheriff, it's me, Carver, US Marshals."

"Can we kill all the lights here, guys?"

"Booth, come on, I'll deal with this…" Carver stepped up to the Sheriff, and Taylor backed up to give the Marshal some room.

"You can come in Carver, no one else."

The Marshal glared at the FBI men who reluctantly acquiesced and stepped back from the doorway.

Taylor shut the door as soon as Carver was through the threshold and turned on the living room light.

"That's quite the look there, Sheriff. No fuzzy slippers?"

"I'm not in the mood, Carver. What the heck is going on?"

"I'm not gonna lie, Sheriff, it's an absolute cluster in the making. We're gonna brief at the airport when the helo gets there."

"What is with all the secret squirrel crap?"

"It's their way."

"No, it's more than that, Carver."

"They don't trust you, Grant. They don't trust you, but they are so short on people they can't really even cover the structure much less make entry. This has all the makings of something going real bad."

"Yeah, no kidding, I've been saying that for a couple of weeks now."

"Well, you really pissed them off going up to talk to him. They've accelerated their timeline and they've got weather moving in they're trying to beat."

"Oh great, a bad plan and they are going to rush it."

"It's worse than that, a bad plan is at least a plan, there is no *plan*, Grant."

They were interrupted by a woman's voice calling from the bedroom.

"Grant, is everything OK?"

"Yes, honey, go back to sleep, just gotta go on a late call," Taylor yelled back to the room.

He turned and looked more perturbed at the Marshal.

"I have to go put some clothes on. My wife is in bed back there, you can wait here."

The Marshal nodded.

"They're just afraid you're gonna call Potter to give him a heads up."

"I have told them all along, they make this a legal and righteous operation, I'm right there with them, but they are making it really hard to trust them."

"I know, Grant. I don't like any of this, and I'm not sure how this Prather kid weaseled his way into this. This should be my case, and you know I wouldn't run it this way."

"That's probably why it's not your case, Carver. Did you think of that?"

"I know, I know."

"I'm going to throw some clothes on and grab my rifle, my raid gear is out in the truck, I'll just be a minute. I'm not going to call Potter."

The Marshal nodded, and the Sheriff looked at him a moment. He wanted to say more, but it didn't matter.

*   *   *

It was cool enough to warrant a fire, but the back rooms didn't heat as well as the front room so he always ran it a little hotter than he needed to. Jeff left his crocs on the floor and propped his bare feet up on the little ottoman. He was just wearing his shorts he called Ranger panties (which always made Jane cringe) and a T-shirt and was plenty warm with the fire.

He looked up from the Bible in his lap, in the glow of the oil lamp across the room to the little scrap lumber tree he built to hold his plate carrier and helmet at the ready. The ballistic helmet was topped off with dual tube Night Observation Devices, ANVIS-9's that had been his preference when he was in, and Active Noise Reducing electric ear protection, stowed along the side.

Jeff took a break from reading. Everything was as ready as it could be. It would happen as it was meant to now. He was trying to adjust his sleep cycle. He'd stay up as late as he could tonight. He tried not to speculate on a timeline, they would come at a time of their choosing now, but it was really too soon. They would want to develop more intel.

Laying the Bible on the wide armrest of the chair, he stood up and crossed the room to the kitchenette to freshen his mug of black coffee. He could feel the cozy embrace of sleep trying to wrap itself around him and the consoling words of the Bible, even Revelations, as it were, comforting him to a level of relaxation that made his body too ready for sleep too soon.

Rubbing his face, he poured the fresh mug.

No sugar, no cream, nothing fancy. Just a bitter taste and heat and caffeine. Crossing the room again he set the hot mug down on the little table beside the chair and turned his attention to the wood stove.

It wasn't quite necessary yet, but he tossed in another round of wood and adjusted the vents. Tending the wood stove was more art that should have been more science, but it had a tendency to befuddle him when he was tired, and he played with it longer than he really needed to for results that would really be negligible to the efficiency of the fire.

Looking at the oil lamp and then back to the fire, he considered returning to the Bible for a moment, but knew reading anymore would put him to sleep within fifteen minutes at this point.

Reaching up, he turned the wick down and blew across the chimney to the palm of his hand. The main room of the cabin flickered in the light of the fire of the wood stove, the light dancing across the roundness of the big logs and reaching out to the dark corners with a nearly strobing affect.

He adjusted the chair to watch the flames TV style. Settling into the comfortable chair he picked up the coffee as he looked for pareidolia in the fire to keep awake. Sipping at the coffee, the sore above his arm twinged. Jeff's mind left the fire for a moment, and he reached up to the spot on his shoulder. Shaking his head, he could feel it was time. He squeezed at the sore until the bone fragment came out. It was a small one, but it gave him that sickening feeling none the less.

He couldn't even look at it.

He stood and stepped to the woodstove, opening the glass door with the spring handle. He flicked the offensive intruder into the heat of the flame, hoping for a sense of purification, but settling for the relief of just being rid of it. Jeff closed the door and resumed his seat and tried again to find entertainment in the lapping of the flames.

Instead the heat and the light and the fatigue carried him back to a place he never wanted to go again. But, he so often wound up there. It was a time he couldn't let go and an event that would never release him.

That dusty village just outside of Konduz.

The Ktah Khas were completing their callouts, and over the net he'd heard they had collected 4 MAMs, three women and two children in the front of the compound's courtyard. Four Military Aged Males. That was the number they were expecting.

He was holding a security point along the backwall, and as the Afghans began their search of the compound a small figure appeared.

He had his NODs swung up out of the way, the Op was taking longer than scheduled, and the Afghans chose to proceed with it despite the increasing brilliance of the morning sun. It was hot already, and the figure appeared to be an adolescent. He looked… uncertain, almost lost. Perhaps he was confused and disoriented by the callouts over the loudspeaker.

When Jeff had a clear view of the boy, he sighed.

"Zero Eight, Zero Five, you got a guy coming your way, you got 'im?" Jeff's earpiece crackled.

The boy had the epicanthic folds and brachycephaly of someone suffering from severe Down's Syndrome, but when Jeff went out over the net all he could think to say was;

"Yeah, I got him… Looks like a retarded kid." Jeff inhaled, that might wind up coming out in the hot wash.

"Dude," The sniper broke radio protocol with palpable urgency. "that kid's fucking wired… I don't have a shot angle. Jeff, you gotta take him."

The sniper overwatch called it just as the Afghan kid smiled at Jeff, who had stepped out from cover to motion him back. The kid smiled wide, like he had just found his new best friend. As he turned a little, Jeff could see the bulk of the S-vest. The wire trailing from the dead-man switch taped to his hand now visible.

"Take him Zero Eight!" the sniper yelled over the net. Jeff didn't think about all the lives behind him and the vehicles and the exfil route that he was positioned to protect. He didn't think about how close he was to the boy who continued walking toward him. He didn't think about the innocence of the boy's smile and the evil treachery that would strap a bomb to such a vulnerable soul.

Jeff didn't think at all.

He thumbed the safety off the HK and planted the reticle on the kid's forehead, offset a little to account for the angle. The trigger squeeze was a whisper of instinct born of a voice of muscle memory of a hundred thousand repetitions. Jeff didn't even hear the discharge of the suppressed 5.56 mm round.

The height over bore put the bullet right between the kid's eyes, obliterating the brainstem and inducing instant, flaccid paralysis.

The kid was dead before he started to fall.

But when he hit the ground, the dead-man switch released, or compressed or whatever mechanism was required, and the suicide vest detonated with a white light and a shock that was the last thing Jeff remembered before waking up in Landstuhl.

There, the doctors informed him of the shrapnel injuries. Of the ball bearing that had dismantled his shoulder to such a degree that it would never be the same. And of the bone fragments of the little boy who had smiled like he had found, in Jeff, just the friend he needed, and that he would carry that shrapnel of bone slivers of a vulnerable little boy inside his body for the rest of his life.

CHAPTER 5

It was after midnight, and the briefing was occurring on the hot hood of one of the Suburbans next to the DHS Astar helicopter, it's turbines still winding down. Under the head lamps, Booth, who was clearly in charge of the raid, was addressing the pilot, looking at various pages of different scales of the Grid Reference Graphics of Potter's cabin.

"If you can put us between the cabin and the flag pole, it will be a lot faster. Can you do it? He has the flag pole illuminated with solar lighting, should be easy to see."

"The other side would be a less confined space, but, ah, yeah I should be able to put you there."

The other helicopter crewman spoke up.

"I'll be able to record IR of the event and can provide you guys real time updates, I'm assuming you're gonna be on the Federal Cooperative Net?"

"Ah, no." Booth said over the headlamp hung round his neck. "We'll be on FBI Secure. You guys don't have that one, do you?"

"No."

"Well, we'll be on your aircraft internal 'till we step off, just update us through the approach. Except for the Sheriff, we'll all be able to communicate with each other on the ground. Marshals will cover the rear of the structure. Prather, the Sheriff and I will make entry."

"What if you can't breach the door?" the Sheriff asked.

"Window two here should be accessible from ground level, that will be our immediate fall back. Good question, Sheriff."

"What if there is movement from the structure on our approach?" the helicopter observer asked.

"Light him up with your searchlight. Blind him. That will really make it easier for us. Take him down outside, then clear the house and the kids. I don't expect a fight from them."

"Why not?" the Sheriff asked

"They're not the type to fight, it seems"

The Sheriff shrugged, but offered nothing else.

"Overhead ISR coverage while we are inbound to target?" The pilot looked up at the moon, threatened by clouds.

"No guarantees, they'll be up on the co-op net, but we're trying to beat this storm."

"You know, we wait a while for this storm to pass, they'll still be there, Booth. They aren't going anywhere."

"We are moving on this because of *you*, Sheriff," Prather said sharply. "We have to keep him off balance."

The Sheriff laughed, what else was there left to do?

"I think we're the ones off balance, *Vince*."

The Sheriff donned his plate carrier.

"What about back up?" he asked.

"We just don't have resources available for a QRF."

The Sheriff snugged the plate carrier in place adjusting the Velcro.

"That's a Quick Reaction Force." Prather said.

"Yeah, Vince, I know what it is. Real cops just need back up, and we don't even have that. If things go bad? If this thing has a chip light or something and has to set down before we get there?"

"Weather should hold for most of our infil," Booth said. "if something happens, we can coordinate through the Pred, call sign Covey One-Two, even if they lose sight of us. Salt Lake Field Office is standing by."

"Salt Lake?" the Sheriff said incredulously as he looked at Carver.

"I let Billings know. We got some guys in Missoula right now, but we'd have to scramble to get lift."

"Let me get the Two Bear Air guys on standby." The Sheriff pleaded as he pulled out his cell phone.

"No, Sheriff. Not a civilian outfit, no way. My field office said we could get the Air Force guys out of Fairchild if things really go sideways. And don't bother with the cell phone, we have an overhead asset that is jamming that location now."

"Are the Air Force guys stood up for this? Are they at least *aware* of this?"

"Salt Lake Field Office is taking care of all that," Prather said. "What is that, Sheriff?"   The Sheriff looked down at the center of his plate carrier where Prather was pointing to the little box with a lens on it.

"It's a body cam, Vince."

"Ah, no Sheriff, that has to come off. The helo's FLIR system will document everything we need for evidentiary purpose."

The Sheriff looked at Marshal Carver who said nothing.

"Well, I'm not taking the damn thing off. Anything else I should know here?"

"Ah, stack order for entry. You'll be in the door first, Sheriff." Booth smiled a little. "Since you have some rapport with Potter, we're hoping you'll keep him from shooting."

*   *   *

The creaking door woke Jeff. In the dim light of the fire's coals, and through sleep filled eyes, he could see Jane trying to slip past him with a backpack on over her shoulder. He sat up straight as he could in the big chair and tried to assess what he was seeing.

"What are you doing, Jane?"

"Um." She looked caught and a little scared, then some anger flared in her eyes. "I guess, I'm… escaping. It's the only thing left for me to do."

"What do you mean?"

"I mean, I feel like I have to flee in the night. Kaylee is down on the road waiting for me. I told her it was going to be a hike, and I had to wait 'til you were asleep." She looked at her phone. "Now it looks like I lost signal… I hate this place."

"I told you, you could go anytime you wanted to." Jeff wiped his eyes. "You didn't need to *flee in the night*. You didn't need to call your ex-*girlfriend*…"

"The hell I didn't. I'm not walking thirty miles to town. And I couldn't talk to you about it. Or Tom for that matter, he's started to buy into all of it. I don't. I'm going, and I'm going on my terms.

Somewhere in the distant darkness of the night, Jeff detected the familiar mechanical pulsing sound that began pushing in from the periphery of his awareness as he dealt with his daughter.

"Always *the drama*, always the *I'm a victim* crap. I tried… your Mom tried… we tried so hard to raise you better than that."

"You've never accepted me for…"

"I've always loved you… would do anything for you…" As the pulsing vibration echoed from the valley and across the logs of the cabin it was thrust to the forefront of his consciousness, and he spoke the word that came instantly to his mind.

"Helicopter."

"It's probably just a medivac, Dad. Geez, you need to mellow out, really."

He moved faster than she thought he could, crossing the big room of the cabin in what seemed like a single bound. Before she could react, he had snatched the iPhone from her hands and stomped it under his bare heel. Picking it up like the carcass of something dead, he carried it to the wood stove, opened the spring handle and tossed it in the firebox, followed by some thinner pieces of wood.

"What the hell, Dad? I'm pretty sure that's illegal, like a domestic violence charge or something."

"They are coming for us. Sooner than I would have guessed, but…"

"No one is coming for us… no one is going to help. That's exactly why I'm leaving." Tears were welling up in her eyes as her well-practiced tough façade began to crack.

Jeff's heart faltered as he stepped into his Crocs by the chair. He then stepped to the body armor tree.

Tom was up and at his door, awakened by Jane's yelling.

"What's happening?"

"They're coming, grab your go-bags, jackets, boots and carbines."

"No one is coming, Tom! Dad has lost his mind… he's really crazy. He hears a medivac helicopter, and he's so paranoid he thinks they are coming for us."

Jeff was slinking into his plate carrier and then strapping on his helmet as he spoke.

"I don't have time to argue, that's not any of our local medivac helicopters, that's something different. Grab your gear, go out Tom's window and get to the mine, I'll buy us some time."

"Dad…" He could hear only disbelief in Jane's voice, and in the next words, she sounded like a little girl again, and he knew in that instant the plan had changed.

"Dad, no…"

*   *   *

The turbines were spinning up in the darkness, the rotors stopped magically as they went through a certain speed by the strobe lights. The machine was in motion. Everything was.

"Come on, Sheriff," the voice said through the David Clark headsets he wore. "We'll be first off."

It was Booth talking, sitting next to Prather on the floor with their feet out the open doorway leaning on the skid with a strap across them.

"You two look a little crowded there, and I'm not nearly as high speed, low drag as you guys. I spent a little time in the Army doing this kind of thing, and I just remember dynamic rollover I think they called it… Anyway, I'm not sure what it was, but it wound up with soldiers in the doors losing legs."

"Brian's a good stick here, Sheriff. Don't need to worry about stuff like that." The helicopter sensor operator's voice trailed off with a bit of a laugh. The pilot chimed in with a matter of fact confidence in his voice as the helo lifted off and started forward motion.

"Nineteen-minute time of flight, gentlemen."

As the lights of the airport and town slipped behind the helicopter, and the cool air bit more with the increase in speed, Taylor looked at his watch instinctively to mark time, then he just closed his eyes and accepted the darkness. His old helmet was in his lap as the intercom wasn't compatible with his hearing protection, and he couldn't fit the David Clark headset over or under it. So, while the others had their NVGs down and were all plugged comfortably into the intercom, enjoying the flight below the mountain tops in various shades of green, he just closed his eyes, eager for the whole thing to be over.

He leaned on his patrol rifle, muzzle down lest a negligently discharged round hit something important overhead, namely the engine.

"ISR just went blind. Drone is reporting they just went one hundred percent obscured by cloud layer," the sensor operator said. "They can't descend through the layer due to icing. They are reporting bases at ten-thousand, so weather shouldn't be an issue for us, and there was no activity at the cabin before the clouds rolled in. What do you wish to do, Special Agent Prather?"

"Press on."

Taylor just shook his head. So many links in the chain that could have been broken to prevent what was about to happen.

"Ten minutes out," called the pilot.

*　　*　　*

"They are coming *here*. They are coming for *us*, Jane. Just go out Tom's window now, both of you. I'll meet you at the southern cache in a few days. But you need to go now and remember to stay under the tree cover, remember everything I've taught you, both of you."

Jeff was standing in front of the door in his helmet, plate carrier, T-shirt, Ranger panties and Crocs. The carbine slung across his chest added to the absurdity and insanity that Jane saw, but as the rumble of the helicopter became a roar, it was clear he was right.

Turning to the door he inhaled and said loudly enough to be heard over the sound of the helicopter one last time;

"Go."

As he opened the door, he held his hands high and was instantly silhouetted by a blinding searchlight. All the things he had ever done wrong, all the mistakes he had ever made, he felt he could now make right in one shining, proper moment, and no one would have to die.

*　*　*

The Sheriff was switching to his helmet as the helicopter drastically slowed forward motion. He just about had the headset off as the helicopter began to flare aggressively.

All he heard was someone say over the intercom one word;

Gun.

Taylor scrambled to buckle the helmet in place and held one earcup of the headset to his ear. Leaning out over Booth's shoulder he saw, illuminated in the Astar's Night Sun, Jeff Potter, framed by the doorway with his hands raised high away from the rifle.

Special Agent's Booth and Prather were shouldering their rifles.

"No!" Taylor yelled into night, then scrambled to get the boom microphone in front of his lips. "No! No!"

But that intercom transmission was lost to the long bursts of gun fire from each of the Special Agent's assault rifles.

*　*　*

After the initial shock of the impacting rounds, a wave of anger flushed through Jeff Potter's very being. It would fire him, sustain him as the blood was quickly departing. By the time he'd hit the ground, he had the safety off and was firing from the supine as fast as he could squeeze the trigger.

The Astar wobbled in its flare. Jeff would never know if he made good hits or if the pilot flinched, but the helo slid back just far enough for the tail rotor to catch the flag pole. Something significant separated from the helicopter and it started a violent spin and rapidly rolled to its right side. The crash of metal and distressed turbines concluded with an unnatural quiet, aside from the few pieces of the machine still falling and hitting the ground.

Tom rushed forward to his father.

"That's a lot of blood, Dad." The boy said nothing further as he ripped open the Bear IFAK on Jeff's plate carrier. He pulled out the CAT tourniquet and quickly set it high on Jeff's right leg where the femoral had clearly been severed by one of the gunshot wounds.

"Jane, you're going to need to get that pressure bandage and packing gauze into that wound in his shoulder," Tom said as he cranked at the windlass.

While Jane's ears were still ringing from the gunfire, she still heard what Tom said, she was just frozen by the scene and what had just happened..

Jeff winced and cried out at the pain of the tourniquet as it seemed to overwhelm the pain of the gunshot wounds. The smell of gunpowder, and blood and dust and freshly splintered wood hung in the air.

"Hurry, Jane. We don't have much time." Jane was shocked at the violence before her, at the gore, and at her brother suddenly seeing through such an event to take charge.

She ripped open the packaging she pulled from the Bear IFAK as Tom locked the windlass and checked the pedal pulse.

Jeff was just conscious enough to be surprised too.

"Good job, Tom… now you both need to go, OK?" He was pleading with them. "Take my helmet, the NODs will help. Leave now before they regroup. Remember, you're not equipped for a fight, but you can *run*. *Run now*."

*   *   *

The Sheriff was amid a pile of bodies as he unbuckled. He could hear the sensor operator up front swearing and frantically running an emergency shutdown hoping to mitigate fire risk.

"Brian's dead," the man yelled up front as he extricated himself from his seat and awkwardly egressed the door now above him. The Sheriff assessed that the front right of the helicopter had taken most of the damage, and there was an overwhelming smell of jet fuel and torn open guts.

He realized the bodies on top of him were moving. The two Marshals were struggling to get out the left door that was now above them. He also realized the one body below him was not moving. Turning on the headlamp around his neck, Taylor realized it was Prather, and he was pinned by the legs in the wreckage. Feeling where the legs and the helicopter came together, Taylor's hand came back bloody. He couldn't see Prather's Individual First Aid Kit so he pulled his own tourniquet.

"Carver, anybody, pass me another tourniquet. Prather's pinned by the legs here and losing a lot of blood."

A hand reached down from above with a CAT into the light of his headlamp.

"You need help in there, Sheriff?"

"I could sure use it, but there's no room." Taylor had the first tourniquet snaked through the wreck and around the leg. He cinched it down tight with the windlass and Prather made some kind of noise and contorted a little in pain. Locking in the windlass, he quickly repeated that procedure on the other leg.

"Hey, I've only got Prather here, we need to find Booth. Are you two OK?"

Carver's voice yelled in response, and Taylor could sense that he and Prather were the only ones left alive in the wreck.

"We're good, Sheriff. The one DHS guy is out and he's good. We're checking on Booth. He's out here, breathing, but unconscious."

"OK, I can't tell if this stopped the bleeding or not, Prather is entrapped, both legs. He's breathing but I don't think he's conscious. I'm coming out."

Climbing up out of the broken machine, he dropped to the ground next to Carver. There was some kind of solar ground light the helicopter had crashed next to, and it provided an eerie glow through the still unsettled dust.

His NODs had detached from his helmet, the lanyard had apparently broken, and he had no idea where his patrol rifle was. Taylor felt for the grip of his pistol on his duty belt and pulled his flashlight from its pouch. The Sig was still there, and he left it holstered.

Pulling his cell phone from his pocket, he flipped it open.

No signal.

"Jamming, brilliant. And with the cloud cover, nobody knows we're in trouble yet."

The Sheriff stood up.

"You guys tend to our wounded. I'm going up and see if I can't talk them out or something."

*   *   *

Markdale looked at the phone, then at the clock, then at the just-opened beer, cold in his hand.

He sighed, it had been a long shift with some overtime. Now the L.T. was calling and really, Craig was done for the day. As the phone rang in his hand, he knew the young Lieutenant wouldn't call like this if it wasn't important.

Pressing the button to answer, he'd wait to hear what this was about before he took a sip of the inviting Coors.

"Craig."

"Yeah, Lieutenant?"

"Sorry to call this time of morning after your shift, but this is kind of important. We got a strange call from a young woman who said she was waiting to give Jeff Potter's daughter a ride from their cabin. She said she heard a helicopter flying really low, then something that sounded like what she described as a crash and no more helicopter noise. She tried calling the daughter, phone wouldn't go through."

"Any missing aircraft reported, or ELT hits?"

"No, I checked for anything overdue and no Emergency Locators going are off. I tried calling Potter's cell number we have on the roster, it didn't go through. Even without the ELT, it seemed strange enough to warrant a check, so I wanted to get authorization to call the Two Bear guys in."

"Sounds reasonable, what'd the Sheriff say?"

"That's where it really starts getting weird. Calls to the Sheriff's cell phone don't go through either, so I call the house, and I wake up Gina and ask if I can talk to the Sheriff. She said he was out on a late call..."

Markdale set down the beer and walked over to his uniform to grab his pen and notebook.

"I never heard him on the radio last night, and I just went 10-7 about half an hour ago."

"Yeah, dispatch has no record of anything the Sheriff was on. I never got anything he was going on, and he handed off to me normally last night."

Markdale rolled his eyes to himself when he realized what must be happening.

"Did the Sheriff say anything about this FBI thing going on?"

"He filled me in on it, but didn't sound like there was anything active, certainly nothing he was planning on doing overnight. It looks like our Sheriff is missing."

"Don't count on it. Sir, I'd say launch the Two Bear guys, I'll meet them out at the airport, probably ought to spin up one of our SAR medics too, if it turns out to be a crash."

"Alright, Craig. You sure you want to go? I know you were late working that DUI."

"Yes, Sir. Getting dressed as we speak."

"Thanks, Craig. I'll be staying on to monitor until we figure out where the Sheriff is."

"Roger that."

*   *   *

The Sheriff approached the cabin slowly, his hands up with his headlamp on illuminating him from where it hung around his neck. In his left hand he held his Streamlight, and his right hand was empty.

"Hey, folks. It's Sheriff Taylor, I just want to talk. I just want to get everyone out of this alive, OK?"

As he approached, he could see the fallen form of Jeff Potter. Drawing closer, he could see all the blood. His step quickened, and he had to remind himself not to rush the scene. Kneeling close to Jeff he could see the shallow, struggling breaths and hear the telling, gurgling, rattle. The eyes were open, but the consciousness that illuminated them was clearly fading. With his Streamlight he was able to find another bullet wound, this one in the chest. It had slipped in next to the plate carrier. The Sheriff tried to seal it with his hand, and Potter's lips moved but he didn't speak.

"I'll take care of the kids, OK, Jeff? I'll do everything I can for them."

And with that Jeff Potter expelled his last breath.

Taylor unbuckled the sling from Potter's carbine, cleared it, put it on safe and set it behind him. He stood up with only his flashlight pie-ing the corners of the door.

"Hey, kids. It's Sheriff Taylor. There won't be any more shooting. Come on out."

Carefully he probed into the main room of the cabin. There were splinters of wood under his feet amid the blood that threatened to take his footing from him. Stepping inside, the smell of the woodstove finally overcame the smell of the blood. The large main room of the cabin was lit only by the red glow of the embers in the firebox.

It was a spartan interior. Clean and well kempt for its age, the doors at the back were swung open, and the Sheriff called again.

"Folks, it's Sheriff Taylor. Let's come on out. There'll be no more shooting."

The first room he checked had very little in it, and the bed had been made. There was a large traveler's backpack, loaded and leaned in the corner by the door.

The next room, the bed was unmade, and the rear window open with the draperies blowing in the gentle night breeze.

*   *   *

She drove the trail through the pale green hues of the NODs and through the tears she couldn't stop. The resolutely composed Tom of the cabin had melted into her back where he hung onto her waist and sobbed into her jacket.

As four-wheelers go, the added suppressed muffler kept it to a reasonably quiet puttering, but it still seemed loud in the mountain night. The machine was overloaded, and so was Jane.

Her grief and sadness soon gave way to a seething anger and hatred. As she tried to remember her father alive, she realized that the last moments when he was really alive were when he was standing, his figure black against the intense white light in the doorway, hands in the air.

He was *surrendering*.

He was buying time for their escape, and they shot him where he stood with his hands up. It should never have happened. But then, they never should have shot a man with his hands up. They never even announced who they were. Was it the FBI as her father suspected, or was it something else? Was it a government hit?

Now she was sounding like him. Was it just because of what had just happened? Or was it because he was right all along?

Jane shook her head. This was no time for philosophizing; this was no time for runaway emotion.

She had to think.

Among Jeff's last words were to meet at the southern cache. She knew where that was, and she knew how to get there. It would be a day's ride on the four-wheeler under normal circumstances, but things would change when day broke. Now with the weather and tree cover, they could move more quickly.

They had only grabbed one of the carbines when they fled. She had grabbed the NODs and her father's Glock 19 from its holster on his plate carrier. She didn't know what the four-wheeler was stocked with, but it was loaded heavier than any she had ever ridden. She kept the machine real slow and easy on the turns and inclines in the trail.

Tom said something into her jacket.

"What?"

Still sobbing, he lifted his head to project his voice more toward her ear.

"Can we stop?"

"No, not yet."

"How far have we gone?"

"I'm not sure, not far enough yet. We'll stop at first light, an hour or so, I think."

She wasn't ready for the painful conversation that would have to happen. She knew the man she loved and hated most in her life was dead, and she knew that Tom wouldn't want to accept that.

* * *

"What do you mean they're gone?" Booth asked.

"I mean, when you lit up their father as he was surrendering, they probably thought it reasonable to depart," The Sheriff said.

"Who surrenders with a gun on?"

"People who don't know who they are surrendering to, or people who feel they maybe shouldn't trust who they are surrendering to… as in this case."

"We need to go after them."

"Not now, Booth, you at least have a very serious concussion, not to mention your partner in there pinned by the legs, and we're sitting here trying to keep him alive until the weather clears so your drones can see we've crashed. Did you have a time when the jamming would stop?"

"When we called them complete."

"You mean from the helicopter that has all its antennas snapped off? Or from everybody's cool little tactical radios that don't seem to be reaching anyone right now?"

Booth didn't say a word.

"Hey," Carver broke in. "you hear that?"

"What?"

"Helicopter." The other Marshal said, and everyone scanned the dark horizon.

"It's all lit up." Said Booth.

"Oh, good, maybe it's someone that knows what they're doing," Taylor offered.

The helicopter arched into an orbit overhead and lit them from above with its search light. The search light played on the crash site first and everyone who could was waving their arms. Then the light hit the larger field below where the flag pole had stood.

The helicopter made a second orbit, then set up into the wind to approach and land in the larger field.

As it came closer the Sheriff began to make out the shape of the Bell 429, then the familiar blue with red and white stripes of Two Bear Air. Ablaze with running lights, it held a stable approach and landed down slope of them. Three figures exited, carefully avoiding the rotor arc and hiked up toward the cabin. The Sheriff went to meet them.

Markdale had his headlamp on, and the Sheriff could see his smile when the light fell on his uniform. The Deputy lowered his headlamp so it wasn't in the Sheriff's eyes.

"Glad you're OK, Sheriff. Looked pretty bad from up there."

"It is bad. We lost the pilot, and we may lose an FBI guy. He's pinned in the wreckage by his legs." The Sheriff realized the other people were one of the Two Bear Rescue Techs and the SAR team medic. Taylor turned to address them. "I think we got the bleeding under control, but he's in and out of consciousness. The other FBI guy is pretty well concussed and marginally ambulatory. The rest of us seem to be OK."

"What a cluster," Markdale said as he looked at the shadows of the wreck just up hill.

"Yup," the Sheriff confirmed. "They killed Jeff Potter, shot him in the doorway with his hands up."

Booth had staggered into the conversation.

"Wait, who are these people?" Booth asked, a little wobbly.

"Two Bear Air, they're a privately funded Search And Rescue outfit in this area, the best in the world. You'll be in good hands."

"No, absolutely not, these people need to get the hell out of here, and I need to NDA every one of them. They absolutely can't talk about anything they've seen here. This is a Federal crime scene."

"You got that right," the Sheriff yelled. "You can take this bird out, Booth. My Deputy and I will conduct the investigation of the murder of Jeff Potter."

"He had a gun."

"Strapped across his chest."

"That's not what the investigation will show, Taylor."

"That's what I saw! That's what the tapes will show."

"This crime scene is closed to you and your men. I'm handling it with the Marshals under the authority of the 2024 War Powers Act."

The two Marshals had walked into what had devolved into a yelling match.

"You can barely walk, Booth. You're getting on that helicopter if I have to cuff you myself."

"Try it, Sheriff."

Booth was surprised at the blur of motion the Sheriff had suddenly become. All Booth could think to do was attempt to draw his Glock.

"Geez, Sheriff." Markdale was going to the ground with both of them. "He's going for his gun here."

Booth was on his face in the dirt.

"You got the right arm? Get that gun."

"I got it, I got it." The volunteer SAR medic had joined the fray and was carefully wrestling the pistol away from the man by securing a handful of trigger finger.

The FBI Agent cried out.

"You broke my finger!"

"Sorry about that. Now just don't struggle so much, and nothing else will get broke."

"Carver, help me! Arrest these men!" the FBI agent cried.

"You're pretty out of it, Booth. You need a medical evaluation. This may be best for you."

The Sheriff looked up at the Marshal as he clicked both cuffs on the Agent's wrists. Carver just shrugged in the darkness as the Sheriff double locked the cuffs. He opened up the dump pouch on his belt and dropped the Agent's Glock in it after removing the magazine and clearing the chamber.

Another helicopter flew low over the scene, lights out. The downwash and sound made conversation impossible for a moment. The Sheriff wrenched Booth up to his feet with the help of Markdale and the medic.

"Craig," the Sheriff yelled to be heard. "Get this man out of here and keep him under watch as he gets medical treatment. Get the Lieutenant in the loop, advise him that I've detained an FBI agent for medical evaluation following erratic behavior after known head injury resulting from a helicopter crash. He'll contact the feds. I'll deal with whoever this is and get things documented as best I can."

"Yes, Sir."

"Leave our medic here with me to aid the agent pinned in the crash. Come back with as many Deputies as you can pack in with extraction equipment so we can get that Agent out of there and on the way to the hospital as quickly as we can. And be sure to tell the Two Bear pilot about this other helo so we don't wind up with a mid-air to add to our problems."

"Got it." The Deputy led the cuffed agent to the running helicopter.

The Sheriff looked up at the mysterious helicopter orbiting overhead. Its dark form caught a streak of light on the far side of the orbit, and the Sheriff realized the first rays of the sun must be peaking over a mountain crest somewhere.

"Well, Sheriff." The SAR medic said "Not the way I imagined starting my day."

The SAR medic was new to the team and the Sheriff didn't remember his name, he was walking a little ahead of Sheriff to get to the wreck and his patient. He hesitated a moment as his headlamp played across the back of the tail boom.

The light caught the bright yellow of fabric laying wrapped around the broken tail.

"That's what they call irony or somethin', isn't it, Sheriff?" the medic called over his shoulder as he started to climb into the wreck.

"It's somethin', alright."

The Sheriff stopped and shined his flashlight over the Gadsen Flag wrapped around the tail.

*   *   *

Jane stowed the NODs in a pack strapped to the front rack of the four-wheeler. The clouds were clearing, and the glow of dawn was penetrating the tree cover.

"How far do you think we've gone, Jane?"

She shook her head.

"Don't know, maybe twenty miles... no, not that much, we were going pretty slow." She looked up at the cover of the tall pines above them. Nothing they would have out now could see them. Her Dad had told her initially they wouldn't have things that could see through the trees. That the first thing they'd have overhead would be visual and IR cameras. He told her they would bring in things like Synthetic Aperture Radar and LIDAR eventually, but those assets were already over tasked and for the first few weeks, just staying in the deep of the forest would be enough.

She looked at the four-wheeler. They were safe enough in this patch of woods. When it was light enough, she could inventory what they had. In the meantime, she saw the wrist mounted GPS strapped to the handle bars.

Jane grabbed it and powered it up.

"It's safe to use, right, Tom? I mean, it just receives. Dad just said not to use anything that transmits, right?"

Tom just nodded.

"What do you think he's telling them, Jane? Or, I guess he's probably still in surgery or something?"

"Tom." She started off looking him in the eye, but couldn't continue that way and just looked down at her feet. "Tom, I really don't think Dad made it. That was a lot of blood."

"But I did everything right. I did everything just like he told us. I did it fast, I did it all right, I know I did."

"There was nothing you could have done different or better Tom. It wasn't you. They did this."

"Who are *they*, Jane?"

"Dad was thinking the FBI. Probably them."

Tom was tearing up, wanting to say more but not finding the words. He kind of just crumpled where he was and started sobbing again, clutching his knees and leaning against a rock sticking up out of the forest floor.

"He can't be dead, Jane. He can't be."

Jane stepped around the four-wheeler, walked over to him, crouched down and hugged him.

"What are we gonna do now, Jane?"

"What can we do? We're gonna do what he taught us, I guess. He really did teach us everything we need to know. Remember all those times sitting around watching TV when he'd throw us a tourniquet and tell us to put it on different limbs our self or on each other. How many times have we put on tourniquets like that before we had to do it for real last night?"

"Hundreds?"

"More like thousands that I can remember, Tom." She stood up and looked at him, and she allowed a little smile through the grief. "And how many times have we played with NODs and driven around on the four-wheeler, just for fun. It's like he was *always* training us for this. And almost beyond training, almost like programming. We were never afraid of the dark, we knew how to see in it."

Jane looked at the GPS.

"Well, I didn't have it turned on at the start, so I don't know how many miles we actually covered, but straight line back to the cabin is twenty-three miles, Tom. We're doing good so far."

*   *   *

When the Two Bear 429 lifted off, the other helicopter broke its orbit and slid into that larger landing zone. In the gathering light, he realized it was one of the new Air Force MW-139s, like what had replaced the old Hueys at Fairchild.

The door slid open, and a man wearing an FBI raid jacket was flanked by two FBI men in ballistic vests carrying carbines at the low ready. As the men cleared the helicopter's rotor arc, it took off and resumed its orbit.

The man in the lead wore glasses and a serious grimace. His head was shaved, and as he got closer, Taylor realized the guy actually managed a shirt and tie under the jacket.

The Sheriff walked toward him with his hand extended.

"Sheriff Grant Taylor." He was met with an appropriately firm hand shake and eyes that first acknowledged him, then sternly scanned the scene.

"Special Agent Luke Tanner, SAIC of the Salt Lake field office. What do we have, Sheriff? And where are my Agents?"

"Special Agent Prather is pinned in the wreckage, one of my SAR guys is tending to him in there. We're waiting for our rescue helo to return with extraction gear and personnel. I had Special Agent Booth sent into the hospital on that helicopter when it arrived. He was clearly concussed and not thinking real straight."

"Thank you for taking care of them."

"I had to subdue and cuff Booth. He didn't want to go, but he was in no shape to really argue." The Sheriff pulled the agent's Glock, it's slide still locked back from his dump pouch. "We had to disarm him, too."

Tanner paused a moment, looked the Sheriff over and nodded as he took custody of the weapon putting it in the pocket of his jacket

"Is Prather conscious? I'm going to go check on him."

"He's in and out of consciousness, and it's a bit of a climb, but we'll get you in to see him."

Tanner nodded then followed the Sheriff to the helicopter wreckage. When they got there, the Sheriff shouted to the medic that the Special Agent in Charge was coming in, then showed Tanner the best foot holds. Despite the shirt and tie, the man showed no concern for getting dirty, and he scaled the wreck with what the Sheriff deemed to be a fairly high degree of dexterity and fitness.

The man emerged about five minutes later with the same serious demeanor.

When he stepped off the wreckage, he turned to the Sheriff.

"Were you able to talk to him?" Taylor asked.

"No, he was unconscious. It doesn't look good."

"Our medics are darn good. We got tourniquets on the legs as fast as we could. We weren't able to get word out right away because the helicopter broke its antenna off, and they had cell phones jammed here."

Tanner shook his head.

"Why has it taken this long? Where was the QRF helo in all this?"

"Ah," Taylor took a moment. "What? Were you the one who signed off on this?"

"Yes."

"There was one helicopter." Taylor pointed at the wreck right next to them. "Five guys, I told them it wasn't enough, I told them this was the wrong guy to mess with like this."

"One helicopter? Five guys?"

"What did you think you signed off on, Tanner?"

"I was told we had your full support and local assets, and personnel would make up for any shortcomings that might need to be addressed."

The Sheriff watched Tanner's facial expression change. From such a serious looking man he was expecting anger, but it was something much different.

"Tanner, I believe you've been misled. I wish you would have called me first. This has been a mess from the beginning, and I always told Prather that. I told him I was *not* going to commit any of my Deputies or any of my material assets to this because they were going about it all wrong from the beginning. I was just here because I was going to try to keep him and our citizens out of trouble. I've failed."

Tanner said nothing, just inhaled deeply and smelled the jet fuel seeping from the wreck and the smoke drifting down from the cabin under the influence of the low pressure system moving through.

"Should we move from the wreck? Fire hazard?"

"Takes a lot to spark off jet fuel, we're good. We didn't want to abandon Prather." The Sheriff looked back at the cabin, then back to the Special Agent In Charge. "Prather was a problem child, wasn't he, Tanner? He made this out to be something easier than it really was, didn't he?"

Again, the FBI man said nothing, but Taylor could tell he wanted to.

"Walk with me, Tanner. That's just part of the story, part of the story of the wreckage of this enforcement action."

Tanner said nothing, just fell in line as the Sheriff walked up the hill to the doorway of the cabin.

They stopped at the lifeless body of Jeff Potter. Despite the smearing of blood and dust, the exposed skin was a vacant pale in the increasing dawn. The eyes were half closed and greying hair disheveled and mop like. One of the Crocs was off, and the first aid pouch on the plate carrier was stripped open. The packed dressing of the shoulder wound, soaked with coagulating blood, poked out of the body like some kind of grotesque stuffing.

"This was Jeff Potter, he was a good man who has dealt with a lot of bad things lately. A veteran special operations soldier in the war on terror. He just wanted to be left alone with his kids, and your men wouldn't have it. They shot him down in this doorway where he stood with his hands up, his rifle slung across his chest. He didn't need to die, neither did the DHS pilot."

Tanner shook his head and remained silent.

A yell calling for the Sheriff emerged from the wreckage, and they both turned back to see Carver straddling the wreckage and waving for them. At a jog they covered the distance quickly.

"Hurry," the medic yelled from inside the helicopter, "Prather's crashing."

Tanner mounted and scaled the fallen helicopter like it was nothing more than a regular work out, and he was inside as Taylor was just starting to recognize the old pain in his bum knee, and the pain he was feeling in his strained neck, that was new.

A few moments later, Tanner emerged, his white shirt and blue raid jacket bloody. His expression had a forced flatness to it that gave away all it was meant to conceal.

Jumping down, the Sheriff met him with consoling eyes.

"I'm sorry, Tanner. I may not have liked the guy, but I didn't want it to end like this for him."

"It shouldn't have ended like this for him." Tanner said. The distant throbbing of the Two Bear's Bell 429 was just becoming clear on its return trip. "But it has. And now he escapes any kind of accountability."

He walked away from the wreck and looked at the sun as it began to peak over the mountainside above. The Sheriff followed, the others, who weren't tending to the dead Special Agent slumped with fatigue among the debris of the crash.

"He was more than a problem child, Sheriff. He was a politically connected problem child. The nephew of a Senator instrumental in the passage of the latest horrendously bad blanket law forced by politicians."

"The new War Powers Act?" the Sheriff asked.

Tanner nodded silently.

"Prather's ambition put him in that wreck, just as much as his lack of skills and abilities. He did this because he wanted to make a name for himself with a big case. He believed this posting was beneath him, he wanted Seattle or Portland Field Offices. He was positioning himself to be inserted in some kind of new legal structure. There are ramifications we can't even comprehend right now about this new law."

"I've got extraction equipment and personnel coming in on this helo, and additional Deputies. We'll get the body out for you, and we'll get our side of the investigation completed quickly. If you could facilitate the Federal side, your investigation and the NTSB response."

"I'm afraid it's not going to go the way you think it should here, Sheriff. You're done here, there'll be no further investigation, and you aren't allowed to discuss anything you've seen or done here. This whole operation was conducted under the authority of the War Powers Act."

The Sheriff smiled.

"I'm going to conduct my investigation and follow on as I see fit. I'll have more Deputies with more guns on scene than you'll have Feds. Don't push me on this."

"I won't interfere with your investigation, Sheriff. I have to respect that, I happen to believe in the law and the Constitution, but those above me don't. I'm warning you, as soon as that helicopter hit the ground this whole thing changed, and they can't afford to lose... and they won't. There will be only so much you can do. Things like this develop their own inertia, and they can't be stopped by a man like you or I, no matter what our beliefs."

"So, what are you going to do, Tanner?"

The question was a challenge greater than Tanner wanted to face, and he could see the anger rising in Taylor.

"I'm going to try to ride out the storm as best I can." Tanner's voice trailed off in an anger that left unsaid the weakness he knew he was showing and he snapped at the Sheriff returning the challenge.

"What are you going to do, Sheriff?"

Taylor slipped his thumbs in his duty belt and gave an intense smile.

"My job."

CHAPTER 6

"They must be looking for us by now, right? Should we get going, Jane?"

"I think we should lie low during the day, move at night. We covered a lot of ground, and I haven't heard any helicopters or anything. We should have heard that by now, right?"

Tom didn't say anything, just sat against the rock, arms wrapped around his knees.

"We'll take advantage of the daylight here to see what we have to work with, do a little inventory."

In full morning light she looked at the canopy of pines high above.

"This is a safe spot, Tom. I can't see anything up, they can't see down, it's not like the movies. All that technology, Dad said they rely on it too much, and it's not a sure thing anyway."

Tom said nothing for a moment.

"We can't underestimate it."

"Your right, Tom. But we can't overestimate it either. We can't let ourselves be paralyzed by fear. We have to keep moving, but we have to be smart."

Tom just nodded a little into his knees. With distraction and exuberance, Jane tried, despite the circumstances, to keep him from sinking into that dark place he so often went.

"We know what we have in our Go-bags." She wrestled a little with the ratchet strap they had used to hold them in place on the front rack of the four-wheeler, over an old green five-gallon jerry can that was already strapped there on its side. "We'll have to find a better home for them though. We just kind of threw them on and strapped them down last night. I guess this must be one of the jerry cans with the new gaskets Dad installed. Doesn't seem to be leaking or anything, still makes me nervous on its side like that. And a big camo net up here too. That's enough to cover the four-wheeler and us in a shelter I bet. We just have to make sure we keep it up off of us and off of the four-wheeler so it doesn't show a heat signature. That will help a lot."

There was a big backpack strapped next to some kind of big ammo can. Jane removed the ratchet straps holding the ammo can down first.

"I bet Dad wanted to go through all of this stuff with us first. He'd been planning a lot of this for a long time, I think. And then I think things happened a lot faster than he expected. I guess we have to kind of look at it like Christmas."

She smiled, but Tom didn't show any response.

The ammo can was about three feet tall. The original military stenciling indicated it was designed to contain some kind of 120 mm illumination mortar cartridges. For a moment Jane was afraid what her Dad might have put in it now.

Levering it open, she sat back when she saw what it contained, and the tears she had been fighting for so long started running again. Slumping down Indian style, she wept inconsolably.

Tom stood up, curious.

He walked over and looked in the ammo can. He pulled the vacuum sealed contents out piece by piece.

The M-1 Garand had been broken down into its three largest components. The trigger group, the barrel and receiver group and the stock group. All vacuum sealed in their own bags. Poking further into the ammo can he produced a sling, two full bandoliers of loaded en-bloc clips, a cleaning kit and cans of grease and oil all individually vacuum sealed.

"Dad said it was his favorite rifle. He said it was the most important one in the family. It was his Grandpa's. Just like the one he used in Normandy," Tom said.

Jane didn't say anything for a long time. She just tried to think about everything it really meant and represented. To her and to her father.

When Tom had finally put everything back and was going to close the can, she stood up.

"Wait… Don't."

She stepped over and he yielded the ammo can back to her.

"If we need this, we need it assembled and ready to go." She pulled out the components and opened her knife to cut open each of the sealed bags. She found each component sufficiently lubricated and the barrel clear and oiled. She mated the barrel and receiver group together and carefully inserted the trigger group. Latching the trigger guard closed, the rifle was complete. Pulling the safety back into the trigger guard, Jane then affixed the web sling. She reached into the bag with a bandolier and took out one of the clips. Locking the operating rod to the rear, she slid the clip in with her thumb. The meat of her hand blocked the operating rod as it tried to spring forward when the clip was fully seated. She let the operating rod fly and the top of the eight 30-06 rounds stripped violently off the clip and chambered.

The girl smiled faintly at the comfort of the familiar action.

"You know why I practiced with this rifle so much, Tom? You know why I did all those high-power rifle matches?"

Tom stepped back a little and shook his head, looking over the assembled piece of history. The walnut and steel that seemed to be a part of the family.

"The first time I shot it… Dad handed it to me and said it was *'a real man's rifle'*
I learned the thing just out of spite at first. But then it was like something we could share. Something that crossed some kind of barrier between us. He respected that I learned to use it well, I respected that he took the time to teach me, despite the fact that he seemed so stuck in his ways. There was a lot he didn't understand about me. Maybe there were things I didn't really quite understand about him. Maybe now…"

She put that thought away.

"What will you do with it, Jane?"

"Whatever I have to."

"Dad said we don't have enough to fight, that we just have to run."

"We may not have a choice. What choice did they give Dad?"

*   *   *

"Why here and why all the… vagueness, Grant?"

"Heard any good rumors lately?"

The Sheriff looked at the waterfall as he waited for an answer. The water was clean and cool looking, and the coins at the bottom of the fountain were bright and seemed to promise something.

"Like what are we talkin' here?"

"Like something that should have made the paper, but didn't."

"Oh, that military helicopter crash north of town?"

The Sheriff nodded and adjusted his collar. He didn't like wearing a tie.

"I mean I heard about it. It was some kind of military special ops training flight or something."

"It wasn't. I was on the helicopter along with two FBI agents and two US Marshals."

"What?" The county prosecutor smiled incredulously. "What happened?"

"They were trying to serve a warrant on Jeff Potter… they shot him in his doorway with his hands up. He returned fire after he was hit and brought us down. Killed the DHS pilot and one of the FBI Agents."

"What?"

"What do you know about this War Powers Act 2024?"

"Hard to tell, it's over twenty-three hundred pages long. I don't know anyone who has been all through it yet, and parts are classified. What is known about it is nasty. Everything the Patriot Act really wanted to be but couldn't at the time. The original War Powers Act in '73 was designed to limit the President's powers, this one goes 180 degrees the other direction. It hands the President the keys to the kingdom, it would appear. Everyone is focused on the conscription component, but there is a whole lot more there, and we're just finding out about it. But this helicopter thing…"

"They're telling me the whole thing at Potter's cabin was done under the authority of this WPA, and that I can't talk about it. Is this legitimate?"

"Well, that's kind of a loaded question. It's passed as a law, as such it is Federally enforceable. We just have to wait and see what all it actually includes, then we can challenge it."

"That hardly seems legitimate to me."

The prosecutor shrugged. He was much more comfortable in a suit, as he leaned back in his chair.

"Did they give you any documentation on any of this?"

"No, tried to have me sign a Non-Disclosure Agreement, which has never happened before."

"So, Jeff Potter, the SAR guy... Army veteran as I recall, is dead? They did an article on him in the paper because of his success rate. He didn't seem like the type to much care for the attention, and the article turned out to be more about the team. That guy?"

"Yeah, that was him."

"What did you do?"

"Not enough." The Sheriff looked down at his coffee and slid his chair in closer. "I'm trying to figure out how I should proceed. His kids are still out there. They escaped."

"What was this warrant for?"

"Draft evasion, warrants for him and the kids."

"That's Title 50 stuff, it's a big deal, especially right now. Those are felony warrants, they aren't playing around."

"Obviously." The Sheriff looked around the lobby of the big bank building, the biggest in the small town. "Look, I want to get those kids out alive. I wanted to get Jeff out alive and I've already failed there. I don't want anyone else dying. I don't want to turn them over to the Feds."

"Whoa, one thing at a time, Grant. What have you done since Jeff and the Federal agents were killed?"

"Well, the first five or six hours, I think it was, we were just trying to keep the one agent alive. He was pinned in the wreckage, and we couldn't get word out for help because they were jamming cell phones. It was just a little luck and good old fashioned cop intuition that my Lieutenant and Craig Markdale were able to put some pieces together along with the report of a possible helicopter crash. But it took a long time for the gears to be put in motion. They got the Two Bear guys called out and arrived on scene finally. We evacuated the ambulatory FBI guy... oh yeah, I wound up wrestling him into hand cuffs. He had a head injury and I'm not sure he was thinking clearly... how's that gonna play out?"

"Just keep going, Grant. Sounds like that's the very least of your worries." The prosecutor pulled out a pad of paper from his brief case and clicked his pen as he began taking notes.

"Anyway, the Feds were relying on drone overwatch, and we wound up clouded in. They couldn't see we had crashed, we had no coms so we were on our own. We secured the scene, confirmed Jeff was dead, and I searched the cabin, kids escaped out a back window."

"How long ago did all this happen?"

The Sheriff winced as he looked at the ceiling some five stories above and ran the math in his head.

"Just under thirty hours ago. I wanted to connect with you sooner, but I didn't want to mention any of this over the phone."

"Really? You think they're... what? Monitoring you?"

"They are going to devote a lot of resources to this now and they're going to do everything they can to keep it under wraps to keep Jeff from becoming a martyr. I've got my report written up on my desk in triplicate, including my press release. I wanted to talk to you before I handled this as a normal case."

"There's nothing normal about this, Grant. This is absolutely uncharted territory. Let me do some research before you do anything else."

"Well, I got a call from Scott Carver at US Marshals. He said FBI has an HRT team in town now. I'm supposed to be interviewed by their team leader today, but I've been officially disinvited from participating in anymore reindeer games."

"Well, that's a blessing, really. How do you plan on handling the interview?"

"Well, I was hoping for some guidance from you, preferably have you there with me to keep me in line."

The Prosecutor shook his head and looked up from his notes.

"Grant, I was barely able to get you in this morning, half the office is out with this new variant, whatever they're calling it… I'll try, but I can't make a lot of promises. You know how hammered we are right now."

"I know, Joe, I know. Just any tips for me?"

He looked down at the table a moment before answering the Sheriff.

"Be *very* careful. It's not just you. This WPA thing opens up a lot of problems for everyone. You've got two dead feds and a Ruby Ridge slash Waco event that has just happened, and they're trying to prevent people from rising up and rallying around the body of Jeff Potter or aiding his kids. The WPA is rumored to be full of all kinds of bad news, Grant. They could come down hard and enact martial law in the county to keep this thing under control."

"Pfft… Come on, Joe." The Sheriff leaned back and smiled. "They've got their hands full with the food riots, they can't commit those kind of resources. We'd have them way out-gunned here anyway."

"Don't bank on that. You have a population of largely law abiding citizens here, people who have always believed in the system, and it's in their nature to comply with law enforcement. This would be the low hanging fruit. They would be happy to let Seattle or Portland burn and reallocate those resources here to lock us down hard and put this down before it gets out of their control any more than it already has."

The Sheriff looked at him skeptically, but with full contemplative respect.

"Look, Grant. The cities always burn, they're always hard to control, it's expected. It's been that way since the sixties... well, maybe all through the ages really. They would crack down harder here now, because rural America has consistently complied. If draft resistance takes off here, then that spreads *to* the cities, what does that look like for them? No more bored farm boys and impoverished ghetto kids to fill the ranks because everyone wants to be like the Potters? That is *exactly* the kind of thing all the bad parts of this new War Powers Act are designed to prevent.

"When you talk to the Hostage Rescue Team guy today, be careful, be smart, be non-confrontational. I'll try to clear up and re-assign a bunch of things today so I can help you with this, but this WPA thing is enormous and it's going to take time to go through and figure out all the implications, then more time figure out work arounds and even more to figure out legal challenges."

"Oh, yeah and that FBI agent that died. He's the nephew of that senator that was instrumental in pushing the WPA through, that might be important."

The prosecutor sighed, deflated in his chair a little and rubbed his face.

*   *   *

Tom handed her the little camouflaged book, opened to one of the beginning pages.

"This one looks good, could you read it to me."

"What do you mean?" She took it with an obvious measure of unease.

"You read it, I'm going to pray."

"Does it work that way? I don't think that's how it works."

"Well, I don't think it counts as a prayer if I'm reading it to myself. That's why they have preachers, I think."

Jane laughed at him, then looked at the open page and stopped.

Prayer When A Comrade Has Fallen.

To herself she read the first few lines and wasn't sure she could read it out loud, despite her personal view on such things.

"I... I don't think... I don't know, Tom."

"I think that's the one we need, it fits better than the others. It's too late for prayer for the dying, and the prayers for loved ones and absent family members don't really apply here. Please, just read that one."

Jane took in a deep breath, and Tom folded his hands together in front of him in a way that seemed awkward and unfamiliar to both of them. He was sitting with his legs crossed in the dirt and his head bowed, waiting for her.

"Lead this, our fallen companion, by your mercy, Lord. Comfort those of us remaining..." She lowered the book and then lowered her head into her hand where she tried to hide the coming tears. Comfort, she thought to herself, what a nice thought, when would *she* ever possibly find any kind of comfort again?

She looked up when she sensed he was looking at her, waiting for her.

"Comfort those of us remaining here and help us seek your kingdom until our life in this age is over, and bring us into your kingdom in the age to come..." She looked up to Tom, whose head was down again. She flipped through a few pages forward and back. "I don't think this is even official or anything, like I don't think it's part of the Bible."

"It doesn't matter." Tom said with surprising resoluteness. "We'll read through all that later. This seems like a good place to start."

She looked at the camouflaged Bible. Its binding was worn white and frayed at the edges. The pages were dog eared and unfolded many times. In the front page, in her father's handwriting all it said was IZ 2009, and she wasn't even sure what that meant.

"Go, on, Jane. Please? You're doing well."

She was sitting side-saddle on the seat of the Four-wheeler, and she flipped back to the prayer for a fallen comrade.

"God, the father of all, whose Son commanded us to love one another: lead us from prejudice to truth; deliver us from hatred, cruelty and revenge; and in your good time enable us all to stand reconciled before you; through Jesus Christ our Lord."

Jane sighed and sat up straight.

"I can't read this. You should just read it to yourself, Tom."

"You're doing fine. Please finish it, Jane."

"I'm the wrong person to be reading this, Tom."

"Please?"

She squirmed a little on the seat and continued.

"Almighty God, kindle, we pray, in every heart the true love of peace, and guide with your wisdom those who take counsel for the nations on the earth, that in tranquility your dominion may increase until the earth is filled with the knowledge of your love; through Jesus Christ our Lord, who lives and reigns with you, in the unity of the Holy Spirit, one God, now and forever. Amen."

"Amen," Tom said, he looked up and smiled a little. "Thanks."

"I can't do that again, Tom." She stepped off the four-wheeler and handed the Bible back to him

"Why not."

"I don't believe in it."

"What do you mean? The parts about love and deliverance from prejudice and hatred and all that, how can you not believe in that?"

"Well… not those parts. The God and Jesus and Holy Spirit parts."

"What do you believe in, Jane?"

"Myself."

"Is that enough?"

Jane looked down, surprised at the whole course of the conversation.

"I believe in nature and the universe."

"Do you ever try to pray?"

"I put my energy out to the universe, maybe that's the same thing."

Tom shook his head.

"I don't think that counts."

"What do you mean?" She gave a little laugh.

"I think it's too generic to be any good. It's like trying to mail a letter by addressing it to Main Street, Anywhere, USA."

"What are you talking about, Tom?"

He thumbed through the pages. They had found the Bible in a pack that had been strapped down beside the ammo can containing the Garand. The pack additionally held a solar battery and crank powered radio, more MREs and a couple of old surplus synthetic fleece jackets.

Tom was a voracious reader and, this being the only book they had, the Bible had drawn Tom in. Before finding the prayers in the beginning, he had started reading at Genesis, because he knew that was the beginning, but found himself getting lost among a sea of 'begats'. As he leafed forward and back, he stumbled across the prayers and thought through some kind of instinct, that it was a good idea even if he was unclear on the proper execution.

He flipped toward the New Testament because he was looking for something. First, he came upon a map labeled The World of Jesus and, he knew he was on the right track. The next page was the beginning of the book of Mathew and reading the little description, he knew he was in the right place.

*   *   *

The man had the physique of an athlete, a clean-shaven face and a scraggly haircut that wouldn't generally be regulation anywhere that cared. He wore an oversized t-shirt that couldn't really hide his svelte musculature or the outline of the grip of the pistol he carried tucked into an appendix carry holster in the front of his jeans.

The two men flashed FBI badges but didn't give much time for them to be examined. The smaller, barrel-chested man was just introduced as John by the bigger guy who did all the talking. They didn't give out business cards, and the Sheriff missed the big guy's name as it was something Eastern European sounding that started with a Z and seemed to end with all syllables.

"Everybody just calls me Z," He said.

"Not going to give us your pronouns?"

"Huh?" Z said. Markdale grinned behind him.

"Last FBI guy we had in here made sure we knew what his pronouns were. Figured it was a Bureau thing."

"Booth did that?"

"No, Prather."

"Ah." Z had the kind of smile that the Sheriff wanted to trust, but he knew better and that made him like the guy even less.

Z looked back at 'John' who showed no reaction, other than following the man with his eyes.

"Nah, we don't all do that, Sheriff."

"So, you guys don't want me to go up and show you around the area up there."

"Much appreciated, Sheriff. We've got one of the Marshals who was actually on board the helicopter, so it really won't be necessary."

That sounded strange and Markdale shot a glance at Taylor who pretended not to notice.

"Are you the Agent In Charge then?"

"No, I'm just team leader on the ground."

"They got Booth in charge then?"

"No, he's got a pretty significant head injury, and he's going to be out a while. We just wanted to ask you a few questions about the young man and woman we're looking for."

"Don't want to know about the man your Agents killed in his doorway with his hands up?"

"What?"

"They're his kids, how he raised them will play a role in this, who and what he was will tend to dictate how he raised them."

"That's not what I mean, where do you get that he had his hands in the air? He shot down a helicopter outside his cabin."

Taylor leaned back in his chair.

"Oh, I'm well aware. I was onboard, and I saw him exit the cabin with his hands in the air. Had a rifle across his chest, but he never reached for it, not until he was shot anyway. Have you not seen the helicopter's FLIR footage?"

"The damage to the helicopter was such that it was unrecoverable."

"*Really?*"

"Yes, what do you mean you were on board that helicopter, Sheriff? There was no mention of that in our brief or any of the paper work I've seen on this."

"That seems a strange omission, doesn't it, Z?"

The perfect teeth disappeared as Z's smile faded. Gears were turning, but Taylor wasn't sure where the machine would go with it.

"Jeff Potter was a good man, a veteran who didn't deserve what he got."

"Just between you and me, Sheriff, I served with Potter in the Army."

"In the Unit, huh?"

"You're familiar?"

"A bit."

"We were in B-Squadron together, did a tour in Iraq and one in Afghanistan with him. He was a good man. I was disappointed to hear he was killed. More disappointed now, to hear how he was killed. If that's true."

Taylor had his elbows on the armrest, and he leaned over a little to rub his beard with his left hand as he evaluated Z's face. Besides being extraordinarily fit, he was annoyingly good looking as well. And he appeared to be the kind of man who could get away with a lot when he flashed a smile, the kind smile that never showed real feelings and only sought to gain.

"I have no reason to lie to you, Z. I was there, and I saw it. I don't claim to have known Jeff well, but I probably knew him as well or better than anyone around here. He was on my SAR team. He saved a lot of lives here. Never looked for anything in return but the next call. His kids are good kids. They don't deserve what you're bringing them."

"We're just bringing them in, Sheriff."

Taylor said nothing and gave a near imperceptible nod.

"What do you know about the kids?" Z asked.

"You ever meet them?"

"Once, fifteen years ago. They were young, and Jeff was one of the few I knew in the Unit that kept family pretty well compartmented away. Most leaned pretty heavy on military family support with our op tempo being what it was."

"I could see that with Jeff."

Z smiled.

"He was a good man, Sheriff, you're right about that… and about him not deserving this. Help me get his kids home alive, ok?"

"What can I do for you?"

"Just tell me what do you know about the kids."

"You know his wife died, right?"

"Yes, I read that. I knew her too. She was a good woman, and they were perfect together. I imagine it was rough on all of them."

"I didn't really know them that well, Z. What you said about keeping the family separate, he did the same thing here. At the SAR team and Department picnics we had, if he came at all, it was always alone. Kinda' got the impression, maybe he had a bit of a hard time getting home."

Z nodded without the smile.

"He had some bad stuff happen. He wasn't one of our magnets for it or anything, but he had more than his share it seemed, and it was nothing he ever brought on himself."

"What can I do to help these kids, Z?"

"Tell me everything you can about them. Would they be armed?"

"In this part of the country? You can count on it. You got grizzlies and mountain lions to consider here. They'll have at least a handgun of a caliber that starts with a four. More likely, they'll have rifles."

"And I can assume Jeff taught them how to use them."

Taylor nodded.

"I would."

"What about wilderness and survival skills?"

"This will all just be conjecture, mind you. Jeff, like I'm sure you are, was a master woodsman. I imagine he raised those kids in the woods. It could all be as instinctive to them as it is to the grizzlies and the mountain lions."

"What could be?"

"Survival."

"No chance these kids are going to just walk out of the woods in a day or two when they get cold and hungry?"

"Nope."

The Sheriff looked grim.

"I don't suppose, Z, there's anyway to get you guys to stand down and let me go in there and bring these kids in?"

"Afraid not, Sheriff. This thing's taken on a life of its own. There are some big politics going on in the back ground. Now, how well do you think these kids are equipped?"

"They'll be equipped for the long haul, Z."

"Do you think they'll put up a fight?"

"Ordinarily, I'd say no. But they've just seen their father murdered in front of them. What do you think, Z?"

"I think that they'll have had a 36 hour head start by the time we get to the field. I think these kids will be very motivated, well equipped, and any fear they have, may well be offset by good training and an unhealthy measure of rage."

*   *   *

They were within an hour or two of the south cache. They would camp here for the day as dawn broke and make sure they weren't followed. Deep in the pines, the sky was a leaden grey of solid overcast that looked like a change and felt a lot like winter. They had discussed whether it would be better to travel at night or during the day, and they decided it would be better to hunker down during the day when detection by hunters or hikers might be more likely. Jane didn't know how the news would play what had just happened, but some people would be apt to turn them in.

In an effort to assess that, she scanned with the little radio using an ear piece, periodically when she could. Mostly she picked up Canadian stations, and they said nothing about her father's death and the destruction of the helicopter.

She had the ear piece in and was thumbing the frequency knob. Of course, the AM reception was more limited this time of day. Jane watched as Tom took the Entrenching Tool from the four-wheeler and looked for a good spot. Pulling his fire starting kit from his Go-bag, he set it, along with matches from an MRE next to the E-tool and the clear spot. Quietly he set about gathering wood. When he returned with an armful, he staged it with other gear in order of tinder, kindling and fuel.

"We can't do that, Tom."

"Sure we can, we're under good tree cover here." He started digging.

"They probably have lots of people looking for us now, Tom."

"It'll be ok, Jane." He kept digging. "This is good, a lot less rocky here than back by the cabin."

With one hole complete, he evaluated the wind and dug a second hole.

"It's gonna be cold again today, this'll be nice. We can cook that can of Dinty Moore that was in the bag instead of just more MREs. And it'll be just like Dad taught us."

When the two holes were complete, he reached in and began digging to connect them, piling the dirt up just outside and in a way that would help guide the wind into the vent hole.

"You're doing the Dakota Fire Hole thing?"

"Yeah." He stopped digging a moment and looked up at her. "You say that like you're surprised."

"Well, just that… you never wanted to do any of this stuff when Dad had us doing it. You'd just sit , and I'd do it all. I don't *ever* remember you digging one of these before, all the times I've dug them, you never did."

He smiled, looking up to her with his arm deep in the hole.

"It was never really important until now."

"Just like the tourniquet, then?"

His smile faded.

"Yeah, I guess."

"So, all those times you were learning this stuff, just absorbing it or something?"

Tom nodded as he pulled the last hand full of dirt out. He placed a flat piece of dry wood he'd found into the hole first, a platform to keep the tinder out of the moist dirt.

"Why didn't you just do some of the stuff so he knew you were learning it, just so he saw you knew?"

Tom shrugged as he lit the tinder. Satisfied with its progress, he fed the fire kindling, then finally fuel.

Jane wasn't sure what to say, all the tension between Tom and their father seemed, in the end to have been so pointless now. But bringing that up would serve no purpose, and Tom must have seen it himself.

With the fire adequately self-sustaining, Tom stood up and walked to the four-wheeler for the can of stew and the little fire screen strapped to the back rack. He started opening the can with the can opener on his multi-tool, with the screen tucked under his arm. Laying the screen across the fire, he set the open can on it.

The sound of helicopters echoed up the valley.

"They're coming this way, Tom."

He frowned, pulled the screen out from under the can, allowing it to tumble into the hole, then shoveled the dirt quickly into the holes. The fire was out with a quick whiff of smoke.

The helicopters, two of them, crossed the ridge across from them.

"Blackhawks?"

"Yeah, Tom."

"Army or National Guard looking for us?"

"No, they were black and shiny. Guard uses green I think, and the ones Dad flew in were a real dull black. I think that has to be somebody else.

*   *   *

"Grab a shovel and you can help, Craig."

"Ha, I officially declare myself off the clock, Sheriff." Craig leaned against the stall, still in uniform. "My folks had horses when I was growing up. Swore I'd never have'em, and I'd never muck another stall. Held to it so far."

The Sheriff just laughed a little.

"You said to be careful what we say, even at the office now, so I didn't mention anything, but I wanted to talk to you about today."

Taylor stood up, set his shovel aside and pressed his index finger to his lips. Digging in the pocket of his Carhart he came up with his cell phone and held it up for Craig to see, then waved for his.

He took both phones silently to his unmarked Tahoe parked just outside the barn and locked them inside.

Craig looked skeptical when he returned to the stall.

"Do you really think that's necessary, Sheriff?"

"If it's not now, it will be before all this is done, I just about guarantee it."

"There were a lot of things you left out telling those Hostage Rescue Team guys, Sheriff. Are you sure that was a good idea? Maybe it's better for those kids if they can just find them in the next day or two."

"Well, first off, they had a mechanical delay on one of their helicopters en route. Seein' as how this all really started with a shot down helicopter, they opted to delay until both helicopters were fully mission capable. They were supposed to insert Z and his team first light." The Sheriff looked at his watch then continued.

"So, they went in about two hours ago. That puts them over 48 hours behind when the kids started their run. I expect they'll be right at home in the mountains, even as this weather moves in. Jeff will have them prepared for this. And those kids' blood will burn for what they saw happen to him. The first few days, I'm thinkin' they'll be most volatile. As they settle into the routine of survival and evasion, that will allow for that rage to cool a little. They'll be thinking more and reacting less. They'll be more rational, more chance we can make contact and talk them out."

"Or that just gives them more time to hole up somewhere and fortify a position."

"If that was the plan, then they already have a bunker built."

"And that girl, you know she's shot high power competitions with an M-1 Garand. She outshoots men three times her age who have been shooting rifles like that twice as long as she's been alive. And her juvenile record, didn't she beat up that kid in high school?"

"Oh, she didn't beat him up. She choked him out. She could 'a done a lot worse if she wanted, the way I saw it she showed a lot of restraint. Near as anyone can tell he'd been saying a lot of things to her for a long time, and that day he finally went too far, and most likely he laid hands on her first. It was mutual combat. More than anything, he and the family were embarrassed he made such a poor showing of himself. They were fresh up from California and wanted to make a bigger deal of it than what it really was. And yes, Craig, the girl can shoot. The boy most likely too, he just seemed like the type with a lot less to prove. Maybe even a little on the bashful side. I'm really hoping with the delay we can get someone into the kids."

"How are you planning to do that? They are going to have that area crawling with feds."

"Not for a while, Craig. They're stretched way too thin right now. If this goes on for a few weeks they'll have more manpower. By then, I expect those kids to be in Canada. In the mean time I have an appointment here with a man in a few hours who is just as good in the woods as Jeff was, *and* he grew up here."

*   *   *

Z looked up at the overcast as the Blackhawks took off and did a sweep to the north. It was a high cloud cover, and he could see Covey one-four, their assigned Pred orbiting, silhouetted against the clouds.

The two agents who had been holding security on the scene were glad to be leaving on the helicopters, having spent more time than they had planned at the shot up old cabin.

146

The wreck of the Astar still smelled of jet fuel, and trampled crime scene tape littered the whole compound, in and out. The evidence techs and morgue guys had come and gone, all under orders not to go beyond the immediate area and spoil the trail for K9.

Of course, that was on hold now, too. No dogs available, give it a week they told him. And no trackers available, they were all working a priority target somewhere in Arizona. The worst of it though was that they only gave him a ten man team. He requested fifty, hoping for at least thirty.

Most of the team posted security while he and John entered the cabin. There was a huge stain of blood on the front porch and wood splinters where it appeared the door way and Jeff Potter took about fifty or sixty rounds.

"They said the back left window was open, and it's assumed they went out there," John offered.

Z didn't bother taking too much time examining the sparse cabin that smelled of stove smoke and the stack of well-seasoned pine beside the wood stove. Instead he walked with purpose to the back room where he found the window open.

He keyed up his MBITR and called out on the team net.

"Guys, just like they said in the hand off, we got window three on the east side, wide open. Looks like some loose dirt out there, that's where we'll start. Chief, I want you on point, see if you can find us a track."

Instead of jumping out the window with all their gear and possibly spoiling any sign, Z and John walked casually out of the cabin to join the team forming up around Chief.

The tall swarthy man was down on one knee with his carbine slung to his side. He had a small tape measure out and was measuring the tracks. Then he documented the tread pattern with his phone camera.

"I got two separate tracks here, Z." He looked up. "They came out here because they knew they had good overhead cover. They're surveillance savvy, for sure. Looks like they continue on this trail west here, but the ground firms up."

Being an avid big game hunter, Chief was the default tracker when none of the pros were available.

"Good tree cover on the trail too," John pointed out.

Chief led the way, and Z and John followed keeping a healthy spacing. The rest of the team spread out in a very loose trail. When they came to the opening of the mine, Z signaled a halt.

"Chief, John and I make entry, everyone else hold security out here. Call Covey and update them on our grid. We're still in the trees so I don't think they'll pick us up, but it'll keep them in the loop."

Z looked with discomfort at the condition of the old timbers buttressing the entrance. He lowered his NVGs and turned on his IR illuminator before crossing the threshold. The others followed suit.

They had their M-4's up as they rounded the timbers and saw that it was only a few meters before the mine appeared to be caved in.

"Clear," called Z.

Chief went to white light and took a knee in the middle of the mine. Z and John hit the white lights on their helmets and looking at Chief, found him smiling as he was pulling out his tape measure.

"Oh, this is gonna be easy. They both loaded up and took off on a quad."

"I'll take it, we needed a break. We're way behind these kids."

Even John was smiling as they stepped out into the daylight.

But Z's smile diminished rapidly outside the mine. He held both hands out to catch the falling snow flakes.

"Damn," He said as he shook his head.

*   *   *

"Tony, Jeff Potter is dead."

"What?"

The Sheriff sat atop his mare and Tony upon his trusty mule. They were watching the snow squall gathering across the lake.

"Shot dead in his doorway with his hands raised," the Sheriff continued. "FBI agents did it. I was with them. They had warrants out for him and the kids for draft evasion."

Tony's perpetual smile was gone for something that steeled his tanned face close to rage. He turned his mule 'Sparky' to face the Sheriff easier.

"I had gone along with them to try to keep things mellow. FBI engaged him before the helicopter even landed. I tried to stop them, but they were already shooting when I realized what was happening."

"I haven't heard anything about this. When did it happen?"

"Two days ago. Feds have a media blackout on this, they are operating under this new War Powers Act law. I'm not supposed to tell anyone about it."

"That's BS, the whole thing. Where are the kids?"

"That's why I called you here. We have to be very careful what we say and where we say it and assume we are under surveillance at all times. I'm sure I am. The FBI is very aware of where I stand on all this."

"Damn, Sheriff, call out the boys. We'll arm up and kick all the feds out of the county."

The Sheriff smiled.

"That was my first instinct, Tony. Believe me. I talked to Joe, the county prosecutor. He kind of talked me down. This whole War Powers Act is a great big can of worms. Right now, the Feds are stretched real thin responding to this. We go hard on them, they could come down on the whole county, just to send a message. That was why they were coming after Jeff and his kids. Didn't go the way the planned so they're keeping it quiet 'til they apprehend them. Then they can send the message that draft evaders will be dealt with harshly, and it doesn't pay to resist, even if you're a special ops, counter terror war hero.

"We have to be smart about this, Tony. And we have to get to those kids and get them out of this county."

"What do I do, Sheriff?"

"You got your trap line out, Tony?"

"Mink and fox the only thing open right now, Sheriff. I usually wait a couple months. Don't have much in the way of fox up here, and the mink haven't been a real big return lately."

"If me or any of my guys are out there, Tony, we'll be targets by both the feds and the kids. Someone like you, who knows those woods like the back of your hand, you can go out there and try to make contact with the kids. You can keep tabs on the feds."

Tony smiled again.

"The feds they got out there now are from the FBI's Hostage Rescue Team. They are very good at what they do, and they aren't messing around. You'll need to be very careful if you run into them."

"And if I catch up with the kids?"

"First, see if they need anything. Make sure they're ok. If you can talk them out with you, we'll figure out something."

"Are you gonna take'em into custody?"

"Only if by doing so, I could protect them from the FBI. I'm meeting with the county prosecutor again soon. We're trying to figure out what we can do within the law. And I'm trying to figure out what I can do otherwise because we may be past that at this point."

Tony's mule snorted.

"You and your mules, Tony."

"They ain't like people, Sheriff." He patted Sparky's neck. "They ain't never let me down."

The Sheriff smiled and nodded.

*   *   *

Jane woke with a start. She didn't remember if she was startled by something in a dream, or something in the real world. At least she didn't wake up crying this time. With that thought, she remembered what it was that brought her here bundled up in the thick Wiggy's sleeping bag staring at a sky obscured by... Camouflage net. Tom must have put it up. They were under significant tree cover, she wasn't sure why he would have set that up.

Then the chill tickle of a cold snowflake settling on her exposed nose made her whole face twitch. She sat up suddenly and looked around. Everything had changed while she was asleep, everything but their predicament.

The snowfall had brought a quiet stillness to the mountains and blanketed everything white and pure.

"You still have an hour, Jane. Go back to sleep."

"When did this start?"

"I don't know, maybe an hour ago? Comin' down pretty good, isn't it?"

"We should break camp now."

"But I haven't slept yet."

"I'll drive. This snow looks like it will last a while. We get going now and any tracks we may have left at this point will be buried, and we'll have our tracks covered by snow while we're moving."

"What if it stops."

"We'll stop before the snow does."

"And the cache?"

"We don't need to restock yet, and with those helicopters earlier, maybe it's better to circle around a bit."

Tom was leaning against the front four-wheeler tire, under the camo net he'd put up over them both for some shelter from the snow. He was looking up from the Bible and looked like he wanted to say something else, but he didn't. He closed the book, put it safely away in his Go-bag and started packing.

"Jane, that Bible has a lot of stuff in it. It explains stuff."

"I remember. When Dad was on that kick to have us all read from it on Sundays, he went through it with us."

"Yeah, it seems different now though."

"So, you're like converted now?"

Tom just smiled awkwardly as Jane slinked out of the sleeping bag.

"Well I'm not, and I'm not going to be. Don't bother trying." She was stuffing the sleeping bag into the compression sack, and she seemed angry. Tom didn't understand why. He wondered if Jane did.

CHAPTER 7

Joe looked disheveled and tired. His tie was loose, and he was gulping at what was probably not his first coffee.

"Why here?" the Sheriff said as he sat down beside him.

"It just had to be anywhere besides the bank."

The beach was empty and cold. Here and all of town was covered with an inch or so of snow. The mountains had more, and it was still snowing to the north where the clouds were darker and lower.

The Sheriff just looked at Joe inquisitively.

"I got a call from the US district attorney's office yesterday a few hours after our meeting. Buddy I have at their office, called me out of the blue. He called me specifically to tell me to be very careful with our Sheriff here. That his office is looking at the War Powers Act and how it *will* be used to prosecute any obstruction by local officials, even that which has previously been legal and supported by precedent. Note that he didn't say how it *could* be used. They are going to prosecute based on this aggressively."

Joe wiped his sweaty face with a napkin, and the Sheriff leaned back and gave as reassuring a smile as he could muster.

"This tramples all over the 10th Amendment, like the Supremacy Clause on steroids and there is no way the Federal Government won't just run amok with it. It's freakin' scary, Grant."

"Does that mean you're in or out, Joe?"

"Oh, I'm in…" The prosecutor tried to force a smile, and there was an underlying confidence the Sheriff could see behind it, but clearly this wasn't easy for him.

"Welcome to the deep end of the pool, Joe."

Joe's smile widened.

"We have to be *VERY* careful now, Grant. Like all that stuff I thought you were saying yesterday that was on the edge paranoid, conspiracy theory stuff… We have to go full on spy level kind of thing to keep us out of trouble…"

"There may be no keeping out of *trouble* as this goes forward, Joe."

The Prosecutor nodded vigorously.

"No, no I get that… this is worth the risk, we have to fight this. But we have to be very smart about it. If they roll us up, we are no good to anyone, and local resistance to this could be crushed before it has a chance to take root."

"They call it OPSEC, Joe. Might want to research it. There are some standard practices that will help you out, might want to look up tradecraft while you're at it. Of course, you want to be careful of how and what you look up online."

"Yeah, I'm familiar with the cyber side of things. After that phone call, I got a laptop exclusively for all this, and I'm going to be careful where I power it up and what VPNs I use. That computer will be separate from anything else I have personal or professional. Got the whole Faraday bag for it and everything. Still shopping around for a quality tin foil hat…

"I was up late in my car using a burner phone with hotspot in town researching the WPA, I downloaded a PDF file of it and joined a legal forum. There's fifty or so like-minded lawyers and legal types on there, and we've divided it into fifty page segments. We're going to come up with summaries and highlights. Then we'll break it down further and really dig into it and figure out how it can be successfully challenged and from what level."

"Is there a chance there won't be a way to legally challenge it?"

"In ordinary times I would say no, Grant…" Joe stopped and looked out at the lake as the implications of what he was starting to say sank in for both of them.

"Look," Joe paused as a bicyclist rode by on the trail in front of them. "What I have read of my section so far, they are laying the ground work for a national, federal police force. This goes beyond CALEA accreditation standards. This is classic Commie style stuff. Cops will be transferred around the country. If you're a cop, you don't work where you've lived for more than five years. They have this position laid out called the DCO. The Diversity Compliance Officer. It's a low-level position but with lots of potential power, basically a Commissar or Political Officer."

"Sounds like a good old-fashioned County Sheriff will be out of a job."

"Grant, I swear, you'll be lucky if that's all it is. I'm thinking I just haven't gotten to the part about re-education camps. None of this will happen overnight, but if this goes unchallenged, in ten years the structure of our country will be unrecognizable. We are on the cusp of a post-constitutional America, Grant. What we are looking at here is bigger than Jeff Potter and his kids. Its bigger than some rural County Sheriff and Prosecutor."

"Then we better get it right."

"How can you possibly be so calm right now?"

"It's kind of part of the job, being cool when everyone else is losing their mind. Just now it's happening on a bigger scale. And what you've just said is really kind of a relief."

"How can you possibly say that, have you actually been listening to what I'm saying?"

"I had a horse once, years ago. A little Morgan. I got a good deal on 'im 'cause the owner just said he couldn't handle him. Well, I never met a horse I didn't like, and I was afraid of where this horse would wind up. Pretty, dark grey mottled coat with an almost silver blaze, and he and I seemed to hit it off. Or, I thought we did. Out of nowhere sometimes, something would set him off... and I never quite figured out what it was. Well, one day I was way out on a trail ride. I didn't have much with me because it was just a day ride, but we were way back there, just he and I.

"And something set him off, and he started to kickin' and buckin' and seriously trying to throw me. No matter how much I thought this horse and I got along, all of a sudden he wanted nothin' more to do with me. And as we were whirilin' around in circles, and I was trying to get him under control, about a million different things went through my mind. I didn't have much gear on me if I had to walk out... if I got hurt, if he threw me, no one really knew to come look for me... and the fear of how much it might hurt if I were to come out of the saddle."

The Sheriff took a break to look out to say hello to an elderly couple walking past.

"So, what happened, Grant?"

"Oh, sure enough he finally tossed me pretty good. And it was really strange. I had just enough time to think 'relax'. See, it was finally made up for me. There was no point worrying in that moment or two before I hit the ground. No point being as tense as I was, that would only make it hurt more. The fact was I was thrown and nothing could change that I was about to hit the ground.

"See, we've been swirllin' around on this wild ride for some time now, Joe. This finally begins to make some things a little clearer."

*   *   *

Z told Chief to set the pace as fast as he could follow sign, and he worked the team on the wide mountain trail at first. An old logging trail cut through trees now at least a hundred years old. They followed the snow encrusted four-wheeler track until the snow became too deep. Then the pace slowed as Chief looked at the ground from different angles when the trail seemed to branch off, or on occasion, disappear in snow laden undergrowth.

The sturdy men of the HRT team weren't equipped for the surprise early snow fall, but they were accustomed to difficult field conditions and pressed on without complaint.

"Hey, Z. Just getting word from air," the radio man called out.

Z brought the element to a halt.

"What they got?"

"Number 2 ship had another chip light, they are down until further notice, looking at possible engine swap."

"Are you freakin' kidding me?"

"They are in coms with command, and their maintenance is trying to sort out the course of action. Command is up, standby."

This wasn't progress, this wasn't beginning to catch up, and it was starting to feel like falling further behind. The snow made everything quiet even under the electronically amplified noise cancelling headsets. It was certainly a pretty part of the country, and Z took the moment to just appreciate that. He could see what brought Jeff here. The beauty, the quiet, the wilderness and the wildness.

A great place to raise kids and make up for lost time. A great place to hunker down and prepare for a fight.

"Z, Command is giving us three options," the radio man said, moving the boom mic from in front of his face. "One, we use the cabin as a base camp and work from there, they'll keep us resupplied. Two, we extract now until lift is fixed. Three, we press on knowing that between weather and being down a helo, we may not have lift when we want or need it."

"We press," Z said. "It's not bad yet, and we'll keep option one open, but that will be losing ground. Just in case, have them drop off a resupply at the cabin and request latest weather. Also have them see about assembling our winter kits."

The radio man nodded, repositioned his boom mic and went out with it.

The team had halted, and most of the men were using the time to hydrate or snack. The steeper parts of the snow-covered path were slick, and one of the men slipped and went down pretty hard. It garnered a brief laugh from the team and cursing by the agent involved.

Z looked at the team, then back out at the surroundings. Things could go sideways with just the weather and no one was even shooting yet. Chief was down on a knee again, looking at the track from a different angle, digging gently under the layer of snow.

"Message passed, Z. And to add to the bad news, air just passed that Covey is out due to icing. Standing by for that weather report."

"Ah, great, no ISR. It's all up to you then, Chief."

The big man was getting up from his knee smiling and smelling something on his hand.

"Smell my finger, Z."

"I'm not falling for that again," Z laughed as he walked toward him.

Chief extended his hand, and Z took a quick sniff.

"Gasoline?" Z said quizzically.

"Yup. Their quad has a leak."

"Must be pretty bad to still be enough there to smell?" Chief shrugged.

"Can't be good, that's for sure. Let's see if we can't get a dog up here, Z."

Z looked back at the radio man who nodded and went out with the request on the command net.

"Request in. And I'll have weather for you in a moment." The radio man had his notebook out and was scribbling quickly.

"Continued snowfall through the rest of the day, trailing off after 6pm local. Expecting four inches in the mountains with temps dropping into the high twenties tonight."

"Maybe we can catch up with these kids because they've run out of gas."

"They're staying under the trees, the trail has gone cold a few times, but as long as we have some path and tree cover, with this gas leak we can stay on it despite the snow."

"What about getting our one helo out here and trying to regain some ground?" Z was pulling out his topo map and orienting it with his GPS.

"There's enough tree cover still that they have some options here, we may wind up guessing wrong if we do that. They are trending toward higher elevation, they get above the tree line that might be a good bet."

"Alright, Chief. We're on your pace. Let's see if we can't have them in custody by dark."

*   *   *

"What?" asked Jane.

"Do you smell that?"

"Smell what?"

"Smells like gasoline, Jane."

She stopped the four-wheeler.

"Oh, yeah. I smell it now too. Damn. I bet it's coming from this Jerry can and we can't afford to be losing fuel now." She swung the NODs up on the helmet out of her way and they shut off automatically as she reached for her head lamp.

Tom dismounted and Jane followed. She took off her glove and felt around the bottom of the Jerry can's cap.

"No sign of a leak here."

Tom took off the seat and looked at the running engine. He was hit with the smell as soon as the seat was off. He shook his head in the darkness.

"It's coming from the engine, Jane."

"That's not good… It's probably that high ethanol eating at the fuel lines and fuel injection, just like the other ones."

"How long do we have?"

"I don't know, but there's nothing we can do about it. We don't have any parts or enough tools to get creative." She was looking at the engine with the green filter of her headlamp and kind of shielding it with other hand as an attempt at light discipline.

"What will we do then, if it quits on us?"

"Then we go on foot."

Tom sighed and slumped a little.

"We get to the south cache, it has better packs and some winter gear, including snow shoes. We can do this, Tom. We have to do this."

It had only been a few days, and Tom was afraid he was wearing down already.

"Let's keep going, Tom. We circle back to the south cache, get what we need and start working our way north. The snow is a little early, but it's to our advantage. It's not too cold yet. This will probably melt in the next week or so, we'll use it while we can."

"How long, Jane? How long do we do this? Do we live the rest of our lives like this?"

"You saw what they did to Dad. You think they won't do that to us? Look at everything Dad did for this country, for this government, and they murdered him with his hands up." Jane's voice cracked, and the tears came faster than she thought they would. She lowered the NODs and looked out to the wilderness trying to hide the show of emotion, but the green light from the devices only served to display her sadness.

"I keep playing that over and over in my head, Tom. That image of him with his hands up in the light. He was buying us time. He was surrendering so we could get out, and we could be free. He was always ready to sacrifice for us to be safe and free. In the end he sacrificed everything so at the very least we could be free. That's what this is, Tom. This is freedom, and it isn't easy, but I think the very least we owe him is not giving up. Really, I think we owe him a lot more, I think we need to make them pay."

Jane's tears were infectious, and Tom spoke through his own.

"With what, Jane? I mean really. We're two kids with an 80 year old rifle and an AR. How does that stack up to whole teams of them and helicopters and assault rifles and machine guns?"

"Remember that book Dad had us read about Simo Hayha, the Finnish sniper in World War II? He killed five hundred Soviet soldiers in less than four months, with a bolt action rifle and a submachine gun. Imagine what he could have done with a Garand."

"He got his face shot off, Jane."

"And he survived the war. He lived into his 90's. You think he wasn't scared, you think he wasn't cold?"

"He had an army supporting him."

"We'll have support."

"Who, Jane? Who in the world do you think will support us?"

"A lot of people in this area will. I bet there are all kinds of people out there upset about the news of Dad's murder, and they'll help us anyway we can."

"There'll be just as many who'll turn us in for a bounty, maybe more."

Jane wiped her face, she couldn't argue that.

"So, how do we know the difference between who will help and who will turn us in?"

"We're a long way from needing that, Tom. We're self-sufficient for now, with tons of supplies to get us through at least winter, even without having to shoot anything for food."

"Dad said we were equipped to run, not fight, Jane. That's not what he wanted from us."

She sniffled before she spoke.

"But Dad is gone, and it's our fight now. When this machine dies, we'll only be able to run for so long then. When the time comes, we'll have to be prepared to fight. Fight smart and fight hard. One shot, one kill, remember, Dad was always saying that?"

"And I always sucked at that," Tom said trying to laugh.

"I didn't." Jane looked through the NODs into the green illuminated wilderness as the tears stopped.

*   *   *

"You do that again, Carver, and I *will* shoot you."

The Marshal's smile melted, and he stopped rocking.

"You're seriously freaked out by these things, huh?"

"You brought me here, Carver, now talk."

The Marshal nodded and let the chair lift settle a little before he started. The climb up the mountain was, in fact, daunting enough. Rocking was a bit much for someone uncomfortable with the ride to begin with.

"The HRT team has a trail, but they're having to start over every day. This early snow is throwing them, and they have no overhead coverage except their helicopters, and they're having maintenance issues."

The Sheriff looked at the man in the Arc'Teryx jacket and snow pants.

"Whose side are you on, Carver?"

The man sighed and slumped a little.

"I don't need to be here, Grant."

The Sheriff studied him a moment, then nodded.

"I get that, Carver. But I also have to be careful of people feeding me the wrong info right now."

The Marshal nodded.

"Grant, you have to be very careful. This War Powers Act is some scary stuff."

"That's what I hear."

The Marshal shook his head into the nothingness of white laced pines and slopes passing slowly below them.

"You have no idea, Grant. This is really bad. They are forming a national police force. This is like Stazi or KGB level stuff, but worse with today's technology. Departments like yours may already be infiltrated, you need to be very careful who you trust with what."

"Says the Fed."

The Marshal sat very straight and looked hard at the Sheriff.

"I've always been straight with you, I don't need to be here now."

The Sheriff nodded.

"I'm sorry, Carver. I'm not in a real good place right now."

"I guess nobody is really, huh?"

The Marshal forced a smile, and the Sheriff returned it.

"So, what do we do here, Carver?"

The Marshal just shook his head.

"I'm just going to try to be a conduit of intel to you, Grant. But I have to be very careful. It's more than just losing my retirement or my dental plan. If they figure me out, I can't help you. This is going to have to happen from the local level. If people like me get spooked, you're screwed."

"You're right, Carver. And I apologize. It's getting real hard to tell who to trust these days."

"You have no idea…"

"My first priority, Carver, is to bring these kids into safety. Do I need to take them into custody for that?"

"Negative, that would be the very worst thing you could do right now. You bring them in, FBI finds out, they come and take them. There'll be no stopping them. Where they go from there is unprecedented in U.S. history. I'm talking worse than Japanese internment camps. This is like something in the Aleutian Islands where no one hears from them again, and that's not hyperbole, that's part of the plan."

"Or they just kill them out right."

The Marshal just nodded silently and the Sheriff inhaled.

"What's the next step then, Carver?"

"They're kind of all in on the HRT guys tracking them down. That team needs to be slowed down, one way or another."

"What can I do to help these kids?"

Carver shrugged.

"I have no idea. I just want to keep comms open between us, on the down low."

"I sure appreciate that."

"We're in a lot of trouble right now, Sheriff. This country, I mean."

The Sheriff nodded silently and pointed at a young bull moose they were passing over as it munched on the local greenery.

"Ah, what a life," the Sheriff said. "Only two things on your mind and eating is the easiest one."

"Yeah, but both of them get us in trouble, eh?"

They both laughed, but only to break the tension. Then they each looked out at the snow-covered mountainsides.

"Should be a good ski season, I suspect."

"I would imagine, Grant."

"Where are the HRT guys now?"

"'Bout three days behind. The weather isn't helping. Between lift issues and ISR weather cancels, they're hurting. Of course, they figure they have the mass and inertia to outlast anyone."

"How will I know who to trust, Carver?"

"Wish I could help you there, Sheriff. I can't, in good faith, tell you that you can trust me."

The Sheriff just sighed as the chair lift approached the summit.

*   *   *

Breske tugged gently on the reins as he crested the rise in the trail. Below, he saw a large man with dark complexion in multi-cams and full combat load out, down on one knee, inspecting something on the ground. The man was focused on a track or sign or something on the ground and had an HK-416 carbine held across his leg. He either heard Breske's steed, or sensed Breske watching him, and he stood up quickly, holding his fist up as if to stop a column.

When their eyes met, Breske gave a big smile and continued riding toward the big man.

"What ya' got, Chief?" Breske heard someone call out from further down the trail.

"Standby," was the curt response.

"Hey," Breske said, holding the smile and nodding his head.

The big man nodded back, obviously assessing the situation.

"What ya' looking for?" Breske asked helpfully.

"Training exercise," was the only response. The rest of the team were shadows of movement amid the snow and trees as they went to cover.

A man even bigger, who carried himself like the team leader, crunched up the snowy trail behind the one he called Chief and he cheerfully returned Breske's smile.

"What brings you out this way?" inquired Z.

Breske held up the Connibears on chains he had draped across the saddle horn.

"Mink." Breske said, and he directed his gaze back to Chief. "So, what tribe are you, man? I'm quarter Kalispell myself."

The big man looked at him strangely a moment before speaking, as if processing what had just been said.

"Oh... no tribe. I'm Italian."

"Oh, I thought I heard them call you Chief."

"Ah... no, I do the tracking, they think I look like an Indian... that's the joke."

Breske laughed.

"Who said you Feds don't have a sense of humor."

"Who said we were feds?" Z asked through a big smile.

"Well, the military guys all do their secret squirrel and survival stuff out Coleville way, and yer' too well equipped for militia types out here."

"Guilty as charged," Z laughed.

"Yer not like a US Fish and Wildlife SWAT team or something are you? I mean I got my license, and all my traps are legal, and mink started a couple weeks ago..."

"No, no man, relax." Z was easy to want to like.

"Cause, it seems like everybody has a SWAT team nowadays and..."

"Yeah, that's the truth. Relax, man. Hey, everybody calls me Z. We're FBI, just doing some training in the area. We're looking for a young man and woman on a quad, and you know how they run these things, they have everything stacked in their favor, so it's kind of embarrassing us, ya know? Any chance you've seen them or their track?"

"Nah, I ain't seen anybody. That's why I like runnin' my trap line out here. Never see anyone until now. Hey, seriously, I'm legit, you wanna see my license and inspect my traps? I got in trouble with the state guys a few years back, and I run a clean ship now, man. I don't wanna..."

Z just laughed.

"Nah, we're good, man. Hey, let me give you my card. You give us a call you see anything out this way, then we can be done here and out of your way, so we don't mess up your trapping or anything."

The man strutted through the snow like a professional athlete. He pulled off his gloves and reached into a pocket in his plate carrier. He looked at the rifle in its scabbard under Breske's leg as he reached out to hand him the card. In return Breske handed him his trapping license anyway.

"Well if you insist." Z pulled a note book out of his gear and made note of the name listed there. Arnold Peters

"Nice rifle, Mr. Peters. Winchester?" Z said as he handed Breske back the trapping license.

"Yeah, my grandfather's 94. .32 Winchester Special."

"Classic, man. That's awesome."

"Mountain lions, Broh. They're thick out this way." Breske looked back to where he thought the last man in the element might be. "They start gettin' hungry this time o' year. They'll grab the last guy in the pack. Be sharp."

That last man broke from cover, eyes widened and Breske kept his cool, skillfully suppressing a smile.

*   *   *

"I don't smell it now."

Jane shook her head in the brightening dawn. The snow was coming down harder now, and that was good. They would approach the cache, get the gear they needed and hide it again. The snow would help a lot. Even now she suspected it was enough to ground the helicopters and keep the drones from seeing them. They could breathe a little easier today as they set their camp.

"Maybe it's not a fuel line, maybe it's something in the fuel injectors or pump. Anyway, we get to the cache, get everything we think we might need in the next hour and come back here to load up the four-wheeler and move a few miles for camp. The snow helps."

"Until it gets too deep."

She replaced the seat, satisfied with her inspection of the engine.

"We have snow shoes here, good parkas. If it gets that deep, we go as far as we can and hunker down in a snow cave. This might be hard for us, but it's harder for them. Their helicopters can't move them around in weather like this, their drones can't see us. This is actually really good, but I honestly don't think it will last long, it's too early in the year. I bet it goes back up into the 50's tomorrow and this is melted by the end of the week. Then we'll have the opposite problem with a lot of soft ground. We should plan ahead for that."

She looked at the GPS she had on her wrist then looked around. In the early dawn light and the snow, everything looked different, but 100 paces north and 100 east should take them from this way point to a position where she would see the boulder, and she could find the cache from there.

Jane's breath condensed like a thick fog in the cold and the heavy snow. With her Garand cradled in front of her, she started her pace count from the waypoint. At one hundred paces, she turned east and started again.

At the end of that pace count, she looked around. It took a moment. With the visibility reduced by the heavy snowfall, it all looked different now.

Covered in a few inches of snow, and the trees and brush, snow laden around it, it took a moment to pick out the boulder. When she did, she realized a flaw in her father's planning.

Jane saw the unnatural flatness in the door to the cache. Maybe if someone weren't looking for it, they wouldn't notice. But she did.

She unslung her Garand and checked to make sure the Gorilla tape was still in place protecting the barrel from the falling snow. Leaning it carefully against the boulder, she shuffled through the snow to the flatness that so concerned her.

Tom was looking around attentively with his AR-15 held at the low ready, but the visibility was so limited, it was nearly pointless. Quickly, Jane was uncovering the snow, then the dirt that covered the door of the southern cache.

Finding the little paracord loop on the door, she lifted it open. While not nearly as impressive as the Northern cache, Tom's eyes widened as he got closer and saw the cinder block and wood construction below the door. Jane had her headlamp out and was shuffling around the contents of the shelves, saying something that Tom couldn't hear. He took his AR-15 and leaned it next to the Garand, its muzzle protected by a purpose made plastic cover.

When he got back to the door of the cache, he noticed it was snowing even harder. Jane was on the steps waiting for him with her arms full of backpack.

"There's a minus 20 degree rated bag in there in vacuum wrap, as well as one of those Wiggy's parkas, also vacuum wrapped, heck, everything in here is vacuum wrapped. Dad went nuts with that vacuum sealer."

She finished her sentence with a smile, the first one he'd seen from her in days, and he smiled back.

170

"More MREs and some Mountain House stuff for a change. Some thermal underwear… he had a pack like this for each of us, so there's a spare one now."

"We don't have room on the four-wheeler."

"Strap them to the sides or something, whatever works. There's still more in here we need to take, especially if that thing is about to die."

"Well, if we can't fit it on the four-wheeler, how are we gonna carry all this?"

She had turned to descend back into the cache and stopped to look over her shoulder.

"What we are getting here is giving us options. We can hunker down, we can pack out… it's good to have options."

Jane stepped back down and grabbed the next pack, then handed it up to Tom.

"Wait a minute," she turned again and stacked two pairs of snowshoes on top. "Go load that stuff up, just have a few more things here."

When Tom came back, Jane's face was more serious. She handed him more vacuum-packed gear.

"If Dad didn't want us to fight, he wouldn't have this in here, Tom. It's a couple of bandoliers of .30-06, Black Tip and a chest rig with six loaded thirty round magazines for an AR."

"Dad probably figured it was good to have options." Tom smiled, and Jane grinned for a moment.

"Hey." The soft, unknown voice seemed to thunder through the valley, and Jane felt her heart stop as Tom spun to look for the source. A dark figure on a pale spotted mule emerged quietly from snow, downhill toward where they left the four-wheeler. The mule's nostrils flared and its breath looked thick enough to be smoke as it labored up the hill in the deepening snow.

Jane looked at the lever gun across the man's lap, then to the Garand and the AR impossibly far away against the boulder. She thought of the Glock in her waist band and for an instant she thought how much they could use a mule if the four-wheeler was about to go down.

"Tom, Jane. I'm Tony Breske, I knew your Dad, and I'm here to help."

Tom looked back at Jane, and she just gave a nearly imperceptible shake of her head, uncertain.

"It's OK. I've heard what happened, and I want to help."

"How did you find us?"

"Took me a couple days. Finally picked up your trail at first light today, heard ya' about an hour before that. It's alright, you're doin' pretty good so far. My family goes back here more than a few generations, I grew up here. It's in my blood.

"You're sticking to the old logging trails because of your machine. It'll work for now, the tracker they have on you ain't real good. They call him Chief, but I think that must be like Chief of the Wannabe Tribe."

Tom and Jane looked at each other.

The rider laughed before he delivered the punch line.

"You know, he *wanna be* an Indian." The rider laughed harder. "Sorry, old Indian joke. Look, this guy ain't great and he ain't no Indian, but you gotta be better to stay ahead, especially 'cause it's the government and they don't like to lose. You got FBI Hostage Rescue Team lookin' for you. I ran into them yesterday. This tracker they have ain't great, but all he has to do is get lucky once. And he may not be great at trackin', but he looks mighty serious. Same with his team leader, man with a fake smile. I bet they're a sight better at killin' than trackin'."

"How many?" asked Jane.

"Twelve. Two helicopters, for now. The longer you frustrate them, the more they'll commit, 'cause, like I said, they don't like to lose. They're staging out of your cabin right now, so they are starting over every day. They weren't equipped for this weather. No real cold weather gear on 'em, no snowshoes or skis. The weather has been on your side, but that changes tomorrow."

"How do we know we can trust you?" Tom blurted.

The rider had gotten close enough they could see his big smile.

"You don't, you absolutely don't. But I am here to help, you have people who know this is wrong, and they want to get you out. You can come out with me if you want."

"No thanks." Jane stepped up out of the cache.

"Is there anything you need, anything I can get you?"

"What are they saying about our Dad in the news? We haven't been able to pick up anything but Canadian news, and they haven't talked about it."

"They have a news blackout about what happened. Officially, no one knows about what happened at your cabin. They're keepin' it quiet so as not to rile folks…"

"You said people want to get us out, if they've kept this quiet, how do they know?"

"Word is gettin' out, they can't keep somethin' like that quiet forever, not in a place like this."

"What would you do if you were us?" Tom asked.

"Exactly what you're doin'. I wouldn't ever get that far from my rifle again though." Breske nodded to the snow sprinkled Garand and AR leaning against the boulder.

Jane sighed, breathing a little easy.

"You got everything you need from there? I'll help you cover it up proper. Your Dad should have consulted a trapper like me about concealing a cache, especially one who may, or may not have done a little poachin' in his day."

"Ick..." Chief grimaced as he pulled his hand up full of muddy beef stew. The two nearly symmetrical low patches in the snow had attracted his attention. The other sign led him to believe this was an encampment. Upon realizing what it was, he looked back up at Z.

"Dakota fire pit." He struggled in the loose dirt a moment and came up with the near empty can of Dinty Moore. "They got spooked while they were cooking."

"We're falling farther behind, aren't we, Chief?"

The man nodded silently while wiping off his hand in the cold snow. The snow was done now, and the world around them glistened a white and silver of slowly melting frozen precipitation as the temperature rose.

"They're circling back, Z." John said looking at his tablet.

"No," said Chief. "They're evading. They don't have a specific place to go other than *away*."

Z just nodded and looked up at the clearing sky.

"Well, maintenance got that engine swap done. We get the third ship and a couple more shooters in tonight and more overhead surveillance. I think we finally start getting ahead as of today and tomorrow. All this snow melts over the next week, and we have nothing but good soft snow and muddy ground for them to lay unmistakable tracks."

"What happens when we catch up with them, Z?" It was the question everyone on the team wanted to ask at this point, but only John was in the position to.

Z flashed a big smile.

"It goes one of two ways. They surrender, and we take them into custody, or they don't and we kill them. That's kind of up to them, isn't it?"

"I know, Z. But... I didn't think these kids could be on the run this long."

"It's not even a week yet," Z snapped. "Look, we got thrown into this from the food riots, then we got this damn weather, they haven't given us the equipment or the personnel… We'll get them, they're just a couple of kids, and we sure as hell don't need to be making them out to be anything more than that. This isn't some hardened haji with his back to the wall in some walled compound in Iraq. This is a couple of typical American kids who just want to get back to their phones and their internet and be left the hell alone. Are we clear on that?"

Z looked around at the gathered team and realized his rant was out of character. He tried to flash his characteristic smile to play it off, but he wasn't sure it worked.

*   *   *

The Sheriff smiled, looking out at the slough.

"Yeah, I'd say they're doin' pretty good. Well equipped, more importantly, well trained and good mindset I think. They let themselves get more distance from their rifles than they should have, but I don't think they'll do that again."

"How far out ahead would you put them?"

The setting sun was nestling into the mountains, and everything around them was dripping with melting snow.

"Well, that could change here, pretty quick. Clear skies, mud and sloppy snow. They'll be leaving a clear track now and won't be moving fast. Fed boys will have the mobility advantage, and the whole eye in the sky thing with those drones. Right now, with whatever progress they were able to make today, I'd put the feds a day behind them and closing fast."

"If it weren't for the Feds, how long do you think they could last?"

"Oh, they could be out there 'til they get tired of it all. It looks like they grew up with this stuff, they're comfortable out there even when it's uncomfortable. It all depends on what The Man brings down on them, Sheriff. They could be done by the end of the week if they catch their fresh track, sooner even."

"They showed no interest in coming in?"

"None, they were pretty suspicious of me. I thought that was good."

"Do you think they'll fight, Tony? Or will they give up?"

"There was fire in the girl's eyes, Sheriff. I didn't get much of a read off the boy, but for a moment, I thought she wanted to shoot me and take my mule. Like, you know, you can just see that in some people. I seen it in her."

The Sheriff nodded grimly, leaning on the flat bed of Tony's old Dodge.

"What do you think we can do best for them? Do they need anything?"

"They need time and distance from those Feds."

"Did they tell you if they have any kind of plan?"

"I think the only plan they have is to run. But they're gonna fight if they have to, and I wouldn't wanna be on the receiving end of the girl's fury. Boy might do his share, too. What they been through, I couldn't blame 'em."

"When can you go back out there, Tony?"

"I'll be back tomorrow. I got traps to tend to. Not doin' any cuttin' right now... deer opens up next week, too. I can be out there as much as you need me... as much as they need me. You want me to run some interference while I'm out?"

The Sheriff inhaled audibly and looked at the man sideways.

"You need to be *very* careful out there, Tony. Remember, you're no good to anybody if you get yourself shot or rolled up by the FBI."

176

"Heck, Sheriff, I been arrested a few times, no big deal... you even done it to me once..." Tony smiled teasingly. "I know, I know, I get it."

*   *   *

Chief looked at the track, then referenced his notes and pulled out his tape measure.

"Yeah, Z. It's the same machine, but they're carrying a heavier load now."

"What does that mean, Chief?"

The big man shrugged and thought a moment.

"I'd say they resupplied, stocked up. That quad was runnin' heavy to begin with, now they put more weight on it and it has some kind of intermittent fuel problem."

"They have help out here? Maybe that guy on the mule?"

"That or they had a supply cache out here somewhere, we could back track and look."

Z shook his head.

"If we had more people we would." Z turned to the radio man. "Go out to Covey with this position, see if they can pick up the track anywhere ahead or behind us. These trees are thinning out a little here. Also see if they can make out some rhyme or reason behind these old trails they're staying on."

"Roger that, going out on air freq."

"How old you think this track is, Chief?"

The big man sunk his thumb in the mud next to the track then grabbed a little hand full of mud from the original track and ran it through his fingers.

"I'm thinking about 12 hours, they're runnin' at night, I think, Z."

"Hmm. Good to know." Z nodded pensively. "Yeah, that makes sense. Probably have night vision, too. So, they run at night and bed down during the day. We got all this snow melt now and all the mud. We got that third helicopter in, we got the additional guys. We start getting on a hot trail we can have those guys sit REDCON 2, and we can get out ahead of them.

"I've got a good feeling about this, Z."

Z smiled and nodded.

*   *   *

"I didn't do it!" She exclaimed.

"What do you mean?"

She dropped it to neutral and hit the starter. The engine wouldn't fire, but the smell of gasoline grew stronger.

"No, Jane, not here."

"It's not my choice!" She was hitting the starter feverishly, but it spun without firing, and the smell of gasoline grew stronger.

"That's it, this thing's done."

Tom looked up at the stars, they were crossing a big break in the tree cover.

"It's really exposed here, Jane. Should we set it on fire or something."

"That would be stupid, Tom."

She raised the NODs and turned on her headlamp with the green filter. She looked at him in the pale green illumination.

"I'm sorry, Tom."

"No, you're right. I'm not thinking straight, I guess. But we need to push it somewhere in cover or something."

"Yeah, we'll push it up over there. Maybe it doesn't much matter with this snow and mud. They're gonna find it. If only it happened back at the stream."

"Should we push it back that way, Jane?"

"I don't think it's worth the time and effort. We just have to assume they're gonna find it, and take everything we need but nothing we don't."

"We're gonna be packin' heavy. We're really gonna be slow." Tom helped her push the machine to the brush she had pointed to earlier.

"Tom, we can do this... all their gear and body armor and all the stuff they have to carry and you heard what that Tony guy said, no snow shoes. It's like we were born for this Tom. Remember all the times Dad had us chasing each other on snowshoes?"

"They have helicopters, Jane."

"We have the home field advantage, Tom." She started stripping packs off the four-wheeler. When she got to the camo netting, she pulled her sheath knife out and cut it roughly in half. "I've got some more ideas, Tom. Stuff Dad told us about, stuff I've read about. We're gonna make them work for every inch of this. Heck, maybe we've been slowing ourselves down being tied to the machine, having to stay under tree cover and terrain we could navigate with it. Now we can really get outside the box."

She was smiling above the green glow of the head lamp around her neck.

"When we can't run any more, Jane?"

Her smile vanished.

"I told you, Tom. Then we fight, get your mind ready for it. Remember how you were with that tourniquet for Dad?"

Tom nodded hesitantly.

"That's how you'll be when the time comes. I know you will, Tom. In the mean time we run, and we run them in circles." A mischievous grin cracked in the dim light.

CHAPTER 8

"Well, I'll be damned…"

"What, Chief? What ya' got?" Z saw the big man looking up from one knee where he was examining the quad track in the mud, snow and slush. Then Z smelled it. "Oh, yeah, I smell it now."

"Not just that, look." Chief was standing up pointing to the nearby brush line. The scattered form of camo netting covering a machine that could only be the quad they had been tracking all week.

"Hell, yeah," Z turned back to his men. "Spread out, we're not gonna rush this. Chief and I go ahead and make sure they haven't set an ambush. Brower call air. I want all three helos and their crews and our additional shooters up Condition 2. Then get Covey one-four eyes on us for defensive scan, and Covey one-two finding and following any tracks away from this grid."

"Rog, goin' out on air support freq with those requests." The radio man was keyed up and talking, and the rest of the team had fanned out and found cover as Z and Chief approached the hidden machine cautiously.

Looking for booby traps and up and down any clear lanes of fire, they found no sign of anything other than quick abandonment of the quad that smelled of gasoline. Scattered around were assorted packs, bags and containers and leading away from the broken machine were two sets of snow shoe tracks.

"How long, Chief?"

"Hours, maybe six, max. Get our lift going and get out ahead of them?"

"Not yet, the helos will spook them, and they can take up better defensive position. If we get Covey's eyes on them, we'll see what we've got to work with. For now, we run them down."

"What about keeping eye steady stare on this, in case they come back for something."

"I'm outa sensors, Chief. Besides, look at how they rifled through everything. They knew they weren't coming back here for anything.

"Gonna be a hard push in this wet snow, Boss. They look like they're carryin' quite a load, but they still got snowshoes, and that's a big help in this stuff."

"This is what we train for, Chief. We got ourselves a bunch of combat athlete studs just chompin' at the bit. I say we end this today."

*　　*　　*

Joe wasn't even wearing a tie. His eyes were baggy, what hair he had was out of place, and his face drawn with concern.

"Grant, this is all really bad."

The trees of the little forest park in town were dripping with the last remnants of melting snow.

"That's all you keep telling me, Joe." The Sheriff tried to give an inspiring smile, but the Prosecutor wasn't buying it.

"We're finding all kinds of bad stuff in this War Powers Act. This Diversity Compliance Officer stuff is really scary. Low level guys with a lot of power and influence. Really the communist commissar position. And doing some basic leg work, we're finding that these positions were already funded as much as a few years ago, before the law was even passed."

The Sheriff just looked at the tired man.

"This means some of these people have already been recruited. These people are already in departments all over the country. They've been studying, taking notes deciding who's on the good list and who's on the bad list. Waiting for this law to go into place. Now all the pieces fall together. All the legal authority is there now. Funding for that facility in Adak, that island in the Aleutians, yeah, that's really happening now, Grant. You may already have a Deputy taking notes about you."

"Joe, this is patently unconstitutional." He tried to pull off the reassuring smile again, but there was doubt there.

"Grant, that's how this Communism and Socialism stuff works. You vote your way into it and then..."

"*Then?*" the Sheriff asked.

"You vote your way into it, and then all you can do is shoot your way out of it."

*   *   *

"Are you sure this is gonna work, Jane?" Tom panted heavily as he looked down the hill they had just run up. "It's really awkward."

"Is that paracord holding up for you?" Jane was also breathing heavy against the cold air, her hamstrings burning.

"Kind of, it's just... It's a lot of work. And I'm worried we're just taking ourselves back and..." He leaned back a moment against one of the cedars, putting some of the weight of the big pack on the tree.

"That's the idea, Tom. Trust me on this, we get there and get back to the stream, then we buy ourselves back any time we lost."

"This is really risky, Jane."

"That's why it'll work, Tom. Just trust me."

"He was doing what?" The Sheriff said as he was reviewing the other reports.

"Sobriety checkpoint, out route five last night," Craig said.

"Out by the Corner Bar, no doubt."

Markdale nodded.

"Roped Larry into helping him with it."

"Larry? That's another conversation… Did you remind them it's pretty clearly outlined in our SOPs we don't do that?"

"I did, Larry knew better and he got it, you know how impressionable he is though. Ted on the other hand didn't seem to understand at first. Said back in his old department, they would get all the stats they needed for the month in a one-night sobriety checkpoint."

"You told him what I think of stats, right?"

Markdale laughed.

"I sure did, the whole do the right thing by your shift mates, and the public and the rest will sort itself out."

"Am I gonna need to talk to him directly? Have Sergeant Perry or the Lieutenant set him straight?"

Markdale shrugged.

"Guess we'll see."

The Sheriff leaned forward, elbows on his desk.

"Is he gonna be a problem child, Craig? One of these; *in my old department we used to,* guys."

Markdale shrugged again, and the Sheriff leaned back in his chair.

"Or worse, what are the chances he's some kind of Federal plant?"

"What do you mean? Where does that come from?" Craig crossed his arms, looked at his feet and laughed a little. "That sounds like some kind of crazy conspiracy theory Alex Jones stuff, Sheriff."

"You think so, Craig?"

The Deputy rubbed his ear and inspected his feet again.

"Just sounds kind of crazy is all. I mean to what end would they do that?"

"Imagine if they were going to Federalize police forces, get rid of County Sheriffs and Deputies… Poof, you are now an ordained Federal agent, and you are now working for the Federal government."

"Aw, well, I imagine that would be found unconstitutional, and it would never go through, right? I mean, where's this coming from?"

The Sheriff shrugged.

"And what if before that happened, Federal Agents were planted in different rural county agencies, especially ones that have a history of contention with the Feds. That way they'd get a feel in advance of who they could trust to play nice and who would resist."

"Sounds crazy to me, Sheriff."

The Sheriff nodded.

"Of course, I suppose that person could be anybody, couldn't it, Craig?"

"I don't know, Sheriff, sounds crazy to me… Hey, what's the latest on the Potter kids?"

"Still loose as far as I know, but maybe we won't even hear if they get taken into custody, I suppose."

"What about getting somebody in to try to find 'em first?"

"Oh, that. Just an idea, Craig. You know I like bouncing all my ideas off you first. Like this Federal informant thing. You're like my voice of reason, Craig. You keep me steady."

Craig smiled and nodded a little.

"Chief, you're killin' me here. You see what's happening, don't you? Look at your GPS."

"What?"

"Yeah, we're goin' in a big circle. We keep going like this we wind up back at their quad."

Z halted his team.

Chief got down on his hands and knees and looked over the snow shoe tracks very closely and from several angles. He rocked back up to his knees wiping his face with hands cold from the snow of the tracks he was probing.

"What, Chief?" Z asked with concern.

"Somewhere, probably back in the rocky stuff, with all those switchbacks, these kids switched their snow shoes around... They're walking backward in their snow shoes to lead us in a big circle. We follow this, it's gonna take us close to that stream. Then the tracks are gonna loop right back to their quad, and then we'll find that they backed out their same tracks to the stream. They either went up stream or they went down stream in that to throw us off. This whole thing was just to mess with our heads and throw us off."

"Brower, I want Covey one-two looking upstream for tracks coming out of the stream, I want one-four looking downstream for the same thing. We rest here a bit 'til they have a look around."

"Rog."

Z looked back at his team. They looked wet and tired.

"Givens, how's that rolled ankle holding up?"

"Ah, it's starting to swell pretty good. I can press for a little while longer."

"This loose, wet snow isn't doing anyone any good, Z."

"I know, John. We are *so* close."

"How 'bout I take half the team upstream, you take the other downstream?"

"No, John, these sneaky little bastards could be leading us into a trap. They aren't worth any of our guys dying for. Time is on our side. When we come across them, I want all guns on them, not half our guns on them."

John nodded and looked up the wet snowy slope to where the distant stream creased upward out of tree cover toward the rocky peaks.

"And Z, what about the flyboys sittin' Condition 2 all this time. They get cranky sittin' there with the APUs running and nowhere to go. Maybe launch 'em, and see if they can flush the kids out, meanwhile we get Givens out of here so he can get that ankle cared for."

Z looked up and down the slope, then back at his men, and he nodded solemnly.

*   *   *

Breske, slowed his mule under the tree cover. He was following the HRT team. They were easier to track than the kids. He put them on the other side of the valley when he realized what was happening, and that the kids had them going in circles.

He could watch from a distance and try to figure something out. He estimated that they had to be getting close now, and it appeared they had abandoned the four-wheeler as the Feds were following trails that could only be on foot. That would mean they were moving slow in the wet snow and rough terrain.

Breske knew if he got too close, it would be too obvious. They'd arrest him for obstruction or some such throw away charge and just hold him long enough he wouldn't be able to help the young Potters.

He looked again through his binoculars. He could see the HRT team still stopped. Vision through the binos was a little dimmed by the mosquito net he had over the objective lenses to reduce flash that might give him away, but the serious men looked to be in consultation as best he could tell.

When the pulsing thunder of rotor blades came echoing up the valley, he was surprised. Maybe they thought they found something?

No, they wouldn't all just be standing there.

Perhaps they were trying to flush the kids out.

Scanning along the mountainside, Breske saw the wrinkle in the terrain to the team's east. At about their level there were thin trees with some good canopy cover, following the wrinkle, which had to be a stream. Downhill, tree cover increased significantly. Working upstream, the trees thinned to nothing but a rocky crag that became more and more rock cover as it got to the snowy peak of the ridgeline.

The sound of the thundering helicopters increased. They were obviously coming this way, and it sounded like more than one of them. Instinctively he tugged on the reins to pull the mule further under the tree cover above.

Finally, he saw them, two of them snaking low up the valley floor… Glossy black Blackhawk helicopters. Breseke smiled, had to be FBI, only they would do something like that.

Then he saw a third ship, flying high along the ridgeline. It seemed slower, but was flying a more direct route than the low ships.

They went to the stream.

It suddenly dawned on him that the FBI didn't know if they went high or low.

He lowered the binoculars and took a moment to put some thought into it. Downstream, into the trees would make the most sense. It would be faster and they could cover more ground protected by the tree cover from overhead surveillance.

Breske grinned, he banked on them doing what he would do. They would go uphill, trying to beat their hunters over the ridge, or even, making a stand among the rocky cover before retreating over. He let the binos hang on their neck strap and slid his Winchester out of its scabbard. It had no real value at this range, but its heft and the cold steel and wood felt reassuring in his grip.

*   *   *

"Covey one-four reporting they just had eyes on two subjects, heavy packs, snowshoes strapped to them and carrying rifles. They got 'em, they continued up hill, and they lost them in the rocks coming out of the stream."

"OK, Brower, make sure the helos have our grid and the last grid where our suspects were seen." Z looked around at his team, then up the steep slope. "Also, I want the helo without our extra shooters to land this location, they'll pick up Givens and Kelley for additional airborne gunnery."

Z smiled at the limping man.

"I assume you're in better condition to shoot than walk?"

"Yes, Sir," the man said with a grin.

"Everyone else, standard, standard. Don't group up and keep good spacing. Also, Brower, need Covey one-four locked on suspect location, prepare to have them give us talk on to include range as we get to one klick and lower. Let's get Covey one-two defensive scan on our movement. As soon as the helo's in sight, we start moving and do our thing."

Smiling as he looked around at his men, they returned eager smiles. Ready to finally be on with it.

With the arrival of the helicopters, the team started moving up the steepening terrain. The trees immediately started thinning out as the helicopters orbited menacingly above. Two low on opposite sides like a reverse circling of wagons, guns pointed inward, looking for the threat to the team. The high ship circled over the rocks near the top of the ridge, the center of the orbit, the grid passed by the Pred as the last location of the two subjects where they slipped into the crags and boulders.

*   *   *

Chili Mac was his favorite, he poured water into the line on the pouch and set the MRE meal aside to let the chemical heater work its magic. Then he looked back to his naked feet.

"Seriously, Tom." Jane looked over her shoulder at him. "Get your socks and boots on, we're gonna need to be ready to move."

"What do you mean? I thought you said we could take a break and eat something here."

Jane half turned, she was behind the stock of her M-1. It rested on her pack on a small flat rock that provided just enough cover beneath the rocky outcropping. Wet and cold from working their way up the frigid mountain stream, she figured they could use some calories. And they needed to tend to their feet, soaked by water rushing well over the tops of their Gore-Tex boots.

"Well, I guess I wasn't expecting you to make a weekend stay out of it." Then she turned back and lifted the small binoculars to her eyes to survey the boulder field they had walked through to here. This place was almost a cave, but not quite. A massive slab of rock hung overhead. The dirt beneath it washed, or shifted clear by some ancient geological mechanism, leaving a few large rocks and enough room for two or three people to shelter.

She had suddenly gone from very happy with herself and her plan, to feeling very wary. Something seemed off, and she wasn't sure what it was. They were both tired, and their sleep cycle was off, having shifted to traveling during the day. Maybe all her plans for evasion and deception wouldn't be enough.

Warm from the exertion of the hike up the hill, Jane stood up and took off her jacket. She laid it across the dirt below the muzzle of her rifle. If she had to fire from this position, it wouldn't kick up a cloud of dust that would help give them away.

Looking at the rifle, she thought a moment.

Jane picked up the Garand and locked the operating rod back, the chambered round spinning to the dirt. Hitting the clip latch release, the en bloc clip and the other seven spilled out of the magazine well on to her pack.

Pulling one loaded clip from the bandolier she wore across her shoulder, she pressed it into the mag well with her thumb, and the operating rod sprung forward into the meat of her hand, eager to feed itself the black tip round. If she were sloppy about it, she would chamber her thumb in a painful phenomenon known as 'Garand Thumb'. But Jane's movements were disciplined and crisp. She let the operating rod fly, and the .30 caliber round locked into the chamber with a loud 'clack'. She pulled out another clip and staged it on the pack. Laying the rifle down, she gathered up the loose eight rounds and en block clip and reloaded it.

"What are you doing, Jane?"

"This was just standard M2 ball." She said holding up a handful of brassy cartridges. "I loaded black tip. They'll be wearing body armor."

Tom put his dry socks on a little quicker now, with the unspoken sense of urgency.

"What are you thinking, Jane?"

"I'm thinking if it has to be today, if it has to be now... here is a pretty good place."

Sitting back behind the rifle she raised the binoculars, but looked over them a moment first. It was a beautiful view, down the snow-covered valley, from here looking over the towering trees of the lower elevation, and across the way, another rock-strewn ridge.

The sun was up and it was warm now. It was a good time, and this was a good place and Jane was feeling the very strangest sense of peace coming over her.

Then she heard the helicopters.

*   *   *

Breske had to take a moment to steady the mule. Sparky seemed uneasy, and Breske wasn't sure if it was the helicopter activity on the other side of the valley or his own sense of foreboding.

The helicopters had tightened their orbit; one had landed and picked two men up, immediately rejoining overhead. The team was taking longer than Breske thought it would take them, but they were moving cautiously, making good use of cover and overwatch.

If he tried to rush across the valley to help in any way, he would be seen long before he got into a position to do any good. The Winchester cradled in his arms was no match for the firepower of the team he was watching across the valley.

This would have to be a different kind of war, it occurred to him. And he was watching it unfold, and that was all he could do for now. He was far beyond the effective range of the 32 Winchester Special, but maybe, he could at least help contribute to chaos that he was sure was about to begin.

As the team on the other side began to slide from a long trail formation to some kind of echelon entering the rocky, boulder field, Breske felt himself tense, and his mule felt it coming too.

*   *   *

"Three of them, three hundred yards, Tom." She whispered as she was snuggled into her cheek weld. She had already estimated the ranges through the boulder field and had the drum sight set for the range and downslope.

"What are you gonna do, Jane?"

"I'm gonna give them the same thing they gave Dad. You stay heads up, make sure they don't flank us if there's more than one element."

"Jane."

"They brought this, Tom. They are *hunting us*."

Tom could see the vague figures of men working their way through the boulders to their position. He could make out three clearly and could see the occasional movement of more behind them. The helicopters orbiting low overhead left no doubt that these men were closing in, and that it could only go a few ways.

"I'll take one shot. Take the leader down, then we can try to escape around this rock up over the ridge, Tom. Be ready," she whispered.

"Jane," he said quietly back, he didn't know what to say. The men were getting closer, and the helicopters seemed louder.

When it came, he wasn't sure which was more shocking, the thunderous report, or the cloud of red that burst from the man's head.

*   *   *

Brower took cover as soon as he heard the shot and saw the back of Z's head explode.

Then he keyed up and went out immediately on the command net.

"Shots fired, shots fired, stand by for immediate nine-line we have one down"

"Where'd it come from?" John yelled.

"Up hill, not sure where," someone yelled back.

"I'm gonna get Z outa' there," yelled Chief.

"No!" yelled John, "I saw it, he's dead."

Chief didn't hear or didn't listen, and the big man was up, out of cover at a sprint. He immediately took a round high on the torso and went down amid a colorful stream of obscenities.

"Damn it," John yelled. He jumped up out of cover, firing a long burst from his HK-416 generally up hill and running toward Chief.

"Any air unit see where those shots are coming from?" Brower called over the net.

"Covey one-two, negative, reviewing tapes."

Brower saw John drop and do a mag change at Z's body, Chief squirming with pain beside him. John came up firing the short HK with one hand, grabbing Chief by the drag handle and pulling him back downhill. Just as he neared Brower's position of cover, he had expended that magazine as well. John let the HK hang on its sling, to drag the big man with both hands from the handle on the back of his plate carrier.

Chief was still cursing in pain, and John dragged him to Brower's cover when the next shot rang out. For a moment nothing seemed to happen, then John dropped, gasping and clamping down on the blood leaking profusely from the side of his neck.

Brower grabbed John and pulled him in behind his rock, then clamped his hand on his neck.

Shots rang out from another direction. Distant but there were a lot of them.

"Command we're taking fire from multiple locations here. We need air to find this fire and suppress it." Brower keyed up with bloody fingers and watched the life starting to fade from John's face. "We have three urgent casualties, need immediate medivac, my location. Marked by white smoke."

Brower took out his smoke grenade, pulled the pin and lobbed it up past Z's body ten yards above him, hoping to help screen them from further fire as well as marking the location for pick up.

He didn't bother with a full nine-line as he too busy trying to clamp down on John's neck, hoping to keep enough blood in to keep the guy alive and calm Chief down, who had taken a round high in the chest just above the plate.

*   *   *

Breske had fired four rounds of 32 in the air as fast as he could lever the action. Sliding the rifle back to its scabbard, he gave Sparky his heels as he drew his Glock 29 from its chest holster. Firing eight or nine rounds of 10 mm while at a gallop, he re-holstered and got some good distance while making sure to stay in the trees. They got off trail, and the mule slowed in the thickening brush.

Tony pulled back on the reins and tried to look across the valley but was obstructed by foliage. Dismounting, he tied the mule to a sapling and walked carefully downhill.

A single smoke grenade had been set off at the front of the team's position, and the firing had stopped. The helicopters seemed an angry swarm of hornets, and now, without gun fire, theirs seemed to be the only noise in the valley.

One of the helicopters slowed, very low over the other ridge. Breske thought it was trolling for fire at first, then it dropped a line of smoke grenades. A second helicopter came in slower and lower than that one and made a one gear landing on the hill side, downhill of the smoke screen. Several men gathered to quickly haul what appeared to be three lifeless bodies to the downhill door of the helicopter.

Breske lowered the binoculars and thought a moment. He looked back at the mule who was now casually munching on something. He wasn't equipped for an overnight, and that was what this was going to take. Then he thought about the kids.

He turned and walked back to the mule.

"They sure aren't equipped for what's coming down on them, I can stretch those tuna packs in the saddle bag there another day or so, huh, Sparky?"

He rubbed the mule's head and untied him.

Stepping into the stirrup, he took the reins and mounted the mule.

"We go north to stay away from all the helicopters comin' and goin', and we work our way around to the back side of the ridge and see what we can do for these kids... Damn, just thought about it. Three for three. Those kids are pretty serious. Those Feds are gonna start comin' down hard. Let's get to 'em first."

*   *   *

"What happened to one shot and we move, Jane?"

"I saw other heads pop up, just like rock chucks. Got greedy I guess."

They were panting against the heavy burden of their packs and running uphill amid the rocks.

"They laid down that smoke screen to medivac their guys. That gives us time to get ahead of the ground team."

"You, like... blew that guy's head off, Jane."

"The first one was a good shot, I pulled the second one a little and rushed the third as he was about to get to cover."

Talking was an exertion so Tom stopped, that and he suddenly found it disturbing that Jane could talk so casually about just killing people.

Jane was only concerned about the helicopters. Two were still preoccupied with medivac, the other one had gone to a wider orbit... and then there were the drones, they had to be out there too. There was plenty of cover amid the rocks but overhead they were exposed to surveillance.

"It's coming back, cover up, Tom."

They tucked under the nearest rocks they could find with gear and rifles banging clumsily against the granite. They froze as the Blackhawk roared low overhead. Jane waited a few moments just to be sure.

"OK, get moving, Tom, we're good."

* * *

"Command, Zeke Zero Eight, we got runners."

"Zero Eight, do you have PID on weapons on the squirters?"

"Yeah, Zeke Eight, affirm we have Positive Identification on rifles on each subject, one with an M-1 Garand, one an AR-15, also appear to be heavily loaded with tactical gear. My gunners request clearance to engage."

There was a brief pause, and the pilot was tightening his orbit, keeping his eyes on the two desperate people below. He was trying to slow down even more, but the closer to the top he got, the more rollers he was catching off the ridge line and the turbulence was making it tough. He was carrying a lot of power.

"Zeke Zero Eight, Command, still working your approval, in the meantime can you talk Covey one-four onto your targets."

"Zeke Eight, standby, break. Covey one-four, we kind of have our hands full here with wind and turbulence so I can't get you a specific grid right now, if you scan the center of my orbit, you'll see'em. They are running up the main crevice in the middle of my orbit."

The two had run into a deep crag that zig-zagged toward the crest of the ridge. The sun was going down, and it was approaching thermal cross over so the Predator's IR sensor would be of limited value. He tightened the orbit more to help out, cognizant of the well-briefed fact that one helicopter had already been shot down at the beginning of this event.

"Zeke Zero Eight, Command Zero Two Actual. Cleared hot, cleared hot, cleared hot."

"Command Zero Two, Zeke Zero Eight, we're in hot."

* * *

"I think they know where we are, Jane. They're circling us now at a pretty steady distance. What do we do?"

"Keep running, we stay in this crag as long as we can. It's pretty good cover unless they're straight over head. If they get straight over head, I can get some shots on them. They know that, they'll keep their distance."

When the shooting started, it took her a minute to figure out where the dust and rock chips were coming from. When a round finally snapped past her ear, she yelled.

"Stay low, Tom. They're shooting at us. Keep moving, quick and low."

Tom instinctively had his free hand over his head. The adrenalin coursing through made him certain his heart would burst. His legs were pumping hard, and his lungs burned. His heart was on fire with a strange mix of rage and fear, and it seemed his soul was lost in some abyss because this new reality was beyond comprehension.

The noise of the Blackhawk shrouded the sound of the automatic weapons fire, but Tom was pelted by rock chips and heard several rounds snap by close overhead. At first the fear seemed to overtake rage, and he felt like a scared, helpless rabbit. As he realized that they were just trying to kill them and how they had just killed their father in front of him, the rage began to rise, and as that happened, he mindlessly thumbed the safety off of his AR and looked forward to a shot opportunity.

He would run until he had it.

* * *

"Geez, guys, come on already." The pilot muttered.

"Well, you're going to just have to hold this thing more steady, seriously."

"Kelley, I'm doing everything I can, the closer we get to the top, the more we get caught in the rollers of wind coming across the ridge. I'm doing everything I can to keep you guys in range and keep us out of the rocks."

"We just can't get an angle on it with all those bends and turns in that crag they are running up. Can we get a direct overflight?"

The pilot sighed.

"I don't know, they've already shot down one helicopter, and they're making it pretty clear we shouldn't be taking any chances that could lead to another crash."

"Look," Givens said over the intercom. "They killed Z, and maybe John and Chief. That'll be four FBI agents alone, plus the DHS pilot. That's five bodies, this has to stop, we can stop it."

The pilot sighed, and it was hard enough that it broke squelch on the intercom.

"Alright, alright. We try this once." The pilot banked hard across his orbit. "Get ready, they'll be out your side in 4... 3... 2... 1, should be in sight."

*   *   *

Battered and nearly blinded by the wind and dust of the rotor downwash and the nearly paralyzing noise of Blackhawk flying low overhead, Tom stood his ground, raised his rifle and as soon as the dark form filled his Eotech, squeezed the trigger as fast as he could. He felt the muzzle blast of Jane's M-1 doing the same next to him.

He couldn't really see after the initial sight picture, his eyes reflexively closing in the blast of air and dust, but each kick in the shoulder of the carbine strengthened his resolve and seemed to diminish the fear to something now inconsequential.

As it passed and as the downwash and noise ebbed, he looked to Jane. For the first time in what seemed like forever, they weren't running, and they weren't in terror. Now something else was there, something else was in that place that had been so afraid just moments ago. There wasn't even any notice of the incoming fire that was raining down around them, although it had been terribly ineffective.

And now there was at least a moment to breath, and connect.

"I got good hits, I know I got hits on it, Jane!" He yelled louder than he needed to.

"Me too! Me too, I hit it, Tom. Maybe it won't be back." She looked into his eyes and saw something she hadn't seen in years.

She saw family.

She shook her head before she hesitated in thought.

"Run, Tom. Run!"

In her eyes, Tom saw respect and acceptance and love and the great bond of a sibling he would die for, and he knew she would do the same for him. Suddenly fear was gone and it was replaced by something he didn't really understand.

He hoped his rounds found something important and brought the helicopter down in a terrible fireball killing all on board. Tom wondered what he had become, he wondered what they had made him.

* * *

It sounded like someone running along the fuselage hitting it with a sledge hammer.

"Gary, watch those engine instruments for me, I got normal control response for now. We seem good there."

The pilot glanced at his instruments then looked back outside, keeping the terrain at bay while fighting the increasing winds.

"Kelley, Givens, please tell me you got something on that pass."

"I don't think so, too fast and too much turbulence we need to go slower next time."

"Ah, hell no, Kelley. In case anyone isn't aware, we took hits on that pass. We won't be doing that again, and we sure as hell won't be doing it any slower."

"This isn't working," Givens said. "We can't get a good angle with that crag, and clearly direct overflight is out."

There was a pause and the intercom was quiet. There was only the ever-present thunder of rotors and whine of turbines. Each crewman was alone in his thoughts for a moment.

Givens broke squelch.

"Put us down, land us up ahead of these pricks. We catch them in this crag and kill or capture them."

"Givens, you can barely walk…"

"I don't need to, I find some good cover in the choke point ahead of them in that crag, and Kelley can maneuver on them as necessary. We keep it up like this and we are just going to Winchester our ammo with no affect. I'm down to only two magazines. How many you got, Kelley?"

"Three mags of five five Six."

"Well, I'm not putting down for that without approval from command," the pilot was shaking his head.

"Let's call 'em." Givens challenged.

"Alright, I'm going out on command net," the pilot said over the intercom.

"Command, Zeke Zero Eight with request."

"Command, because of terrain features here, we are unable to properly engage from the air. My shooters are just going to run out of ammo if we keep this up. Givens and Kelley are requesting to be dropped off out ahead of them to engage from the ground."

"Zeke Zero Eight, standby on that request and say play time remaining."

"Command, Zeke Zero Eight is at fifty-five minutes to bingo fuel."

"Roger, standby as we run this request up."

The pilot deliberately left out the fact they had already taken rounds. Everyone on board knew this had to stop, and right now they were the only ones in a position to stop it.

*   *   *

When Breske heard more shooting and saw the helicopter maneuvering so drastically, he cut his corner across the valley much earlier than he wanted to. He was risking detection, but by the volume of fire, he was afraid he might already be too late.

Imagining their fear, he got Sparky up to a gallop on the flat terrain of the valley floor. Plunging through the rushing stream full of fresh snow melt, they ignored the discomfort of the cold and wet. Even the mule sensed the dire urgency.

Pointed in the right direction, the mule sure-footedly found his own path and kept the gallop up as long as he could until they got into the trees on the other side. Even then he kept his speed up without having to feel Tony's heels.

Tony meanwhile, was calculating his ammunition situation. As the ride smoothed out a little, he slid the Winchester from its scabbard and pulled rounds from the butt cuff carrier. Topping off the magazine tube, he had five rounds at the ready. He knew he had a fresh box of twenty rounds in the saddle bag. Putting the rifle back in the scabbard, he grabbed the fresh 15 round magazine for his Glock 29 from his Denali holster. Using the interchangeable Glock 20 mags gave him an extra five rounds. Carefully hitting the mag release on the pistol holstered on his chest, he pulled the magazine that extended from the grip. Inserting the full 15 round magazine in the pistol, he looked at the partially used magazine.

Breske wasn't sure how many rounds he'd fired for his distraction, and now he was cursing himself because it was probably just a waste of ammo and didn't help in anyway.

He leaned forward in the saddle as Sparky was climbing an ever-steepening incline in the trees. Breske realized he was going to have to be smarter about these things, not so impulsive. This wilderness was his second home. He was a master of this place, and he could own them here. He didn't have the guns to fight them anyway. If he played it smarter, he wouldn't need them.

*   *   *

"I think they left, maybe we caused enough damage they had to, Jane."

"No, I still hear them, I think they are over the ridge waiting for us."

"Ah, I think they're starting that circle again, Jane."

"They know they can't get us in here... Tom, maybe they dropped someone off over the ridge, waiting for us. Waiting ahead in this."

"We can't stop. We can't go back, Jane. We have to keep running, we just have to clear our corners real careful. We get to the other side of the ridge and drop down into the trees on the other side. It's gonna' be dark soon, we'll have that working for us too."

"I'm not sure the dark really helps now, Tom. They all have night vision and thermal."

"We just have to keep running."

Jane nodded and smiled a little, realizing the role reversal.

They had paused a moment to assess the changing helicopter sound, and they took off at a run again. Nearing the top of the ridge as the sun was setting, they were taking their time around the blind spots and curves of the crag, guns up and pieing the corners as best they could. Fatigue was now overriding the original surge of adrenaline that had fueled them up the mountainside. The downhill, with such a heavy load, wouldn't really be any easier.

The crag was deeper on this side and offered more protection from the still orbiting Blackhawk. They were a little at ease, but they were backlit by the setting sun.

As they carefully rounded a particularly sharp corner, they heard a commanding voice yell;

"Stop right there and drop your weapons! Do it now!"

Jane just barely saw the helmeted figure of a man taking cover ahead of them in a V in the rocks. She ducked back quickly.

"No!" she yelled back. She turned to whisper over her shoulder to Tom. "watch our back, I see him... I think I have a shot."

"Do we have to kill him, Jane?"

"Are we going to surrender, Tom?"

"No."

"Then we're gonna do what we have to. You watch our back for anyone coming up behind us or over the crag here."

She paused, then yelled around the corner.

"Let us go, we just wanted to be left alone…"

"There's no way that's happening. You're boxed in now, you have nowhere to go. You throw your guns out, and come out with your hands up, and you'll get a fair trial. That's a lot more than you gave my guys."

"You murdered my father."

"I wasn't there, let's take this easy, drop the guns, come on out, and this will all come out after an investigation in the trial."

"You're FBI?"

"Yes, come on out, hands up, OK?"

"So, you'd be investigating yourselves?"

"Yeah, that's how this works."

"You're kidding, it doesn't *work* at all."

A burst of automatic weapons fire sounded behind her with Tom answering with several shots simultaneously.

"We OK back there, Tom?" She whispered cautiously.

"Yeah, I don't know if I got him, but he backed off."

"This guy up here was just buying time until his guys got into position. I'm going to take him."

Snapping quickly around the corner, the helmeted man started firing immediately, and she felt herself clip the rocky corner hard with her ribs. With bullets snapping around her and rock fragments and dust filling the air, she found her front sight through the rear aperture and settled it on the base of the V where she saw the muzzle blast and squeezed the trigger. With the report of the big Garand and settling from the recoil, the V in the rocks was now empty, and the firing had stopped.

"MOVING!" Jane yelled. This was why Dad always had them communicating when shooting. He always said the two-way range was different, and now Jane was running forward to deal with the man she put down.

"Moving!" Tom acknowledged, and she could hear him running behind her.

Then they heard someone else yelling.

"Givens, answer up! Givens!"

The helicopter was moving in low, preparing for an overhead pass. Jane approached the V quickly with her rifle up. On the other side, a man sprawled in agony and with difficulty breathing.

Jane leveled her rifle at his head.

"Don't, Jane. You don't need to kill him."

"Get his rifle and his pistol away from him."

Tom flicked open his folding knife and cut the sling on the man's HK-416 and threw the weapon out of reach. He struggled a moment with the thumb release on the kydex holster, but came up with a nice 1911 with a weapon mounted light that he slid into his waist band. He grabbed a few spare magazines while he was at it and pocketed them.

"He needs a chest seal, Jane."

"Hold on…" The helicopter swept in very low blowing dust and making it impossible to communicate. She continued when it past. "He doesn't get one of ours."

"No, it's OK he's got an IFAK here on his kit."

She yelled over the edge of the crag to anyone who might listen.

"Anybody out there, throw down your guns. I've got your guy at gun point and I'm just four pounds of trigger pull away from blowing his head off, so don't try anything. He's got a sucking chest wound so we're gonna put a chest seal on him and keep moving, and you're just gonna come down here and take care of your guy while we move on."

"I'm not dropping my weapon, you guys really don't need to add another murder to the charges you've racked up, just let him be," responded a voice.

"We're trying to keep him alive here, but if you come at us now, I swear I'll kill him. At this point, what's one more? And radio your helicopter to stay clear, that crap's annoying." Jane was looking around the crag edges while Tom was tending to the wound. The Black Tip 30-06 round had penetrated the man's rifle plate low on his chest. He was trying to talk but was just letting out this gasping sound. When the chest seal was in place, the man took a few deep breaths. Then spoke softly.

"There's no way out of this. You surrender or die, those are the only outcomes."

"I don't want to kill you, but it won't bother me if I have to."

"You have nowhere to go," the man said.

"Stop talking and conserve your energy. Don't be stupid, and you won't die."

Jane started moving down the crag slowly, rifle pointed at him. "Come on, Tom. That's good enough, leave the rest for his buddy. Grab his rifle too, that's going with us."

Tom stood up, scooping the HK on the way. He pulled the charging handle back to confirm a round was chambered then, stepped back to grab a magazine from the man's plate carrier. It was his last one.

As they approached the next bend in the crag, they saw the other man in full gear creeping slowly toward the edge where his fallen partner lay. Jane was still watching her target, just over her sights. Tom was in the lead with the 416 at a high ready, leading Jane until they rounded the corner. The helicopter sound was getting louder again as they lost sight of the FBI men.

They started running again and when they found a muddy spot, Tom looked for just a moment at his carbine and the 416, then jammed his AR muzzle first into the mud and kept the Heckler and Koch.

A sharp pain jolted Jane from where she had hit the rock coming around the corner. She had to stop a moment and held her side. Her hand was instantly wet with warm blood.

"Tom..." She hadn't clipped the rocks, she had been shot with one of the very first rounds the man fired.

"Oh, no, Jane."

CHAPTER 9

"Sorry to call you so late, Grant. But I know you would want to know this right away."

Carver was looking out from the bridge over water glistening in the rising full moon.

"Alright, what is it Carver?"

"All hell has broken loose in those mountains, Grant."

"The Potter kids were holed up in what amounted to a natural pill box, FBI guys closing on them. They lit them up at 250 yards, shot Z in the face and he was DRT. The Chief guy took a round through the chest and is expected to be OK. The guy John was trying to drag Chief to cover and took a round through the neck. It's not looking good for him, I don't think they expect him to make it."

Dead Right There. DRT. The Sheriff thought to himself. It had to be the girl doing the shooting for those kind of results. He kept that to himself. Either way, the ramifications were clear. Another dead FBI agent and this time the kids were clearly responsible. Things were about to change for the very worst.

"The guys on scene were reporting they were taking fire from multiple locations, at least four, maybe five guns. The effective fire came from this rock formation the kids were in. Two of the three helicopters medivac'd the wounded and dead out, third stayed on the scene. One of the Preds spotted the kids working their way up the mountain to the top of the ridge. They have two shooters in the helicopters, so they engage the kids. Well, the Potters find this little gorge or something that takes them up over the ridge and the FBI shooters can't get an angle on them to get hits. So, these two FBI guys get dropped off by the helicopter to cut them off and engage them from the ground. The girl drills *another* FBI agent through the front plate with an armor piercing round. They get up on this guy, and buy themselves some time by threatening to shoot him in the head. The boy treats the FBI agent for a sucking chest wound, and they continue on while the other guy and other helicopter lands, and they medivac *that* guy. I think he's gonna be alright. Oh, and that helicopter came back with bullet holes in it."

"What's the status on the kids?"

"Last I heard a Pred was tracking them leaving the scene."

The Sheriff shook his head.

"This has instantly gone from really bad to even worse, Grant. And that's just the beginning. That Tanner guy, Special Agent in Charge of the Salt Lake field office, he's been recalled to Washington for some kind of temporary duty. He's being replaced by some guy nobody has ever heard of direct from the Hoover building, *and* as of tonight they are launching some kind of special Joint Task Force. My guys at the FBI are saying that whatever is coming is huge. An absolutely massive response. Nobody knows what though. This is classic 7th floor FBI stuff. With a JTF, you'd expect our SOG guys would come out to play. I know a bunch of 'em, they haven't heard anything about this.

"And I've got an old contact with FBI HRT. The backstory on this team they fielded here, it was a mix a few HRT guys and Regional SWAT guys. They are stretched so thin with the food riots and all the special details they are running from Portland and Seattle to New York and D.C. that they couldn't spare a whole HRT element. So, it was three HRT and the rest were Regional SWAT drawn from all over the country. And of course, guess who two of the first guys she smokes are?"

"HRT guys?"

"Yup, Z and that guy John. Not just HRT but long time Operator types, like old school CAG guys."

"Yeah, Carver, they knew Jeff Potter."

"Oh, well that whole community is pissed off with Z and John getting killed."

"Not a good group of people to have pissed off, but they probably don't know anything about the fact that Jeff Potter was killed with his hands up either, do they? Does anyone know the truth to how this started?"

"The truth is, Grant, that a lot of people see these kids, and their war hero father as slackers, shirking their duty when the country needs them most. That's how it's being sold to us in briefings. If Potter had just let the system run its course, maybe those kids wouldn't even have seen a shot fired in anger. Now they have their own war, and they've brought it on themselves."

"Is that what you believe, Carver?"

"What is the old cop saying about domestics? There's three sides to every story; his side, her side and the truth. I don't know what the truth is a lot of times these days, I just know it's not a real good idea to get too invested in any one side because you may not have all the information."

The Sheriff sank his hands in his pocket and kicked at a rock he saw near his feet in the moon light.

"You, know, Carver, sometimes you have to hold onto the truth you've seen. You have to anchor to it so it holds you steady. The truth I know is from talking to Potter before the raid, he didn't want to kill anyone. The truth I know is that when the helicopter was coming to a hover, he had his hands in the air, and he never reached for his gun until he was taking incoming rounds. I know those kids sure don't want to kill anyone..."

"Are you sure about that? You sure this girl isn't some kind of psychopath? The last FBI agent she shot said the boy had to talk her down, that she was amped up and looked like she wanted to kill him. Be careful where you hang your hat, Sheriff. You have a lot of responsibility beyond these two kids."

The moon was silhouetting the surrounding mountains and beginning to cast shadows.

"I love a full moon like this, Carver."

"Full illum is what they call it, the kind of folks they're bringing in now. One-hundred percent illumination, a *gunners moon.*"

"Well, I guess I don't know about all that, Carver. I've just always liked when the moon casts shadows like this. Light in the darkness. But not a lot of people ever bother to see it. They just turn on a light, that's what everyone does. It's easier, and it's always easier to just go along with what everyone else does, isn't it, Carver?"

"I don't need to be here feeding you the latest info, Grant. It's dangerous for me career wise."

"We all have our lines we won't cross, right, Carver? What's yours, losing your dental plan? Losing your retirement? Jeff Potter's line was further out than most of us. The man died for what he believed in."

"Look, Grant. I'm no good to you if they pull me off of this for some reason. If I keep my head down I can feed you intel, right?"

"I know, Carver," the Sheriff sighed. "I'm sorry, I have a bad habit of sometimes saying things to other people that are meant, really, for myself. Wife points it out all the time."

Carver smiled and tried to relax a little.

"Grant, they are monitoring you and your department. They may have an informant inside your agency." The Marshal had saved it for last because he really didn't want to be the one to break that news to the Sheriff, and he wasn't sure how the man would take it.

"I know, Carver. I know."

CHAPTER 10

"We've just got to make the tree line, OK?"

She just nodded; he could tell she looked pale even in the moon light. She unbuckled the waist band of her pack and started to slink out of it after leaning the rifle on a rock.

"I'll take it, Jane."

"No, leave it, it's too much."

"No, I can do it, just to the tree line." Tom leaned his AR against the rock and slipped the straps of big pack over his shoulders so he wore it on his chest, and for a moment it felt more balanced. When he started walking with it, the doubled weight sank into him.

He held his AR in one hand and was holding Jane's hand with the other, pulling her along. Tom had packed the wound quickly, as well as he could, but with the darkness lit by the full moon he felt exposed and was waiting for the helicopters to come back at any moment. They assumed they were always under the watchful eye of the Intelligence, Surveillance, Reconnaissance Drones overhead. ISR, Dad always called it, and it seemed insidious now. The relentless threat that they had to try to thwart every day. And they had, for how long now? He didn't even know. And he didn't know what they had done wrong to get caught. Maybe there was no escaping it in the snow.

And now Jane was shot and bleeding, and now he could swear he could hear the drones, and wait, was that a helicopter? And why aren't the damn trees getting any closer.

Tom paid for every step with nearly two-hundred pounds of packs and gear, but that wasn't the real burden that laid so heavy upon him. He fought the frustration, and he fought the tears.

"Come on, Jane. You can do it, I'm with you."

"I know, Tom."

When they finally reached the trees, and thought they were deep enough in, Tom found a flat place on a bed of pine needles free of snow. He let go of her hand and started dropping the packs. Inhaling deeply, he took a moment just to breathe. Jane had dropped the M-1, which was something she had never done. She wobbled a little on her feet, and before Tom could catch her, she collapsed across her pack.

"Jane... Jane." Tom helped roll her over, reclining back against the pack, then he repositioned the other pack so it was under her legs. "Jane, I'm going to pack that wound some more, OK?"

She waved him off as he started to fuss with the jagged hole in her jacket.

"It's really bad, Tom. Something inside is really wrong. It's more than you can fix. I don't think anyone can at this point."

"Don't say that, Jane. We can patch you up and figure something out, maybe we can find that guy Tony, and he can get us some help."

"Tom, I've got some things I have to tell you... first off, the northern cache is on here." She ripped the GPS off her wrist by the Velcro strap. "It's listed as North Point in the way points, remember this; One-hundred paces south, one-hundred paces west. Now say it three times."

He did, and she continued.

"Take the helmet and the NVGs, you'll need them. I've got Dad's Glock in my waistband."

Then she was quiet for a long time, and Tom thought he should say something but didn't know what, so he just stayed quiet. The night was warm, and they could hear the tree frogs and snow dripping off of everywhere. The moon light seemed to grow stronger as their eyes grew more accustomed to the light. They were amid shadows of tall Ponderosas through the tops of the trees further down slope from them, they could see a lake glittering under the full moon and the outline of more mountains.

"It's very pretty here, Tom."

"Does it hurt, Jane? A lot? Can I do something?"

"At first it didn't really hurt at all, then all of the sudden, it felt like the most pain I'd ever felt. Now it seems to be back to not hurting, but I'm real cold, Tom. Could you get my sleeping bag out and cover me?"

Her pack was the one under her legs and he tried to pull it out without moving her as best he could. Opening up the compression bag, he stripped it out as quickly as he could and covered her.

"Thanks, Tom. That's nice."

He shook his head and hoped she couldn't see his tears coming.

"It's so beautiful here, Tom… Tom, do you think Jesus is here?"

Tom nodded and tried to collect himself as the words came out.

"I know he is, Jane."

"Do you think he loves me? After everything I've done now?"

"I know he does, Jane."

*   *   *

"So, you haven't seen this either, Grant?"

"No, almost watched it back at my office the next day, something told me not to plug it into any of my computers."

"Probably pretty prudent. Two weeks ago I would have called it paranoid. Not now."

The prosecutor adjusted the computer on the picnic table so there was less sunglare and then inserted the SD card.

"Well, when you said you had a burner laptop, that sounded like the way to go."

The Sheriff was watching over his shoulder.

"It'll be the only file on there. I had it running the whole time, gonna need to fast forward to when we're in the helicopter."

When the file came up with the video player, Joe fast forwarded and looked for the helicopter.

"So, what is your plan, Grant?"

"Well, if this provides evidence the FBI shot first, I'm going to the press. This has been suppressed far too long, and if we get our side out first, it will be good protection for the kids and the county. Heck, it may go further than that. Folks see how this War Powers Act is already being abused, maybe they'll start to see the light."

The Prosecutor gave a skeptical sigh.

"Here, we go, Grant."

"Yeah, you're getting there... whoa... too far, that's into the crash, go back..."

Glued to the screen, Joe looked around the park a moment and adjusted the volume.

"No... No, no!" And the video revealed only the dark backs and backs of the FBI agents heads, and then the muzzle flash of their assault rifles firing full auto.

"Nothing, Grant. That doesn't show anything. It was below your sightline and it's not tied into the intercom on the helicopter so all we hear is you, the helicopter and the guns. Darn near worthless."

The Sheriff stood up straight and crossed his arms. The park was nearly empty, and it was a nice warm morning.

"Maybe not completely worthless."

"How so?"

"You and I know it doesn't show anything. No one else does."

*   *   *

Breske eased back on the reins.

"Whoa, Sparky." He was looking up slope through the trees. It was the line that continued naturally from the crag the kids had been running over the ridge. It was predictable.

Tom was dirty and bloody and tired, and he was alone. He didn't show any sign of concern of Tony being there, and he just continued on his chosen path. Breske wheeled the mule around to be directly in front of him and waited for Tom to come to him.

As he was approaching Tony and his mule, he looked up to check the canopy of trees overhead. Tony looked up, too. It was thick, and no one was seeing through it. Looking back at the stream behind him Tony was afraid of the answer to the question he was going to have to ask Tom on his approach.

Tom's grubby face showed no emotion, and that didn't help.

"Where's Jane, Tom?"

Tom pointed behind himself with his thumb and didn't speak for a moment.

"Back there... I buried her last night."

Tony sighed, leaned on his saddle horn and bowed his head. Should he have taken a faster, more dangerous route? Should he have risked exposing himself to surveillance? Should he have rushed directly to the sound of the guns?

"I'm sorry, Tom."

"I didn't do it very well. I just had my knife and my... hands." Tom looked down at his filthy and bloody hands, the first time he had really seen them in the daylight.

"It's OK, Tom."

"I mean I got her deep enough to keep the buzzards and the coyotes out but, not the bears I imagine... Will they... I mean they're gonna come across her as they follow our trail. Will they take good care of her body? I mean they'll be respectful, right."

222

"Yeah, Tom. They will. You done good. Are you ready to come out?"

"There's no comin' out of this, Tony."

"Look, Tom. It shouldn't have been as easy for me to find you as it was. You been through a lot. Hop on back with me, buy you some time, get you some distance from all this."

Tom scanned all around him, and he snapped back a little into himself again.

"Look, Tom. Just get to the stream here. Walk down stream and hop on where we cross."

"But what about your tracks?"

Tony looked back at the line of tracks his steady mule had left in the last of the snow and smiled widely, very proud of himself.

"Oh, you don't need to worry about those."

*   *   *

"So, I'm not going to beat a dead horse, Ted. You get why we don't do those sobriety checkpoints, I mean Craig made it pretty clear right?"

"Yes, Sir."

"Relax, relax. This isn't about chewing you out, this is about educating you. How long were you with that other department? Five years?"

"Seven, Sir."

The Sheriff smiled.

"There's always a readjustment period, had it myself. I came from a big city department a lifetime ago now, it seems. Look, you have that pocket copy of the constitution I gave you, right? I just have a homework assignment for you. I want you to write me a five-page essay on why the Fourth Amendment is important, and how you would want it applied to you."

Deputy Ted Zites squinted a little, not expecting a homework assignment as he sat across the desk in the Sheriff's office.

"But that's not the only thing I called you in for. This next thing is something that might interest you. Your last department had helicopters, right?"

"Yes, Sir."

"Well, we just have Bob."

"Bob?"

"Bob Lewis. Retired doctor. Very wealthy man and rather generous. Old Bob has his own helicopter, and he makes it available to us free of charge for things like Search And Rescue and fugitive pursuit. Bob's a funny guy in ways and very Constitutionally minded, he won't use it for any drug stuff, and if he doesn't think we are following the Constitution, like the Fourth Amendment, for example, he says he will take his toy and go home."

Deputy Zites tilted his head a little.

"Ah, OK. I'm getting ahead of myself or maybe behind myself or something. Let's start with this. Heard any good rumors lately? Law enforcement related? Maybe an investigation we aren't participating in?"

Deputy Zites looked down at his feet, then came up with a shrug and shake of his head.

"Maybe something the Feds are working in the area?"

"Oh, yeah. I heard the FBI is pursuing some fugitives in the mountains out past Chisel Ridge, Carbon Valley area. Is that what you mean?"

The Sheriff nodded with a smile.

"What else do you know about that, Ted?"

"Just that they're after draft dodgers or something, rumor that some FBI agents have been killed, and that they shot down a helicopter. They are keeping a lid on it because they're afraid all the locals will help the fugitives."

"What if I told you that I was on that helicopter that was shot down, Ted?"

Ted didn't look too surprised, but Ted seemed to be the type that really liked controlling his emotions around others.

"What if I told you I saw the FBI murder the father of the two *fugitives* on the run?"

Zites just shook his head, not sure what to say.

"What if I told you I'm going to call old Bob to get his helicopter and help us find those kids so we can get them the heck out of here before the FBI kills them?"

"Ah... I don't know, Sheriff..."

"What if I told you, I'd like you to be one of the observers on that helicopter? I figure you might have spent time on helicopters back in San Francisco, and this would also help you learn the area better, be good experience for you and give you a break from patrol."

"I'm ah, I'm prone to air sickness... Really bad, Sheriff. Like, a lot of vomit. Not a good idea."

*   *   *

They had ridden for hours deeper into the mountains, Tom giving directions based on the GPS. He didn't trust Tony enough to take him directly to the North Cache, and it would be a couple day ride anyway, but he figured he could start working that way.

He reminded Tony a few times the importance of staying under tree cover, and when they finally got to a good place to stop and rest, Tom had his big sheath knife out diging a hole in the ground.

Tony was tending to Sparky, but when he saw Tom immediately digging with the big knife, he turned to watch. He had his AR laying close beside him, he didn't let it get far from him now.

"Hell of a knife there, Tom."

"Esse Junglass. My Dad gave it to me for my birthday a few years ago."

Loosening the dirt with the long blade, Tom shoveled it out with his hands.

"What ya' diggin' there, Tom?"

"Dakota fire hole. Gotta dry out after walking in those creeks."

"Right on," Tony said with an impressed grin. Finished tending to the mule, he grabbed his last two packs of tuna out of the saddle bag.

"Want some tuna, Tom?"

"No, I got food."

He was digging feverishly, already into the second hole.

"I'll go get us some wood, Tom."

"Tinder, kindling, fuel, dead wood higher off the ground the better."

"Yeah, I ah, I know, Tom."

By the time Tony came back, the Dakota fire hole was complete, and Tom was sitting with his boots and socks off, feet drying in the 50 degree air and indirect sunlight through the trees. He had dismantled an MRE and was eating something Tony didn't recognize and had the matches and toilet paper staged near the hole. Tony dropped his arm load of firewood next to Tom, and it was roughly organized in the order or tinder, kindling, fuel.

"Thanks," Tom said as he took the tinder and toilet paper and arranged in the hole, then lit it with the match.

"So, you headed for Canada then, Tom?"

"No, why would I do that?" He was down on all fours, ready to breathe life into the fire if it didn't take right away.

"When I was a kid, during Vietnam, all the guys draft age who didn't want anything to do with it ran to Canada. Maybe it's different now, maybe that don't even help no more."

The meager supply of toilet paper that came with MREs was really only good for starting a fire, and Tony had selected dry wood very well. The fire was taking off with very little effort.

"This is my home, Tony. This is where I belong. Not Canada. Not Ukraine, not Taiwan. Do you think I'm a coward, Tony?"

Breske couldn't help but let out a little laugh.

"Are you kidding? You come out here where very few people can survive anymore, and you get into firefights with the FBI, and you wonder if I think *you're* a coward?"

Tom pushed up from being low on the fire with a big smile and reached into his waist band handing Tony a big 1911 grip first.

"Pulled this off the last FBI guy Jane shot. She wanted to kill him, but we kept him alive to get us time to get away. She shot him one time through the chest plate with an armor piercing round. Sucking chest wound. I sealed it up and convinced her not to kill him."

Tom laughed a little thinking about it.

"Anyway, I got the pistol and this HK off of him. Check it out. It has one of those little red dot sights and high-power flashlight on it and everything."

Tony felt its heft and looked through the Rugged Miniaturized Reflex Sight at the little holographic red dot.

"That's a real nice piece there, Tom."

"And look at this thing, Eotech and all, I haven't zeroed it yet but..." Tom presented the HK-416.

"And a silencer too, Tom!"

Tom smiled in the firelight.

"Dad always called them suppressors, he said silencers was Hollywood stuff."

"Ahh..." Tony nodded in acknowledgement.

With the extra wood, Tom fashioned a simple rack to dry his socks.

"My last pair," he said.

"How can I help you, Tom? I'll carry you as far as you want."

"No, no Tony. You've helped a lot, I'm good. I just want to be left alone now."

"They won't ever do that, Tom. They'll always hunt you." He handed the .45 caliber pistol back.

"So, I guess that's what I do now. Some people work in grocery stores. Some people drive trucks. Some people are doctors and help people for a living. Me, I run from the people that hunt me, and that's my reality now. There is nothing else for me, no other way, so I just have to embrace it. Dad always said, *embrace the suck*."

Tony looked at the kid across the rising heat waves from the fire as flame licked out of the mouth of the hole.

"Tom... Are you OK?"

Tom just smiled a little and said nothing for a moment.

"I don't know, Tony."

"Tom, you're a good spirit. I see that, and others do too."

"Good? What good do you see, Tony? I mean, really, I just helped kill a bunch of people. What good is there?"

"You didn't do nothin' to them they weren't tryin' to do to you, Tom. So that ain't got nothin' to do with good. Ain't no shame in defendin' yourself and what you believe in. And the only good out there right now is good people tryin' to do good things. Don't give up on that, Tom. We'll get you out of here."

"I don't want to get out of here, Tony. I just want to be left alone here. Is that really too much to ask? I can feed myself, I can take care of myself, and no one will even know I exist."

"It's nice today, Tom, but winter is coming."

"That's been planned for, and I've been trained to live in this. I can do it, Tony and if I can't and I die here, what does it really matter? Either way I'm not hurting or affecting anyone. Can they really just not grasp that? I know you can, Tony."

"Is bein' left alone doin' any good, Tom? I get you, I get what you're sayin'. But at some point you need to be out there in the world, and that's where the good happens, not here. I've spent most my life out here, but you still have to go back to town once in a while, talk to people, talk to girls... Go back and help people sometimes. Get it?"

"No, Tony. I guess I don't. I guess I never got that. I just want to disappear now, that's what I really need. I need to go away and never be found, and maybe that's what was always meant for me. What else is there?"

Tony shook his lowered head and wished he knew what to say to help. He sat in front of Tom, cross legged and searched for some kind of special deep wisdom that might matter to the kid, but he found himself at a loss.

He stood up, and walked to his mule and reached in the saddle bag. Returning to Tom, he dropped four or five wire snares next to the fire.

"You know how and where to use those, Tom?"

"Yeah, Dad taught us."

"Good. They're a good way to quietly take food, doesn't take much energy to do it."

He sat back down next to Tom, wondering if there was anything else he could do for him.

"Tony, you keep finding us... me. If you can, they can, what am I doing wrong?"

"This snow made it easy. This snow will be gone in another day or so, you'll have a few weeks before it comes back. Be easier to hide your tracks then, Tom."

"You said not to worry about your mule tracks, Tony. Why's that, just as bad as my tracks, right?"

Tony smiled, held up his finger and jumped up. He walked back to Sparky and wrestled his front hoof off the ground, showing the bottom of it to Tom.

Tom rolled over next to the fire laughing, laughing in a way he really needed.

*   *   *

"Just had a little talk with young Deputy Zites about the importance of the Fourth Amendment, Craig."

"How'd that go?"

"Guess we'll see now, won't we? Maybe he's not long for work here, maybe this isn't a good fit for him. Or maybe there are lots of changes on the horizon."

The Sheriff was quiet.

"What have you heard about the Potter kids?"

The Sheriff just shrugged and shook his head a little.

"I'm thinkin' I should go to the press with my bodycam footage. You know, to prove that the FBI is lying about the whole thing. Show the world Jeff Potter came out of that cabin with his hands in the air and that the FBI shot first, unprovoked."

Craig raised his eyebrows.

"You got body cam of that?"

The Sheriff just nodded.

"Can I see it?"

"I got it back at the ranch. If something were to happen to me, Craig, it's in Betsy's cob bin in the barn, buried in a little pelican case."

"Well, it would be kind of out of context for the press right now, wouldn't it? I mean they don't know anything about it yet, do they? Maybe oughta wait on it a bit?"

"Wait for what, Craig?"

"Well, I don't know, 'til some of the story gets out first. You show that video, and people won't really know what it's about."

"Hmm," the Sheriff pondered.

"I'm just thinkn' Sheriff, I don't know."

"What do we do if these kids start killing the Federal Agents tracking them, Craig?"

"Smart money would be to stay the heck out of it. Feds don't want us involved anyway."

"That would be what smart men would do, Craig. What should we do?"

Markdale laughed.

"You mean what is the right thing to do, Sheriff? I don't know, that idea you had about getting someone in to help them. Someone who knows their way around those mountains. Get out there and help the kids. Find 'em. Find what they need. Get'em some help."

"If it comes to it, Craig. If we needed to intervene, come between those kids and the Feds, could I count on you to be there, Craig?"

"Absolutely, Sheriff."

*   *   *

Tony Breske's old trailer sat on a small farm just a few miles outside of town. He rented the trailer and small barn and corral from an old man who gave him a cheap price in return for taking care of some of the heavy labor around the farm. It was run down and dirty but it was what he could afford, and when he couldn't the old man would cut him a break on rent for extra cords of wood cut.

The Sheriff pulled in and parked next to Breske's old Dodge pick-up with the homemade flat bed. Taylor was in uniform, but drove his personal vehicle. Breske was at the corral waiting for the Sheriff.

Breske looked tired and trail weary, which was unusual for him. Tony Breske's little spread was really a base camp, and he spent more time in the mountains than he did at home. He was in tune with the wilderness and was part of the wildness. To see him looking like this after being back from the woods worried the Sheriff.

"How's it going, Tony?"

"Not good, Sheriff. Jane is dead. They shot her dead, but she got some of 'em first. Four by my count, I don't know how many dead, but I saw three carried away, and Tom told me about another one."

The Sheriff swore. They were leaning on the corral gate looking out at a pair of mollies. Breske gave the Sheriff some of the handful of carrots he carried, and they fed the female mules through the gate.

"Tom is still alive then?"

"Yeah, I got him outa' there as far as he'd let me. Got him some distance from the scene, bought him some time so he wasn't leavin' tracks for a while. He got himself a fire goin' dried out and we talked for a good while, but I didn't know what to tell the kid. He'd just been through hell. I saw it from a distance. There was nothin' I could do, right, Sheriff? It was just me and my old Winchester and a Glock. Should I a' rode right into the middle of it, just to be some kind of help?"

"Tony, I absolutely trust your judgement out there in the woods. Maybe not so much in town in some of the bars and I sure as heck question your taste in women," the Sheriff gave big smile and continued. "But out there in the woods, you are an expert. If you don't think you could have helped, then you couldn't. Like you said, you and your Winchester against their helicopters and their firepower… well, you'd a likely got yourself killed, and maybe had it escalated in such a way that both the Potters would a died, and we'd never know what happened. Now you're providing intel and you're a link to Tom. Tell me what you saw and what you did."

Breske told the Sheriff about watching the fire fight unfold from the other side of the valley, about firing his own rifle for some kind of futile distraction. He told him about all the helicopter activity and the smoke screen and the medivac, and then the one lone helicopter chasing them up the crag, shooting at them as they ran.

"It was first light the next morning I found Tom. He was filthy, and I think in shock after all that and buryin' his sister."

"He wouldn't come out with you?"

Breske shook his head.

"Not a chance, Sheriff. I thought maybe he was headed for Canada, seems to be the traditional way of handlin' such things. He said he just wants to be left alone out there."

"Well, there's no way they'll leave him alone out there, no way at all after all that's happened."

"I don't blame 'em, Sheriff. Saw their Dad murdered in front of them, hunted like dogs…"

"Oh, I can't say as I blame 'em either, Tony. Just… we gota' look at the realities of the situation here and be as prepared as we can be for them."

"What are you sayin', Sheriff? That we just leave him out there for the Feds to finish off?"

"Oh, no. Don't you worry about that, Tony." He'd fed the last carrot to the big grey mule then turned to pat Breske on the shoulder. "What I'm saying is that they are going to come down hard on that boy. They've been plagued with a lack of resources to commit to this, but that all changes now. With a couple dead Federal agents out of this so far, they will make it a priority, and they'll draw every asset they can into this to find Tom. I just have to ask you, are you willing to stand between the Feds and Tom Potter? You understand you could risk jail or worse?"

"I need to redeem myself, Sheriff. I shoulda done more."

"Now, don't talk like that, Tony. You're bein' smart, and that's what we need. Right now, you are Tom Potter's only life line, the only person he'll likely approach out there. That's a real critical piece in this, and we need it to continue to keep Tom potter alive and free."

"Well, I was hopin' you'd be thinkin' along those lines, Sheriff. Come over to the barn, I wanna show you my secret weapon for this." They walked to the barn door and Breske looked around carefully to be sure no one was watching. The Sheriff was just a little concerned about what he was walking into.

Tony stepped in first and left the door open just enough to allow the Sheriff in.

Sheriff Taylor sighed and wiped his face.

"What is this, Tony?"

"He's undercover, Sheriff."

"An undercover... mule."

"Yeah, this is his disguise."

"I'm a little inclined to believe, Tony, that there may be a special place in hell reserved for a man who would strap moose antlers onto his mule. How did you even manage it?"

"Oh, it takes some doin'. But we finally came to an agreement. Keepin' the feed bag on a while seems to help too. And look, it's more than just what they call 'visual signature', this'll work against thermal heat sensors too." Breske was pointing to a wire that ran from the saddle to the rack. "Antlers are wrapped with the rear window defrost wire from an '88 Subaru. Got a little six volt in the saddle bag, gives it just enough heat that someone runnin' thermal will see what looks like real live antlers."

"Tony, I think the saddle is gonna give it away."

"We're gonna run mostly at night, Sheriff. You seen all those thermal videos from Iraq and Afghanistan. They're all kind of fuzzy, can't make a lot of detail at night a lot. Plus, it's gonna be run by some guy in Nevada or somewhere, probably never seen a moose in his life. But there's more, check this out…"

With some coaxing, but more muscle and leverage, Breske got Sparky's front left foot up to inspect the shoe.

The Sheriff laughed almost uncontrollably when he saw it.

"Been runnin' these for years, made 'em myself, got a set for each mule and a few spares."

"Moose print shoes for your mules, that's pretty good, Tony. Of course, I won't ask what you use those for."

"Oh, I just do it so other people don't find my favorite hunting spots."

"What if they're hunting moose, Tony?"

"Yeah, they have to be off for moose season."

"And, Tony, with those antlers, what happens if you and old Sparky there come across a real bull that wants to challenge you on the trail?"

Tony ran his fingers through his hair.

"Well, Sheriff, I hadn't actually considered that."

Breske shrugged.

"Guess we'll find out."

*　　*　　*

Sometimes they would slip below the low clouds on days like this, and you could see them easier. He sat at the tree line watching for a while and finally decided to chance it. Tom knew he would need to get to the northern cache soon, he was running out of food. He was glad for the snares Tony gave him. And Tony had taken him several miles from his last tracks. It would be like he disappeared in that stream. All they'd find was his tracks ending at the stream and some random moose tracks that crossed it at one point.

The low clouds looked like more weather coming in. It was just cold enough it would probably be snow again. Tom was tired and hungry. He had one more MRE left and some Mountain House stuff.

His legs felt weak and shaky from the fatigue, the exertion and trying to stretch his rations. Finding a nice spot among some large cedars, he stopped between two large boulders. Leaning his carbine against one, he stripped himself of the heavy burden of the pack and stretched his neck and shoulders for a moment.

Tom dropped to his knees and drew his Junglass and started digging his fire hole. He wished he brought an E-tool, but they were too heavy and his pack had to be over eighty pounds as it was.

It was rocky and full of roots so he had to restart the hole twice, but finally he managed to complete it, a little shallow, but with the trees and the big rocks he figured it would be safe.

He collected enough wood to start the fire and keep it going for a few hours, for company more than anything. Once the fire was self-sustaining, he reached for his pack.

236

As he routed in his pack for his water and metal canteen cup he came across a loose bag of Mountain House, rice and chicken. That would be dinner, and maybe he would stay here a day or so and give himself a good rest.

He felt so sure of himself when he talked to Tony about just staying out here forever, but now, alone in a vast wilderness, even though he felt he could, he wasn't sure he should.

Jane said the north cache was huge, bigger than the south cache he had seen, and they left plenty of food there. He imagined making it there; he would be set for the winter, even without snaring hares or trying to discreetly shoot a deer. When he got there, he'd make that his base camp. There, he should be far enough away he could just sit it all out until he was forgotten.

There was no helicopter activity today, that was good. Maybe, he thought, they were tired of helicopters getting shot. And he smiled to himself knowing he'd shot one.

As he filled his canteen cup with water and set it on a little grate of green wet saplings, he thought that maybe being out here shouldn't really be his plan. But he couldn't go back *there*, and that meant this was the only place left.

Here and now was all that really mattered.

There meant injected and conscripted or persecuted, never just left alone.

His father was right, it was a war of their making, let them fight it. It was worth just standing up and saying no. Was it worth Dad being dead? Jane being dead.? Was it worth running for your life, every day for the foreseeable future?

What else was there? Prison now. Or some other modern form of slavery. Just listen to what they tell you. Just pay your taxes, just take your shots, just fight our wars, just believe what we tell you, ignore what you think. In return you get to watch your football games and drink your beer and smoke your weed, in a home of your choosing... because we let you.

Dad and Jane were truly free now and that had to mean something.

And I'm free right now, too. Tom thought. It's not easy. It's not pleasant. And he's always got to consider himself being hunted. But now he listened to the birds and the wind in the trees and the smell and even just the presence of the big cedars that surrounded him.

The big trees, the two big boulders on either side of him. They had presence, and they had meaning. The trees had to be over one-hundred years old, the rocks here for thousands of years. Surrounded by the works of nature, the works of God.

What was it to surround yourself with the works of man? Tom was never comfortable in such a place. And really, being honest with himself, he hadn't been comfortable here before in the wilderness. He had spent a lot of time in the woods because his Dad made him. And then he spent time there because he could get away from everything else. Now the getting away was a kind of destination in itself, and he folded himself into the embrace of the wilderness, of nature, of God.

He suddenly felt more at home here than he had anywhere since he could remember.

It was certainly better than prison, and prison would be a certainty if they caught him.

Had he killed anyone? Tom wasn't sure. He'd shot at some, but he wasn't like Jane. What she shot, she killed. There was never a question with her hitting what she was shooting at, even when she was a kid. But Tom would be an accessory for sure, and they would pile on all kinds of charges so he would never see the outside of a prison cell ever again.

Tom leaned back against the rock and looked up at the enormous cedars swaying with the wind. He would stay here in the wilderness. He would fight here if they made him, he would die here if that was meant to be.

He pulled out his self-inflating air mattress and laid it out, followed by his sleeping bag. Tom fed the fire then pulled out his stuff sack that had a spare set of BDUs and under wear and t-shirt all rolled up, and that was his pillow.

Then he pulled out his Bible. He would read and eat his chicken and rice and fall asleep next to the crackle of the little fire.

He had last pulled it out in the dark when Jane was dying, reading it under his headlamp, trying to find words to comfort her and himself. Now, seeing the Bible in the daylight, he realized it was dirty and blood stained.

*   *   *

"See, Sheriff, See? Those big Army trucks showed up first, then all these helicopters out of nowhere, and they've got a huge TFR East of the field that just went active. Center actually called a Gulfstream that was setting up for the approach and told them they couldn't make that approach and had to stay south and west of the field. They diverted. Do you know how much that is lost in fuel and parking fees?"

"What's with the TFR?"

"Oh, there's this rumor that there's some kind of manhunt going on and that some local pilot was going out to help some fugitives or something and so they've got this Temporary Flight Restriction up, guy could lose his license flying into that."

A line of four dull black Blackhawk helicopters sat idling with their lights on as three AH-6 Little Birds took their turns hot refueling from large eight wheeled HEMTT tank trucks. Amid a blur of motion of rotors and green and red navigation lights, the refueling personnel worked with a practiced precision.

"Gary, what the hell is going on?" Another man approached the Airport Manager from the main entrance door. "I just got turned around on airport road by a guy in a black suburban that said he was FBI, and that the airport was on lock down and I needed to stay here for the time being."

"See, Sheriff. They can't just shut down a civilian airport like that, what's going on? Is that fugitive thing true?"

"Well, the FBI guy let me through because I was in uniform, he said he would have whoever was in charge come talk to me, but I don't see anyone, so I'll go out and talk to them."

"They won't let anyone near that operation, Sheriff. They showed up in that Suburban earlier, one guy in a suit and a soldier in uniform, said they needed to park some trucks on the ramp, that they were going to need a little corner of the field to quietly refuel some helicopters for a training exercise, then all of the sudden they've taken over the whole airport! They can't do this, Sheriff, can they?"

Taylor had opened the glass door, and Gary's last words were drowned out by the sound of turbines and rotors. The men standing perimeter guard wore the latest and greatest in high speed low drag gear, with NVGs and ear protection mounted to their helmets. They carried M-4 type carbines decked out with the latest in optics, lights and lasers. He saw that they had different types of accoutrements which suggested some operator choice in the outfitting of their weapons.

Taylor hadn't gone far when one of them ran quickly despite his heavy load out.

"Sir, Sir! You need to stop." The man got between the Sheriff and the helicopters and stood with one hand up and one gripping his weapon. The man yelled to be heard over the sound of the helicopters. "Sorry, Sir, for your safety I need you to stay inside the airport office over there."

The Sheriff shook his head.

"I'm Sheriff Grant Taylor, Sheriff of this county, and I need to talk to someone in charge to tell me why they are shutting down my county's airport." He yelled as his hair was blown by the rotor wash.

The man hit a button on his gear and talked through a throat mic.

"Standby, Sir, I'll get you someone."

The Little Bird helicopters took off in sequence holding a tight trail formation and the Blackhawks, with long aerial refueling probes, powered up just enough to snake up to the fueling trucks in proper orderly fashion. They had wing stub mounted external fuel tanks giving them a muscular appearance.

"I don't want someone! I want the guy in charge!"

"Yes, Sir, just wait right here."

A man in full tactical gear came trotting over, obviously more encumbered by his gear. His uniform was different, and it took the Sheriff a moment to recognize him.

"Grant."

"Carver. What the hell is this?"

With a nod of the head, the Marshal led him away from the flightline to the other side of the building where it was a little quieter.

"So, you're in charge of this?"

"No, Grant. I'm just the badge."

"These guys aren't U.S. Marshals, this is the U.S. military, a Special Mission Unit."

Carver said nothing.

"How, Carver? How do they get around Posse Comitatus? Or are we already that far gone already? Is the Constitution meaningless?"

Carver mumbled something.

"What?"

"We deputized them. They are deputized U.S. Marshals."

"Are you kidding me?"

Carver shook his head, he'd never seen the Sheriff so angry.

"How many, Carver? How many do they have here? Will they be maintaining presence here at the airport?"

"There's a lot I can't say here, Sheriff. All I can say is that they couldn't get their tanker support here in time tonight, they'll be here tomorrow. You won't need to worry about them in town anymore."

"How many shooters, Carver?"

Carver looked away.

"Those Little Birds, the rocket tubes and miniguns, are they loaded?"

Carver said nothing.

"What about this Temporary Flight Restriction, what sparked that, this military activity?"

Carver hesitated and finally spoke.

"They have an informant, said you had a guy who was going to go look for Tom Potter in a private helicopter... Sheriff, I can't talk to you anymore. I helped as best I could as long as I could, they sent me to talk you down."

"Who is they?"

"This is the Joint Task Force I was warning you about. They call it Task Force Z."

"You have to be kidding me. They don't know anything about how it really went down at Potter's cabin, do they? I bet these are some of his guys too."

"Too young. They're doing what they're told."

"They aren't the only ones, Carver. *Just following orders.* We'll see how that plays out in the end."

"It's not worth it, Sheriff. One kid isn't worth what they'll bring down if you try to do something heroic. Just let this happen."

"JUST LET IT HAPPEN? Listen to yourself, Carver. This isn't you."

"They have CONPLANS in place if there is significant resistance from the county. They bring in National Guard from metropolitan areas, we're talking CCP, Tiananmen Square level stuff. If you want to start the next Civil War here, Sheriff, they'll be happy to oblige you. Is one kid worth that?"

"What if it was your kid? Oh, never mind, your kid would just follow orders, your kid won't think for himself any more than you will."

Carver looked down, then held his earpiece close.

"They're rolling, I have to go." Carver started running back around the building toward the flight line, he yelled back over his shoulder; "I'm sorry, Sheriff."

Sheriff Grant Taylor walked to the flightline. It was awash in the blue lighting of the taxiways and the red and green and white position lights of the helicopters. As Carver hurried aboard the first helicopter, it taxied promptly out. Turning smartly out to the runway in sequence, the lead ship turned on its landing light and the last ship turned on its strobes.

The formation lifted off with a thunder and wind and Taylor noticed the HEMTTs and a HUMMV all leaving the airport gate. The four Blackhawks held a tight trail formation as they flew east into the darkness, and the Sheriff noticed the little white slice of the moon peeking over the mountains. Somewhere just a few miles east of the airport, all the Blackhawk helicopters went dark at the same time, and all that was left of them was a rapidly diminishing roar and the smell of jet exhaust that still hung in the air.

Sheriff Taylor looked at his watch. It was getting late, and he had a lot of phone calls to make.

*   *   *

Tom rolled reflexively out of his sleeping bag. He never zipped it up in bear country unless it was the dead of winter. But, what startled him awake now was a rolling, pulsing thunder that struck his core, a vibration he felt through the ground and in his chest.

It was dark, and he had slept longer than he anticipated. Dumping dirt in the fire hole, he grabbed his HK, his sleeping bag and tucked in as close to being under the big rock as he could get.

Helicopters, a lot of them. Very low, right on the trees, he could feel their wind, smell their exhaust. He didn't get a count of them but it was several, and when they had passed, he slipped out of cover, unstrapped the bump helmet from the pack, then pulled the NODs out.

This wasn't the FBI, this was something different, he knew. He wondered if it was the helicopter guys that his father had talked about, they transported his Dad and his men all over, and he said they were the best pilots in the world. What did he call them? Tom had to think a moment as he listened to the sound of rotors and turbines fade to the north.

Night Stalkers…

It had become *the U.S. Army versus Tom Potter*, he thought with a tightening in his gut. He trembled a moment and tears started. How could it come to this, how could this possibly be? Did they not realize what they had done to his father? How could his own people do this? Sometimes his father laughed and talked about them like they were his family. How could they be a part of this?

Then the rage started rising. How *could* they do this? He thought. And what exactly were they doing? They were going too fast to be looking for him…

They were sending him a message, he realized. It was a show of force, meant to intimidate him, to flush him out, to make him do something stupid. To make him afraid.

But there was another message that he took from it.

They had no idea where he was, and he was winning…

CHAPTER 11

Ted Zites walked through the Sheriff's open door looking a little concerned.

Sheriff Taylor smiled, but it wasn't to alleviate that concern.

"Working late tonight, Sheriff?"

"Mm hmm."

The Deputy pointed at a chair, dispatch had just called him in off the road.

"Don't bother sitting down Ted, this won't take long," the Sheriff sighed. There were so many things he wanted to say, but he kept it short. "You're fired, Ted. I need your gun, your badge and ID, your radio and the keys to your patrol vehicle."

"What?" Ted looked absolutely astonished, and then angry. "Why?"

"Just not working out."

"Well, you're gonna need more than that. I'm gonna appeal this with the County.

"Well, I wish you luck with that, maybe I'll see you back here someday. But really, I'm sure you've considered working for the Feds and that would be a better fit for you wouldn't it? In the meantime you're still fired, and I need that sidearm, badge, ID, radio and keys. You can turn anything else over at your convenience, and I can get one of the guys to give you a ride home... unless you want me to give you a ride..."

Ted stammered, then hesitated a moment at the grip of his pistol. The sheriff slid back a little from the desk to give himself room.

Craig Markdale poked his head in the open door.

"Sheriff, did you want to see me?"

Ted looked back at him as the Sheriff spoke.

"Well, I thought you might be here a little earlier than this."

"I was out state line when I got the call from dispatch, they didn't say it was urgent."

"No, no problem, Craig." The Sheriff watched carefully as Ted slowly unholstered and laid his Glock grip first on the Sheriff's desk without bothering to clear it, then came the badge, ID and badge wallet, the keys and the radio.

"I'll arrange my own ride."

"Good, get out."

Craig watched, a little perplexed, as Ted stared at him on the way out.

"Make sure he's out of the building." The Sheriff nodded at Craig and he dropped the mag and locked the slide back on the Glock and laid it on his desk.

Craig came back a moment later.

"He's gone. What happened?"

"I fired him."

"Yeah, but, why?"

"Not really a good fit."

"That gonna be enough?"

"Nope. He'll appeal it, maybe win, but we'll deal with that later. Right now, I just need him gone the next few weeks, and I needed him out of here immediately."

"Well, there's a department issue Glock for you, Sheriff."

Taylor looked down at the stainless Sig 220 with custom grips in his holster.

"Yeah, I'm a wood and steel kind of guy, Craig."

"In a plastic kind of world, huh, Sheriff."

The Sheriff chuckled.

"So, what is really going on, Sheriff? With Zites and everything."

"Long time ago I heard somebody say; *the only thing worse than the enemy is a traitor.* Hopefully we now have that all sorted out. I'm making a bunch of phone calls tonight, gonna have a big meeting at the indoor corral at the fair grounds tomorrow night at midnight. I'd sure like you to be there."

"Sure, Sheriff, what's it about?"

"You hear anything about what went on at the airport tonight?"

"Heard dispatch got a bunch of calls about low flying helicopter and such, like I said I was working the other side of the county, so I didn't get any calls or see any of it."

"Jane Potter has been killed, she took a couple of federal agents with her. Tom Potter is on the run, and they've got a Joint Task Force stood up and they are going after him with the very best of the United States Army."

"What are we going to do, Sheriff?"

"Well, we're gonna stop them, of course." The Sheriff rocked back in his chair and smiled, happy that the decoy SD card in pelican case was still in Betsy's bin full of Corn, Oats and Barley.

*　　*　　*

The line of helicopters was working a south track, and when Tom heard them coming, he worked his way downhill aways to see out under the tree cover. He couldn't see them at first, they were low enough to be in and out of the tree tops and didn't have visible lighting. In the NODs he saw they had all kinds of IR lights on. Seven of them, he counted. Four Blackhawks and three smaller helicopters. They were close together and incredibly close to the trees. He was watching them from behind one of the big boulders, hugging it like cover with just enough of his head sticking out to see over with the NODs. The rock was cold but a kind of solid reassurance. He leaned against it and said a little prayer.

God, can't they just leave me alone. I don't want anyone else killed. I just want to be alone now, I won't do anything to anyone here.

He was still tired and knew he could sleep. It might be best to stay the night here, let things settle a bit. With the military presence, he assumed there would be more surveillance assets so he would have to be careful. Reaching down to his pack, he found the snares that Tony had left him. Looking around with the NODs, in the nearly full moon, he could see little game trails through the underbrush in what remained of the snow. He figured he'd set a few snares out overnight and have a hare or two available to cook up the next day.

Getting down on his hands and knees he threw his jacket over his head and it spilled out on the ground allowing him to turn on his headlamp and confirm the tracks of his quarry while maintaining some light discipline.

Confirming hare tracks, he found a good choke point, then set and anchored the first snare. He repeated the process another time. When he returned to walk back and look for more tracks, his foot snagged a log in the darkness and he came down on his ankle with a twist. It was hard enough he cried out and went to the ground in pain. The bump helmet hit the ground and the NODs detached from their mounting and skittered into some snow.

Gathering up the helmet and NODs he reassembled them and cleaned the lenses of snow as best he could. They functioned fine, but when he went to stand up and put weight on his foot, he realized he might be in real trouble.

*   *   *

"I'd like you to be there tonight, Joe."

"Where?"

"Indoor corral, at the fairgrounds. I got old man Sorensen letting me in."

"For what?"

"I'm callin' up the Posse. We're goin' out to help Tom Potter."

"What?"

"He's all alone, Joe. And they've brought in the Army. It's not right. We're going to stop them."

"What do you mean they brought in the Army?"

"Do you know what 160th Special Operations Aviation Regiment is, Joe?"

The Prosecutor shook his head.

"They call them the Night Stalkers. They're the helicopter guys that carry Special Forces, Special Mission Units and the National Mission Force around. They showed up at the airport last night with seven of their helicopters, and they were loaded for bear. They are hunting Tom Potter, an eighteen-year old kid and they have no idea what the FBI did to his father, who was one of their own."

"And what do you possibly hope to accomplish, Grant?"

"I hope to stop them."

"I get that, Grant, but how?"

The Sheriff leaned forward on his knees and looked down at the cracked sidewalk. He shook his head, inhaled and leaned back on the park bench, then spoke.

"I'm not entirely sure yet. I've got a list of over one hundred men I've squirrelled away in the event I needed them. Some are former military, some former cops. Some EMS or Fire guys. Some are just men I've heard about or talked to that impressed me a certain way. A lot of those men are a darn lot smarter than I am. I don't have to figure it all out myself. And I don't know all the circumstances yet I have to work with.

"I've given a basic brief on the Jeff Potter situation to all the Sheriffs in adjoining counties. I know Steve Baxter will stand with me, I know he has a similar list, probably similar number. Not sure about Devan or Rieger yet."

"So, those guys in those helicopters, you're talking like Green Berets and Delta Force?"

Taylor nodded.

"How can you possibly think you can do anything against the best in the U.S. Army?"

"Well, with that attitude we'd all still have English accents and be having tea and crumpets now wouldn't we?" The Sheriff smiled sideways at the Prosecutor.

"This is serious, Grant. You don't speak for the whole county."

"No, but I'm certainly obliged to protect it."

"But are you really protecting it at this point? Are you just bringing more potential havoc down on the county, just in an effort to protect one kid who is breaking the law?"

The Sheriff thought for a moment.

"So, when does it stop, Joe? When do we finally stand up against this? If not this kid, why the next? Maybe we just live with it. Maybe some people want to go along to get a long, but it doesn't work that way and you know it.

"A few months ago, this kid hadn't done anything wrong. Then a few pen strokes in Washington D.C. make him a criminal, they kill his father and sister and they bring out the U.S. Army against him. Why is that, Joe? It's a Federal crime, Joe, but it's still just a Class A misdemeanor. They're bringing out the best the Army can field for one kid accused of a misdemeanor…"

"Well, Grant, don't forget the whole *murder of federal agents* thing, I think that plays a little role in how this has all developed."

"It didn't *develop*." The Sheriff half turned on the bench, and he was angry. "It escalated, and *they* escalated it from a misdemeanor that is a new law that hasn't faced sufficient debate in congress or challenges in the courts. *They* did this all, *they* got all those men killed and don't you forget it."

Joe sat back a little.

"Sorry, Joe. I was more yelling at myself there, I think. I shoulda put this posse together a long time ago and stood between the Feds and the Potters, and maybe none of these people would be dead."

"Or they still would be and even more would be dead when your posse shot it out with the FBI."

"When I was talking with Jeff Potter that last time, trying to talk them down, we were talking about standing up to this... Federal Government. He said to me; *If not now, when? If not here, where?*" and that really made an impression on me. I thought it was a Kennedy quote or some variation thereof, but I couldn't find anything for certain to pin it down. Doesn't really matter though, it's one of those things that doesn't matter who said it, 'still holds true. We need to stand with Tom Potter. To stand against this one law that is part of all the other laws that are stacked on one another that are not just the erosions of individual liberty, but are ultimately the foundations of tyranny. People in Germany didn't just wake up one morning and Hitler was in charge, he manipulated and exploited the system and the laws to get there."

Joe put his face in his hands a moment, then took in a huge breath.

"My Dad's side of the family had people die in the Camps, Sheriff. A long time ago, a side of the family we don't really keep in touch with, but…" he shook his head. "This whole WPA thing, it goes too far. It's beyond declarations of war and conscription. It's just all about control and all about laying a groundwork… What the Patriot Act couldn't do, this does. I should be there with you tonight, but I won't be. Grant, we need to start setting this up like a resistance movement. The more we do that early on, the better off we'll be. We need overt and covert sides to this. I read about how Al Qaeda did it in Afghanistan. They would have overt regional figure heads that would talk to U.S. Forces, then they had covert Shadow Governors who ran things behind the scenes. Whole command and communications structures that *they* don't know about. You start working the covert side, I'll work the overt side. At this point I don't even want to know what you have going on. Make sense?"

The Sheriff smiled.

"See, I don't have to think of everything, I just have to pick good, smart people to hang out with."

Joe smiled.

*　　　*　　　*

The yipping of the coyotes woke Tom up after he'd finally fallen asleep. The ankle was swelling and made it impossible to get comfortable. He'd kept it elevated and iced for as long as he could bare, then wrapped it and hoped for sleep. When he had finally drifted off, the coyotes started singing and woke him, and he cursed them quietly.

He then heard the quiet distant crunching of many footsteps in the snow in the still night.

Quietly he reached for the NODs. He donned the helmet, strapped it on and lowered them to turn them on. He reached for his carbine.

He couldn't see them, they were on the other side of the rocks, but they were coming closer. The ankle put maneuvering out of the question. He couldn't run, whatever was about to happen, was going to happen here.

Tom's heart raced, and he had to consciously fight to control his breathing. Thumbing the safety off of the HK, the footsteps continued to get closer. Leaning out a little around the big rock he finally saw them, four of them, close…

A bull and what had to be three cows, but something seemed off about the moose.

Eyes squinting in the pale green light he tried to make sense of what he was seeing. He knew he was seeing moose antlers, but it appeared that the bull carried… *a rider?*

At a safe distance the animals stopped, and the rider dismounted. He was being quiet and cautious, apparently inspecting tracks with a small low power flashlight that shown like a beacon on the NODs.

The figure used the light sparingly and walked toward Tom's little haven amid the rocks with only his natural night vision under the bright nearly full moon. The footsteps of the man walked closer and Tom's grip on his AR tightened, left thumb ready to flash the weapon mounted light.

In range and rounding the big rock, Tom lit the subject up.

"Whoa!" Breske's hands went up reflexively to shield his face.

"Tony?" Tom turned the light off immediately on recognition and lowered the carbine. "Tony?"

"Yeah, yeah. Darn kid, you scared the crap out of me, I thought you'd be long gone by now, I left you here a couple days ago. I figured I'd pick up your track here, wasn't expecting you to still be here."

"Tony, are you riding a moose?"

"Na, that's just Sparky, he's under cover."

"He's undercover as a moose…" It was more statement than question.

"Yeah, pretty good, huh?"

Tom laughed a little.

"So, not just the shoes, you got sparky fake antlers too?"

"Ah, no man, real antlers. Even gave 'em a heat signature so they'll look more real on thermals. Pretty slick, huh?"

"Yeah, Tony. Pretty cool. Fooled me."

"You seen the helicopters, Tom?"

"Yeah."

"I think that's the Army, Tom."

"It is, Tony, it's the Night Stalkers. They fly guys like my Dad around. He used to talk about them sometimes. He said they were the best pilots in the world."

"That sounds right, they'd flown in the night I was loading up. Talk of the town, they fueled up at the airport, real deal black helicopters."

As if on cue, they heard the distant throb of rotor blades.

"See, there they are again, I seen 'em pretty close last night, silhouetted by the moon light. Bunch of 'em, no lights."

"They use these, Tony. They have lights you can only see with 'em on."

Tom unstrapped and handed the NODs to Tony.

"Oh, cool, NVGs. I've heard about 'em but never looked through any before." Setting them on his head he looked around, like a blind man seeing for the first time. "Whoa! No way, this is amazing."

"If the helicopters come by again, you'll see the lights I'm talking about. I've heard them the past few nights and during the day."

"Is that why you been hangin' tight?"

"No, I twisted my ankle."

"Oooh. Bad?"

"Bad enough. I've been doing the RICE thing, you know, Rest Ice Compression Elevation, that and poppin' Ranger Candy, that's what my Dad always called ibuprofen."

"Damn, Tom," Tony sat thinking a few moments. "I brought more food with me if you need it."

"Thanks, Tony. I ran out yesterday. I think I snared a hare over there, but I didn't want to try getting over to it."

"Where?"

"Over that way."

"I'm gonna use these to go find it OK?"

"Yeah, be careful, they're not focused for up close stuff."

Tony walked off muttering in amazement at his new found super power.

"Found it!" Tony whispered loudly.

Tony walked back, slowly, holding the frozen hare by the ears.

"Like shopping the freezer section." He said with a smile. He handed the NODs back. "You better take these or I'll get spoiled, and I won't want to give'em back. Well, this thing's frozen all the way through. I got some peanut butter and a fresh loaf of bread for you in my pack. We probably shouldn't be doing a fire with the helicopters up."

They could hear the Blackhawks maneuvering in the distance.

"Why'd they bring the Army out after me, Tony?"

"I don't know, Tom. I think you guys done a good job of holdin' off the Feds, they figured they needed to bring in their real heavy hitters."

"Do you think they know what they did to my Dad?"

Tony shrugged in the dark.

"I don't know."

"They can't know, you said they were keeping a news blackout, right?"

"Yeah, Tom. Word is getting out around town, but I don't know what they're telling these guys."

"But if they knew, they wouldn't be doing this right, Tony?"

Tony sighed because he could hear what sounded like a pained naiveté in Toms voice.

"They'll do what they're ordered to do."

"But they aren't supposed to use the Army against American people, right, Tony?"

"I'm afraid they'll just follow orders, Tom."

Tom was quiet as the helicopters sounded closer.

"Tom, I can get you up on my mules, and we can move you further. Where would you like to go?"

Tom was silent a moment more.

"I think I should stay here another night or two. I'll be headin' north out of here, but I think I need to let this ankle heal a bit before I move. This seems a safe place for now."

"OK, you want me to bring you anything else?"

"Some kind of fresh food would be good, something that doesn't have a real strong smell to it. I think I'll be here another two nights."

"Tom, I been talkin' with the Sheriff. I think he's tryin' to figure a way out of all this for you. What else do you need?"

"I just need to be left alone, Tony. I may need some higher power pain killers, something I can still think with, ya know."

"I'll get some stuff for that ankle, and I'll talk to the Sheriff and I'll see you back here in two days, I'll go get that other food for you."

"Tony, tell them I don't want to kill anyone else. I especially don't want to kill soldiers 'cause of my Dad and all. But I'll kill anyone I have to at this point."

"Yeah, I'll tell 'em, Tom."

*   *   *

Sheriff Taylor looked at the big, noisy fan. He was standing facing the bleachers of the big corral. It was too loud and a hundred men or so on the bleachers would preclude just talking to them. Markdale was the first man there.

"Craig I gotta run back to my truck and grab the bull horn, I thought this might be a problem."

Outside, in the parking area, vehicles were filtering in. Pick-up trucks, work trucks, beat up old Subarus, brand new Volvos. An interesting cross section of men started filing in past the Sheriff as he held the door and smiled for them.

There wasn't as much small talk as there might have been other times. The air carried a weight of seriousness to it, and although the men had no idea what this was about, they all sensed that much.

Shuffling into the big corrugated metal building, the Sheriff was glad of the bull horn. The acoustics were horrible and made worse by the murmur of the small crowd.

Looking at his watch, most of the men were there by five 'til the appointed hour. A few more shuffled in, and the Sheriff waited until five after to start. The kind of men he called wouldn't be late for the cryptic call he had made to each of them. There were no messages left, only direct calls to each of the men, with the time, the place and the instruction to leave cell phones and all electronic devices at home.

"Gentlemen---" The bull horn squealed with a loud squelch issue, and the Sheriff looked at it and held it a little differently;

"Gentlemen, thank you for coming tonight. I really appreciate each and every one of you being here despite the fact that I couldn't tell you much over the phone. I have been thinking of all kinds of things to say tonight, things that harken back to places like Lexington and Concord, but I don't want to get too dramatic. I'm just going to get right to it. It's late, and some of you may not want to sit through all of this.

"So, if you have a problem with standing up to the Federal government, with facing arrest and all the consequences we've seen with standing against the regime in power in Washington D.C., I won't think anything less of you, but please go now."

The Sheriff lowered the bullhorn and looked at the men, then over at Markdale beside him.

"Next, what I'm about to discuss, doesn't leave this building. It doesn't get discussed with wives, it doesn't get texted to girlfriends, it doesn't get put up on Facebook. For this to work, and for everyone's protection we must maintain the highest degree of Operational Security.

"Men, I hate that it has come to the point that I have to ask you to be here to be a part of whatever is coming. That being said, I'm confident that each of you would feel a little cheated if you weren't included in this. Again, if for whatever reason, you can't commit one hundred percent to this, it's OK to leave...

"Alright, enough of that. Like I said, I've thought a thousand different ways to talk about this. First, I'm just going to update you with what is happening and what they've blacked out of the news.

"Some of you knew Jeff Potter. For those that didn't, he was a member of our volunteer SAR team, he was a good hand. Heck, he was excellent in the woods. And he was damn good at finding people. Part of that, I'm sure, is from the fact that he was a Special Operations veteran of the Global War On Terror. He had certainly done his part, and bled for this country. We are fortunate that when he chose to retire he came to our county, where in his own, quiet way, he made his contribution.

"For reasons I couldn't argue with, Jeff Potter chose to stand against the draft. He didn't want his kids going to fight what he saw as a rich man's war. That's where all this starts. If you have a political or philosophical problem with that, I understand. Again, if you wish to leave now, please do. I won't hold it against you, and I don't want any other man here to have a problem with it."

The Sheriff lowered the bullhorn and looked at the ground. A part of him didn't want to see who was leaving... but no one was.

"Nearly a month and a half ago now, Jeff Potter wrote a letter to the Draft Board telling them his children would not be participating. It was carefully worded but of course the Feds saw it as threatening, and ultimately telling the Feds *no* is always problematic. But Jeff Potter had the guts to do just that, whether you agree with him or not, you see where this is going."

Sheriff Taylor lowered the bullhorn, a little unsure of how to continue because of what he saw as his failings in all of it. He didn't want to get emotional in front of all these men, that wasn't his way, but the fact was, he carried some guilt like a very physical load.

These men deserved the very straightest story he could tell them.

"I have to say, I fantasized about calling you men out around that time. That we'd ride up to Potter's cabin and stand between him and the Feds. I was afraid of going all *John Wayne*. I was afraid of getting people killed.

"Instead, I tried to talk Jeff and his kids out and work with the Feds, I was trying to keep the peace in our county. Well, Jeff wouldn't come out. And when the Feds decided to raid his cabin, I went with them to try to at least be a good witness to whatever happened.

"That night I saw the FBI murder Jeff Potter in his doorway with his hands raised."

There was a collective gasp and hum from the stirred crowd. The Sheriff gave a moment for it to settle.

"I tried to stop it, it was too late. When I realized what was happening, they weren't listening, and they gunned him down with his hands up. Of course, they've kept all this quiet. They've also kept quiet their manhunt for Jeff Potter's son and daughter. Against all the FBIs greatest technology and some of their best Agents, those two young people... ha..."

The Sheriff lowered the bullhorn a moment to cut off what he thought was going to be emotion getting away from him.

"I keep reflexively calling them kids, 'cause that's how I always knew them.

He shook his head and continued, the men in the stand feeling that this was difficult for him.

"But Tom and Jane Potter are a young man and young woman, worthy if anyone is of that title. They were running for their lives, having seen their father murdered. Jane Potter gave more than they took I suppose. She accounted for at least one dead FBI agent and three injured and out of the fight. Like her father, who's last act was bringing down the helicopter I was on with the FBI and Marshals tasked with bringing them in. Jane didn't go down without a fight. Jane is dead too, now."

He lowered the bullhorn again and shook his head looking to Markdale.

"Yer'd doin' good, Sheriff," he nodded. "just keep given' them the truth, and they'll see."

"Young Tom Potter is on the run, alone. As far as we can tell, he hasn't killed anyone. He is only guilty of breaking a law that was signed into effect two months ago. And all this that has happened is because the Federal Government has pushed too hard. This isn't the boy's... this isn't that *young man's* fault.

"Now they have brought in the U.S. Army. The very best of the best as they say. To hunt Tom Potter. Again, if this is too much for anyone, I understand. If you wish to leave, please do. And again, I want no one to hold any judgement against anyone who might leave. Just please remember, none of this leaves this building."

Sheriff Taylor looked down then back up to Markdale who nodded reassuringly. Again, no one left.

"Among you men, we have a whole lot of experience in military and police matters. I'm going to count on you to come up with good courses of action. I'm counting on you to not shoot when we can talk, but I'm counting on you to shoot when talking no longer matters. That's why you are on my list, it's a matter of experience and judgement.

"Understand, what is happening to Tom Potter, clearly isn't happening in a vacuum. It's a symptom of a sickness that has taken over our country. This is part of the continued erosion of individual rights. I think some men may prefer to have decisions made for them, some men prefer to have someone else tell them what to think. When I moved here twenty years ago, it was because I wasn't one of them. When I moved here, it was because I thought this was the last, best place. This was a place a man could still be free.

"So, I ask, given what we know now, knowing that we're not yet sure where we're going, who will ride with me?"

The bleachers erupted with unanimous applause. The Sheriff looked at Markdale who was smiling and clapping.

*   *   *

"Sheriff Taylor."
Taylor hit the button on his phone.
"Yes, Mary?"

"There is a Lieutenant Colonel Cavanaugh and Sergeant Major Hinson here to see you."

"Send them in, Mary."

The two men entered his office wearing well-worn ACUs. They were both very fit and strapped with some kind of high-end rigger's belts with Glock 19s with the latest in reflex sights. They were both very serious looking men with the Lieutenant Colonel wearing hair that had to border on being out of reg, while the Sergeant Major's head was shaved clean.

The Sheriff stood and shook hands with each of them, they seemed to try to smile but just couldn't quite pull it off.

"Sheriff Taylor, I'm Lieutenant Colonel Cavanaugh, this is Sergeant Major Hinson. I command Task Force Z that is operating in your county."

Taylor said nothing, and the two soldiers stood for a moment, seeming to expect more than Taylor was willing to give.

"Sheriff, I'm not sure what details you are aware of regarding this operation, but we are working with Federal law enforcement to apprehend a dangerous fugitive in your county."

"I may be more informed on all this than you think or would like me to be, Colonel. You're old enough, did you know Jeff Potter?"

"Yes, we served together in Afghanistan."

"I imagine that the FBI didn't brief you on the fact that he came out of his cabin with his hands up when the FBI agents shot him? Did they brief you on that?"

The lite Colonel laughed.

"We're not here to deal with local rumors and legends, Jeff was a good man but…"

"I'm not talking local legends, Colonel." The Sheriff's tone suddenly went flat. "I'm talking about what I saw. I was on the helicopter that went down, and Jeff Potter had his hands raised away from his weapon when the FBI shot him dead. Ask them for the sensor footage from the helicopter. They'll tell you they don't have it because the hard drive was damaged in the crash. I'm here tell you they don't have it because it incriminates the FBI. I'm here to tell you that if you saw the truth, this would be Task Force Potter, and you would be going about this in an entirely different way."

"There is a lot of misinformation going around, Sheriff," the Sergeant Major offered with full conviction.

"I'm telling you what I saw with my own eyes, I have no reason to lie. Jeff Potter was a good man, he raised good kids, they don't deserve this. You men are on the wrong side."

"Sheriff, we have recovered the body of Jane Potter, we have our K9 teams working on the trail of Tom Potter. We have reason to believe he is receiving assistance from locals. We are concerned that you may be part of facilitating assistance to this fugitive. We believe he was involved in the murder of Federal agents."

"What evidence do you have that Tom Potter murdered anyone? Maybe Jane was the one who killed them. And are you going to just ignore the fact that the FBI is lying to you? Are you just going to follow orders? How did that work for the Nuremburg Trials?"

The Colonel and the Sergeant Major were both stone faced, and the Sheriff couldn't tell if he was getting through to them.

"Sheriff, we have at our disposal a lot more assets than have been previously available on this tasking. We will apprehend the fugitive, and we will apprehend anyone assisting him. They will be turned over to the FBI for DoJ prosecution under the new War Powers Act. Tom Potter was involved in the murder of law enforcement agents, and he is in violation of the new draft laws. As a law enforcement officer, you should be able to appreciate this, and you should be ready to assist us, not block us."

"Well, I guess that's where you're mistaken. I'm a peace officer first. I'm here to protect the citizens of this county, and if that means I have to stand between them and the Federal Government, I will. We need to stop this before it gets worse."

"I agree we need to stop this before it gets worse, Sheriff. Tell us where Tom Potter is, and we're done. I'll stop looking as soon as I have him."

The Sheriff shook his head.

"Are those rocket tubes and mini-guns on your Little Birds loaded, Colonel?"

"I'm not discussing that."

"You don't have to, not with me. But maybe you two should discuss among yourselves what the hell you're doing here hunting Americans on American soil. Why you, why now, why this? Doesn't it bother you a little, especially now that you know the real circumstances of Jeff Potter's murder?"

"I think we're done here, Sheriff."

"I think so too, Colonel, you can see yourselves out."

The soldiers left, and the Sheriff picked up his phone and dialed.

"Yeah, Craig. I need you to take yourself out of service and start the phone tree, we'll meet the same place tonight after dark."

*   *   *

The Sheriff rolled up just as Tony was getting the last mule out of the trailer and leading it to the corral. He walked up to Tony while carrying a folded topographical map.

"Tony, where is he?"

"Hey, Sheriff, I was gonna come see you."

"We need to get him out now, one way or another. If we don't, they will."

Tony sighed, something had changed, and it probably had to do with the helicopters.

"This about all them helicopters we seen?"

The Sheriff nodded.

"It's bad, Tony. These guys know their business, and they're going to find him if we don't get him out of there.

"Well, I got more bad news, Sheriff. He's hurt. He twisted his ankle. I saw him two days ago, got him some fresh grub."

"Damn. How bad?"

"Bad enough. He's in a safe spot for now restin' up. He's out way of Kruger Pass, in the foothills to the north."

"I've got the posse called up, I'm thinking we roll in heavy, and pull Tom out right now. We've got over 100 men, we'll ride within the hour."

"Oh, no, no, no, Sheriff. That's too many and too fast."

"Too many? They have seven helicopters by my count, only four of them can really carry any real number of men. I figure they can field about forty at a time, no telling what kind of reserve they are holding. We go in full strength, and I may have backing of Sheriff Baxter, he said he can field at least seventy-five. We go in force."

"Sheriff. Tom and I talked, I got an idea who's on those helicopters, I got an idea who is runnin' the show now. You go in with more than a handful of guys, and they get out ahead of where ever they see that mass of men going, they still get Tom first where he is now. We gotta slow down a little here, Sheriff. Gotta think this out, and we gotta put the sneak on 'em."

Taylor put his hands on his hips and looked at the mules in the corral.

"Walk with me, Sheriff, I gotta get'em some good feed and water. They rode hard the last couple of days. He doesn't want to go nowhere, he wants to be left alone in the woods. I reckon he's kind of earned that at this point."

"It's not going to work that way, these guys are going to find him. They aren't going to leave him alone. More people are gonna die, at the very least Tom."

"He said he don't wanna kill nobody, Sheriff. But he said he will if he has to, and I believe him. Lit me up with a flash light and I reckon I was just a trigger squeeze away from bein' dead myself. He's got himself wired pretty tight out there. I was gonna let the mules rest a day restock and get some more fresh food out to him, head out tomorrow."

"No, you need to get out there as soon as possible, Tony. You say he's a two day ride in?"

"No, I just take two days. I follow the elk heards, and their trails, lose my tracks in theirs, make as much use of tree cover as I can. Just bein' careful. I can get to him faster if I have to, and I can ride tonight if I need to. Just let the mules have several hours and I'll get some supplies."

The Sheriff nodded.

"Let's get under some cover here, and I want you to show me where he is on the map."

Taylor unfolded his map under the awning and flattened it on the work bench.

"Alright, Tony, here's Kruger Pass."

"Yeah, Sheriff, he's right about here." Tony pointed to a contour line near a stream.

"Can he walk at all?"

"Don't know, he wasn't walkin' while I was there. And if he can, he sure can't carry no pack."

"So, there's no chance of him getting' to Sundog Pass, here?"

Tony laughed.

"Not under his own steam."

"You know the old abandoned rail tunnel up that way?"

"The one that comes out just about on the Canadian border?" Tony asked.

"Yeah, that one. I need him to get there. I've been tossing some ideas around, and if you can get him there, get him close, I'll have the posse assembled there. You're right, they'll detect that many men, but if he comes to the posse, we can protect him without compromising him. We can get to the tunnel from the trail head in forty-five minutes by horse, faster on four wheeler. By the time the Army figures what's up there, we should beat them."

"He has no interest in going to Canada, Sheriff, if that's what yer' thinkin'. And there's a lot of open ground without tree cover up that way, don't know I can safely get him all the way to the tunnel"

"All the better, we just have to keep the Army guessing, and that would be an international incident, a minor one, but they might not be ready for the exposure that would bring. You just get him close, Tony. And as far as a pack goes, I just need him, we can re-equip him once he gets to us. You have 48 hours to get Tom into position."

"Not sure I follow, Sheriff."

"Yeah, it's still a little cloudy to me, but it's comin' together. You just get to Tom. You get him as close as you safely can to that tunnel, the posse will take it from there. He won't need to go to Canada, and maybe we can help him get lost after. Oh, and Tony, I'm gonna need a description of what he's wearing and he needs to keep wearin' it. And I need to know which foot is hurt."

"Huh?"

"Like I said, it's still cloudy, but it's comin' together Tony."

"He's always wearin' a black knit cap, brown fleece jacket and old camo BDU pants. Not sure he has much else. And it's his right ankle that's hurt."

"OK, that's a start."

*   *   *

"Things are getting critical, Joe. I've got the posse assembling tonight, they'll be fielded first light day after tomorrow. Army came to my office this afternoon. They are gonna find Tom Potter if we don't get to him first."

"How are you going to protect him, Grant? Protective custody in the jail? That won't work for long."

"He's done a fairly good job of protecting himself, he just needs a little hand. We're gonna give it to him. What do you have going on?"

"Well, I went in person to file suit for that hard drive of the helicopter video of the Jeff Potter shooting. Of course, right now they're hiding behind the WPA and claiming that it didn't happen. If you look at the paper today, I think you'll find it an interesting headline. I went to the Daily a few days ago and leaked the story of his shooting. They did some poking around and realized no one has been in contact with the Potters for weeks, they interviewed Jane's girlfriend who talked about hearing the helicopter crash. Whether Jeff liked it or not, he was a bit of a local celebrity, people will take notice and start demanding some answers. They can try to keep this all hushed up, but if we get out ahead of it with the truth, people are going to demand answers for what is going on. That and all the *black helicopters* flying around."

"Does the girl know about Jane Potter's death?"

"No, Sheriff. I didn't include any of that in the information I leaked. I mean we only have that second or third hand, right?"

"I'd say it's reliable but, yeah, we don't have all the facts surrounding that really."

"I've also got appointments with senators and congressmen. I'm going to get them in the loop so they can be exerting pressure from their end."

"Well, this is all coming to a head, one way or another this should all be over in a few days."

"Grant, here's how I think this has to work. I can tell you what the overt side is doing 'cause it's all coming out in the news any way. I recommend you not tell me anything about the other side, at all. OK?"

Taylor nodded.

*   *   *

The Sheriff stepped in under the raised bi-fold door. Half the hangar was appointed like some kind of gentleman's lounge, the rest housed the green and grey helicopter. Bob Lewis had a cowling open and was working on something near the turbine engine.

"Bob, seems like you spend more time workin' on it than flyin' it."

"Nature of the beast, Sheriff." Bob stepped down off the step ladder and returned his wrench to the big rolling tool box. He wiped his hands off with a rag and shook Taylor's hand.

"Got the message about tonight, Sheriff and you know I was there the other night."

The Sheriff nodded, thumbs resting under his Sam Browne.

"Well, one concern. You probably don't want me bustin' this TFR they have up covering half the county, and I'm not the young buck most these other guys are. I can't ride anything like they can be it four-wheeler or horse. I'd be kind of a liability if I'm not in my helicopter."

"You flew these in the Army, right, Bob?"

"Well, not these, this is an old British Army machine, the Gazelle. But I flew helicopters in the Army. OH-58s back in the day, I was a Scout pilot."

"So, you know what the 160th is then?"

"Oh, sure. I tried out for them a long time ago. Didn't make it through assessment though."

"What do you think you and this old helicopter of yours could do if you went toe to toe with them today, Bob?

The old man laughed.

"Well, not much, Sheriff. This thing is nearly fifty years old, and I'm quite a bit older than that myself. And like I told you, when I was in my prime I wasn't good enough for them. No way I could out fly them today with this."

"Well, you're good enough for me, Bob. And what I have in mind it would be better if you *don't* out fly them. Now about bustin' that TFR. What would be the consequences to you if you did?"

"Well, at the very least, I lose my license." The old man shrugged. "I'm sixty-eight years old and you're right, these days I spend more time working on her or just hanging out here than I actually do flying. It's not as fun as it used to be." He shook his head and thought a moment.

"All these new rules and regulations, and if it's not for that then I'm getting taxed with some new tax. Probably, I wind up in jail now with this War Powers thing for going into that TFR. You tell me what you got in mind, Sheriff. My level of give a damn is kind of bottomed out at this point, and one last really cool flight might just make it all worth it..."

*   *   *

"You're here early, Tony. I was expecting another day or so."

"Things have changed, Tom. The Sheriff's really worried, he's met with these Army cats, and they ain't foolin' around. We need to get you moving. How's that ankle?"

"I can put some weight on it to get to the latrine pit, but I have a tough time getting further than that, and I sure don't want to be carryin' a pack right now."

"Look, Tom. I told the Sheriff all you told me. He gets it, but he has a plan. I can move you on the mule tonight and get you into position. Then you wait for the posse to come back you up. Can you ride for a while?"

"It's gonna hurt, Tony. I could but... I'd rather do this all on my own."

"Tom, I get that, and so does Sheriff Taylor. But the Army ain't gonna leave you alone. You ever been to that old rail tunnel north of Sundog Pass?"

"Yeah?"

"I need to get you there, I can get you in a little hide in the tree line there, and you can wait for the Posse to take it from there. The Sheriff's plan is to get you some place you can be alone somehow. I don't know all the details, but he's workin' it."

"I think I know the place if the Sheriff can help me get close."

"I'll let you work that out with him. Brought you some fresh carrots, what you don't eat, I give to the mules and we don't leave any sign that way." He handed Tom the bundle of carrots, and he started munching on them without peeling them. "We should get you packed up and move you in the next hour here, Tom. You been icin' and elevatin' that ankle today?"

"Yeah, much as I can stand."

"Well, I didn't have time to figure out anything about pain meds for you. Brought you a little Jack for the ride, should take the edge off." Tony handed him a little silver flask. "This all yer' stuff here?"

"Yeah, it's not much. Basically, just gotta stuff my sleeping bag and close up the pack."

"OK, well, have some carrots, you want anything else to eat?"

"No, I ate just before you got here. Couple of peanut butter sandwiches." Tom unscrewed the flask and took a long drag from it.

"Whoa, Tom. If yer' not used to it..."

Tom coughed and gagged a little, the fire hit his belly and warmed him all through. He laughed.

274

"I'm glad I didn't bring you too much, just do me a favor and sip at the rest of it, should last you the night if yer' not a pro. Get dressed in your warm gear, and I'll get your pack all set."

Carefully pulling his BDU pants over his ankle, he wore them over his thermal long underwear, then added a few layers of thermals before he put on his brown fleece coat and black knit watch cap.

Tony was stuffing the sleeping bag into the compression sack and Tom took a more careful sip from the flask.

"Slow down on that, Tom. I don't need you pukin' all over my mule."

Tom smiled.

"Oh, and don't change your clothes."

"Huh?"

"Don't ask me, it's part of the Sheriff's plan. He needed your clothing description and I told him you been wearin' that the whole time."

"OK."

He took another sip.

"Seriously, man. Slow down on that. I'm gonna go strap this to a mule. No more whiskey 'til you're on the ride. Before you put those boots on, we're gonna wrap that ankle nice and tight. I'll help you if you need me to."

"Tony, you want the NODs since you'll be leadin'."

"No, Tom. I think I'm better off usin' my natural night vision if I don't have any practice with those things. I might just lead us all over a cliff lookin' at all the pretty stars or somethin'."

Tom laughed and assembled the helmet.

It took Tony a few minutes, but when Tony returned to the rocks, he could hear Tom stifling a cry as he cinched the Ace bandage tight.

"You OK, Tom?" he asked as he was rounding the rock.

Tom was taking another swig. Tony just rolled his eyes but didn't say anything more.

Tom didn't say anything either. He put his Merrill on his good foot first, then took time to loosen the laces of the other one as much as he could. He grimaced as he slid the injured ankle into the boot.

"OK, I'm gonna need a minute here, Tony, before I get up here." Tom strapped the NVG helmet on but left the NODs in the up position powered off.

"Ya know, Tony, my Dad asked me once; He said, what are deer and squirrels and hare? Well, I didn't know what he meant. But he said, ' they are prey and they know it and they are tuned for survival as such'. Then he said 'we, men, are predators, and we *don't* know it. That we've been deprogrammed from that reality by our cushy existence.' He said we can learn it again, to be predators. And I haven't had a very cushy existence these past couple of weeks. Dad said that God didn't give us sharp teeth and claws or incredible strength, instead he gave us John Moses Browning... And I'm feelin' like a predator now."

Tom drew his trophy 1911 from his waist, pointing it at the rock and looking through the red dot sight.

Tony moved quickly and carefully grabbed the pistol from his hand, his finger between the hammer and the firing pin.

"Tom, you can't even be feeling that whiskey yet and yer' bein' a fool. I'll keep your guns tonight, I'll give them back to you when we get to the hide. You can be a predator all you want then, but tonight yer' just a passenger."

*   *   *

"Gentlemen," the Sheriff said through the bullhorn. "In thirty-six hours we head into the field to help protect Tom Potter. We have 105 men here tonight, committed to this. Sheriff Baxter promises a Posse of 87. That gives us a combined strength of 192. I estimate the Army to have brought about 120. They can only field about 40 at a time. I'm assuming they have three groups of 40 because they seem to be operating nearly around the clock, but they may not even have that many.

"At any rate, we will go to the field to initiate blocking and diversionary actions to protect Tom Potter. Right now, I need you men to separate into groups based on horseback, ATV or UTV and my long-range precision shooters. When I say long range shooters, I'm not talking about somebody who goes to the range and shoots from the bench at 100 yards. I want former snipers, long range hunters and long-range competition guys. If you don't know what you need to do when shooting long range down a slope, you don't belong in that group.

"Deputy Markdale here will be briefing those men in the ATV/UTV group. I'll brief our horsemen and snipers.

"Before we break off into our groups, I wanted to show you this in case you might have missed it. It's our daily rag here."

Taylor took the folded newspaper out from under his arm and held it up to display the large headline.

"So, for you guys in the back who can't read it, it says WHERE IS JEFF POTTER? Jeff Potter is dead, I saw that myself. I have reliable information that his daughter was killed in an exchange of fire with FBI/HRT. Some of you guys may remember Jane, she may have out shot some of you at local high-power rifle competitions. Jane put the hurt on them with her M-1 Garand. She died fighting for what she believed in, and now Tom Potter is all alone.

"Tom Potter is running for his freedom, and he's not asking for any help. Tom Potter is running from the U.S. Army that is hunting him on U.S. soil. I have been asked why I would risk so much for one kid. Why would the Federal Government employ so much against one scared kid who wants to be left alone? And I have to stop calling him a kid at this point. He's a young man by any measure, and do you want to know why he's worth protecting?

"Because if the Federal Government will go through all of this for one young man, what will they do to keep all of us in line? And how many more terrible policies and oppressive laws do we put up with before we say *no*. What is going on now, whether by accident or design… that doesn't matter much, the outcome is the same. This is the foundation of tyranny, we do what we can to stop it now, or we suffer living with it later.

*   *   *

Colonel Cavanaugh leaned back in the cheap business chair. The conference room in the little rural Army Reserve center had been stood up as a temporary Tactical Operations Center. It was three in the morning, and the Colonel was just starting his day. There were four large screens at the front of the room digitally labeled COVEY 12, COVEY 14, NIMBLE 15 and   NIMBLE 18. The display for Covey one-four was a dark and shadowy, grainy image that seemed to show a part of the Predator drone's fuselage. Its sensor stowed, Covey one-four was Returning To Base. Covey one-two was scanning a streambed. Nimble one-five and Nimble one-eight were the feeds from two of the Little Bird helicopters. They appeared to be orbiting some animals.

"Hey, Bob. What's Nimble got?"

"Not sure, Sir." The S2 said, squinting a little at the screen. "They just started that orbit."

"I think they just found the moose, Sir," the civilian analyst chimed in. "Covey one-four passed that as the only thing they'd seen all night before they went RTB. The DHS Pred guys have seen two herds of twenty to thirty elk and there's these four moose. That's all they've seen in this Killbox all week. That one moose has pretty big horns, I guess that's the male."

"Antlers, Mike," the Colonel smiled.

"Sir?"

"Moose don't have horns, they have antlers. Antlers fall off and grow back every year, horns don't fall off."

"Really, Sir?"

The Colonel nodded and smiled.

"What kind of intel guy are you, Mike?"

"Well, Sir, it's intel analyst, not wildlife biologist."

The radio broke squelch.

"Command, Nimble one-five. Is Zero-one with you by chance?"

The Colonel keyed up the microphone at his station.

"Nimble one-five, Zero-One Actual, go."

"Yes, Sir. We, ah, happened to pass over these moose a few seconds ago. We took up a two-mile orbit, and they don't hear us out here, we're gonna close to one mile, and we want to see if you see what we thought we saw."

"Nimble One-Five, I'm watching your feed."

The Colonel sat up in his seat. The pilot of the AH-6 tightened his orbit, and his co-pilot tried shifting the thermal image from black hot to white hot to see if there was any change in definition. Disappointed, he switched back to black hot as the four moose traveling in trail grew larger on the screen.

"That's a helluva rack on the bull," the Colonel said to the two intel men. As the image grew the Colonel stood up. "I'll be damned... that's how they're doing it."

The Colonel keyed the mic.

"Nimble One-Five, good catch, are you seeing riders or packs?"

"Zero-One Actual, Nimble One-Five, we think we're seeing both here."

"Nimble One-Five, maintain that stand-off for now, we've got Steady Four-Three, patrolling a few keypads south. We'll get them headed your way for the interdiction. If it looks like you'll lose them in the trees, interdict yourselves, and we'll have Steady there as fast as possible to put a stick on the ground for take down."

"Nimble One-Five, wilco."

*　　*　　*

Tony smiled to himself and patted Sparky on the neck. The two little helicopters went low overhead in a shadow of blur only visible because they were darker than the rest of night. They were close enough he felt their downwash and smelled the jet exhaust.

"Good job old boy! I knew it would work." He was surprised how quiet they were, there was a bit of a wind but even cupping his hands behind his ears, he couldn't hear them very soon after they had passed.

The tree line was just a few hundred yards ahead, and he resisted the urge to hurry the mules along. They startled only a little by the overflight, then settled quickly again. The wind was following the helicopters, favoring a quiet approach if they should return from that direction.

*　　*　　*

"Command, Nimble One-Five, can we get an ETA for Steady Four-Three."

"Nimble One-Five, Steady Four-Three with you showing a twenty-three minute ETA your grid."

"Rog, Steady Four Three, these guys are gonna make the woods in the next ten minutes or so, we're moving to block."

The Colonel leaned forward on his elbows nodding in concurrence with the crews' coordination.

*   *   *

The little egg-shaped black helicopter swept in quickly and quietly, hovering just a few feet off the ground, it's rotor plane just a little above Breske's head. Even though it was at least thirty yards ahead of him, it was frightening. It was suddenly loud now as the helicopter pivoted to look at him head on. Tony could see the faces of the pilots illuminated green by the NVGs they had on their helmets.

"Easy, Sparky, easy. Guess we need to just stay here. It was sure a lot of fun while it lasted."

Tony looked up and down hill and didn't see a good avenue of escape for the string of mules. Looking back at the rockets and miniguns, he wondered if they were loaded. Then he wondered if it would be quick for the mules. He wondered how they'd be treated if he just gave them up. And how would he be treated now?

He'd been arrested before, scuffled with the law on occasion, but now things were different. Now America was different. Would they just disappear you now? Would they torture him to find out where Tom was?

Tony smiled and wondered if the pilots could see it.

"HOKA HEY MOTHER FU…"

He drew his Glock 29 from his chest holster and fired at the menacing machine.

*　　*　　*

"Nimble One-Five, taking ground fire."

"Nimble flight, Zero-One Actual, cleared to return fire, rifle only, One-Eight, move in for the shot if you need to."

"Yeah, One-Five, we took a few rounds through the canopy and we've got some temp spikes in the engine, we're putting down for precautionary, it's One-Eight's shot."

"Nimble One-Eight in hot."

*　　*　　*

Tony didn't see the second Little Bird moving up on his right side, he was fixated on the helicopter in front of him settling to the ground, he knew he had good hits on it. Tony didn't see the muzzle of the suppressor on the M-4 poking out of the left door of the Little Bird positioning beside him. And, of course, he couldn't see the invisible IR laser that was painting a dot on his right side just below his armpit as he was still pointing the Glock at the first helicopter.

Out of the corner of his eye, he caught the flicker of muzzle flash, but it was too late. The multiple 5.56 mm impacting his side felt like he had taken a hammer blow sufficient enough to knock him out of the saddle.

Falling to the muddy snow, he had never known such pain. And so much blood. Aspirating it and choking and convulsing, he knew for only a moment, that this was what dying must feel like.

CHAPTER 12

The Sheriff had arrived an hour early to the office to review and sign off on paperwork and anything that needed attending to before he was going to be gone for... who knew what would happen tomorrow. He was hoping to leave at noon.

"Aubrey Harries to see you, Sheriff."

"Send him in, Mary"

The older man limped in, and the Sheriff stood and shook hands.

"How can I help you, Mr. Harries?"

"I hear you're forming a posse."

"Well, not sure where you heard that from, Mr. Harries."

"I know he was supposed to keep quiet about it, but he's an old hunting buddy, and he knew that Jeff Potter rescued me."

The Sheriff nodded and gave a grim smile.

"And now I saw in the paper they're saying he might be dead, that the FBI might have shot him."

Inhaling, the Sheriff took a moment to formulate what to say.

"Mr. Harries, I'm afraid I was there, and I know for a fact the FBI shot Jeff Potter. His loss was a loss for the whole community."

"I want in on the posse. I can't ride, but I can hitch a ride in a side by side or something, I can handle myself if it comes to it."

"I appreciate that Mr. Harries..."

"I know I'm old, I know I'm still hobbling from the surgery on this broken leg, but Jeff Potter put me back in touch with my kids. I kind of gave up on me that way because I wasn't the father I could have been. He helped me see past that and my kids too. So even if something goes bad here, if I didn't make it out alive, I at least get to be the man my kids can look up to. There has to be something I can do to help."

"Your limp is on your right leg?"

"Yes."

"How tall are you?"

"Five foot eleven, last time the Doctor measured. Used to be six foot one, guess I shrunk a bit..."

"Do you have any BDU pants? Brown fleece coat? Black wool knit watch cap?"

"Well, I can't think of right off hand..."

"Go to Ed's surplus store in town, you can get all that there pretty cheap, but get it. You've just been a big help to me, Mr. Harries, this cloudy plan I've had swirlin' around in my brain, you just gave me the last piece, and it all seems to fit now. We meet at the North Gate Trailhead, first light tomorrow. If you'll excuse me, I've got a bunch of phone calls to make."

*   *   *

Craig let off the accelerator as the Tahoe passed the trailhead; he almost hit the brakes and pulled in when he saw the activity. Instead, he made mental note of everything he saw and reached for his cell. Turning off at the next cross road, he pulled off a bit before turning around as he hit the speed dial for Tony Breske's cell.

The call went right to voice message. He tried once more with the same result, then he called up the Sheriff's personal cell and hit it.

"Craig, what's up, I'm just finishing up here at the office, headed back to the house to pack up."

"Hey, Sheriff. I'm on Welton, just past the Lazy Forest Trailhead. Tony Breske's been parking his rig here for the last few weeks, wanted me to keep an eye on it for him. Well, I just went past it, and there were a bunch of government vehicles there, bunch of FBI lookin' Suburbans and pick-ups and a flatbed wrecker with US Government plates. They were hitchin' up his four-horse trailer with what appeared to be his four mules in it to a black Ford three quarter ton pick-up. Looked like they were positioning to put his Dodge on the flatbed."

The Sheriff's demeanor suddenly went heavy, weighted by the implications of what Craig had just seen.

"Sheriff, you want me to go back and ask questions and poke around?"

The line was quiet as the Sheriff was thinking a moment.

"No, Craig. Get out of there, now. Get back to town, go 10-7 and start getting ready. I'll make a call."

"Yes, Sir."

"Thanks, Craig. Good job."

*　　*　　*

"Grant, I shouldn't really be..."

"Where is Tony Breske?"

"Grant..."

"Carver, did they take him into custody?"

There was silence on the line, and the Sheriff didn't like it but didn't know what to fill it with.

"Tony Breske is dead, Sheriff. You deserve to know that. He put a couple ten millimeter rounds into one of their helicopters and took it down, so they lit him up. There, that's all I can say, Grant. More than I should be saying. You're a good man, Grant, whatever you may have started, it needs to stop now before anyone else gets hurt."

"Do they have Tom Potter in custody?"

"I've already said more than I should, Grant. Goodbye."

The line went dead, and Taylor looked at the handset.

The Sheriff sighed and sank his face in his hands.

*   *   *

The analyst stood in front of the Colonel and his staff at the long table. Clicking the remote for the power point, he made sure he was at the first slide.

"Gentlemen, what we have been able to put together so far is this." Clicking, it showed an image of Tony Breske's body, bloody in the snow and mud where he died. "We have finally been able to ascertain that this is one Tony Breske through state motor vehicle records, and we have it confirmed through picture match. The only ID Breske had on him at the time of his death was a current trapping license in the name of Arnold Peters. We're not sure of the whole story there.

"Steady was able find his horse trailer and pick-up truck at what is known as the Lazy Forest Trailhead. Ground force element was able to get his horses there this morning, and FBI took all of them in for impound."

"Mules, Mike," the analyst had been cycling through pictures of the different evidence collected thus far and the latest images was of the team and FBI loading the trailer.

"Sir?"

"Those are mules, Mike," the Colonel said nodding at the picture. "Relax, Mike, go on, animals just aren't your thing."

"Ah, yes, Sir." The analyst smiled nervously and continued.

"So, ah… Mr. Breske had been contacted by the HRT element a few weeks ago, and he had presented his trapping license. They made record of the contact, ran him for warrants but apparently the fact that Mr. Arnold Peters is deceased went somehow unnoticed. It was just noted that he was trapping in the area and said he had not seen the fugitives in question. We're not sure what the deal is with the false trapping license. Breske's criminal record is fairly old, a few assault charges and DUI, but those are all old, last one being over ten years ago. He also had some state wildlife convictions right about ten years ago, some kind of hunting thing.

"Anyway, the meat of this, and it's really embarrassing. Breske apparently affixed moose horns… ah, antlers, to one of his *mules*. He also had shoes fashioned to imitate moose, ah… hooves, Sir?"

Colonel Cavanaugh nodded with a patient smile.

"Well, Breske would follow elk herds to help hide his tracks in and out of the operating area, following known paths as much as possible. With this new information our two K9 units were able to back track a bit and find a bed down location for Tom Potter. There was a buried Dakota Fire Pit, and some buried garbage consistent with his M.O. He apparently spent some time there and from the tracks there our trackers were able to determine that he has injured his right leg or ankle. It is clear that Breske was providing Potter with material support and transportation. Trackers were further able to determine that Breske took him out on one of the mules and went North. At this point the K9s were really fatigued and lost the trail, and the trackers lost good track amid elk and what were real moose tracks. Trackers are hoping to pick up the trail today with improved light conditions. The good news is we know he is at least an entire killbox further north than anticipated..."

"Canada?"

"Yes, Sir. We assess the fugitive is trying for the Canadian border. Given his movement and the history of people fleeing such crimes."

"Well, this is some progress. We'll shift all our efforts one killbox north and see how our coordination with the RCMP and Canadian government is going."

*   *   *

The Sheriff looked at the sky, the dark foreboding clouds building to the south and the wind in his face. The men were assembling at the trailhead. He was getting Betsy out first and saddling her up. He'd get the big palomino out second and get him saddled once Betsy was settled.

The weather was due to turn bad later in the day, after noon. The first real snow of the season, they said. That could help or not depending on how the day developed.

He left unmentioned to anyone his concerns that Tom Potter might already be in custody. The uncertainty of the full circumstances surrounding Tony Breske's death were hard enough, thinking that all this might be too late was terribly troubling.

Tony wouldn't have shot unless he felt threatened, or someone threatened his mules. And if it was true and he hit and took down a helicopter, it had to be real close if he used that 10 mm Glock he carried.

The Sheriff snugged the billet a little and shook his head.

Tony was a good man and didn't deserve it either way. Just like Jeff Potter.

It would be easier to be intimidated by the reality of good men dying. Easier to just decide to quit and cut these other 105 good men loose so no more good men died. But, really, that wouldn't be fair to men such as these. Like Tony, they would want to be informed, and informed, they would want to be nowhere else.

The true test of whether or not Tom Potter was still on the run, would be if this gathering of over 100 men and the other one that was Sheriff Baxter's muster, nearly the same size, got the attention of overhead surveillance.

Baxter and his men were rallying at the Fire Ridge Trailhead. They would work the ridge and the north end of the old rail tunnel, just shy of the Canadian border. They were a critical part of the plan, and the contingency if things went sideways.

After getting Betsy saddled and settled with some feed, he brought out Tiger, the big gold and white palomino. More spirited than Betsy, he was an honest ride as long as things weren't too unpredictable. At the same time, he was more powerful and faster if the situation warranted it. Betsy was surefooted and steady, and she trusted Taylor as much as he trusted her.

As he saddled Tiger, the Sheriff looked at the other men readying their rides, be they wheeled or legged. The men were a mix of solemn and jocund, and of various degrees of outfitting. Some appeared as cowboys, fresh off the range from another time. Others equipped with the very latest AR-15s and optics and suppressors and body armor. And he found it a little humorous that he didn't always match the ride correctly with the rider. One man with ballistic helmet and plate carrier and black rifle stepped into the stirrups of a giddy pony, another in a duster, a worn cattleman hat and carrying a Henry, mounted a Polaris.

He had picked them well, and if this was his day to die, he wouldn't want to be among any other. As he finished with Tiger and had them both enjoying some buckets of COB, he turned back toward the men.

Waiting a few moments until he thought most of them seemed done, with some effort, he used the push bar on the bumper of his Tahoe to climb onto the hood and address them.

"Guys, gather in close, I don't have the bullhorn today. I think you're all pretty well briefed on the plan and our Rules Of Engagement. I'll repeat the ROE at the end here. I just want to update you and reiterate my appreciation for your being here." The Sheriff was yelling to be heard, and the men crowded close, especially the older ones.

"I'm gonna keep this short, just our assembly here will likely get a lot of attention. We'll let Deputy Markdale and his ATVs go first, they'll get our snipers into position sooner. We'll be close behind, figure this to be about a half hour ride. Remember, no cell phones, no Baofengs or radios of any kind, nothing that emits a signal. Make sure your license plates are removed here at the trail head. We're not gonna hand them anything.

"Last night I was informed that Tony Breske was engaged by helicopters of this Task Force Z. I'm told he shot at them, they returned fire and killed him. This was heartbreaking news to me, and I know it will be to many of you as well. Tony wasn't always the easiest guy in the world to get along with, but despite some rough spots in his personality, his heart was always in the right place. And if you were in trouble, especially out here, there's no one else in the world you'd want helping you. And I'll tell you now, he has been our contact to Tom Potter. He thought Tom was worth helping and risking his life for.

"I think it's appropriate to take a moment of silence and prayer now for Tony, and for the Potters, and take a moment to pray for peace if we can have it."

Hats were removed, heads were bowed. Taylor tried to pray, but there was too much running through his head. All he could manage was a quiet *God help us,* to himself. As he replaced his Stetson someone yelled from the back of the crowd.

"Did he get any?"

The Sheriff cupped his ear.

"Did Tony take any of the bastards with him?" the voice yelled louder.

Sheriff Taylor bowed his head and came up with a little grin.

"He allegedly took one of their helicopters out of the picture. I have no other details."

There was a laughing cheer from the crowd. Task Force Z wasn't invincible.

"One last time, our Rules Of Engagement come from our history books, gentlemen. They should be pretty easy to remember; *Stand your ground, don't fire unless fired upon, but if they mean to have a war, let it begin here.*"

*   *   *

Tom estimated it to be a half mile of open terrain from the hide. But with his ankle the way it was, the distance didn't matter. Scanning with the binoculars Tony had left him, he could see the old rail tunnel opening clearly, the old rail bed cutting through the lower elevation. He was just barely back in the tree line, but nestled among some fallen cedars with good thick tree canopy overhead. It seemed like he'd been here forever now, since Tony had dropped him off. Was it two days? Today was the day, wasn't it? Or should it have been yesterday? Had something changed?

It would be this morning, he reassured himself. But looking to the south, he saw weather developing. That could change things, too. Whatever plan the Sheriff was putting together.

Looking at the GPS he was a long way from the north cache, which was where he really wanted to be. Jane had talked of it often, that it had so much more than the south cache, that he could totally replenish there, and there was lots of different kinds of food and duplicate gear to replace anything lost...

He heard it first, four-wheelers, a bunch of them. Binoculars up, he saw they were coming in from the trail to the west, dozens of them it seemed… Was it the Army? The panic quickly subsided when the only uniform he recognized was one of the Deputies from the Sheriff's department in the lead. This was part of the Sheriff's plan. Tom smiled.

The assorted ATVs fanned out in front of the tunnel, some men dismounted side by side vehicles carrying long guns and packs, and they started up the mountain side above the tunnel. He saw another group of ATVs approaching from the east along the ridge. So many men, all armed, all there to help him.

Could this really work?

He couldn't run to them, how could he get them to come to him? And he was so far from where he wanted to be. He looked back to the GPS face, and it flashed in sun rising above the peaks in the east.

When Tom saw the first horses show up, he could see the man in the lead was Sheriff Grant Taylor, riding one horse and leading another.

Tom held his fingers in a V at arms' length, putting the distant figure of the mounted Sheriff in the notch of the V, he raised his GPS.

*   *   *

The Colonel walked into the TOC with a sense of urgency, Covey had something, and the analyst was smiling when he said it.

Two of the big displays up front were dark, the other two labeled COVEY 14 and COVEY 12. The displays showed large gatherings of people, vehicles and horses. The Colonel stood behind his S2.

"What've we got here?"

"Something big is happening, we've not seen this large an assembly of people in any of the wilderness areas at all. This is something really big. They're all armed, and this is *very* close to Canada. These are the Northgate and Fire Ridge Trailheads. We are assessing a total of approximately one-hundred fifty military aged males. In between the two gatherings we found what we believe is an old abandoned rail tunnel and rail bed. It exits less than a quarter mile from the border."

"This is gonna be it then, they're running for the border. Are Steady and Nimble flights fueled up from the night missions?"

"They're finishing up now, team is advised and standing by."

"Load and launch as soon as they're fueled. Do we have the diplomatic clearances for Canada?"

"Negative, still nothing from State on that."

"What about RCMP?"

"We notified liaison of the activity and location, they're pushing it up to them."

"Estimated time of flight after launched?"

"Forty-five minutes, Colonel."

"Well, we better stop them before they get through that tunnel."

*　　　*　　　*

As the Sheriff arrived at the tunnel entrance he looked around at the positioning of the men. ATV's idled and horses snorted with anticipation, they could sense something was about to happen. Everyone seemed properly positioned in and around the tunnel, he could see the top of the ridge where some of Baxter's posse had taken up overwatch.

He looked at the tree line far across the open terrain. Now he had to figure out where Tom was, if he had made it this far with Tony. The clouds were closer now, and the occasional icy snow flake was spit out in front of them. The sun would be obscured soon.

Then he heard the helicopters.

Damn.

"Alright men, it's about to be show time..." as he was yelling that, something caught his eye in the tree line, a flash...

Another, three flashes. A pause, then three more...

"There he is. You three men on me." The Sheriff nudged Betsy with his heels and quickly got her to a full gallop. The other three assigned horsemen followed suit charging across the open plain.

* * *

"Colonel, Covey one-two is reporting sensor bent, possible icing, they're RTB, Covey One-Four is trying to get below this weather."

The big screen for Covey One-Two was a worthless opaque blur. The other screens were showing feeds for Steady Four-Three and Steady Four-Five and showed them en route over the forested wilderness. They were only a few minutes out with Nimble flight in the lead.

The screen for Covey One-Four suddenly showed a shift of the sensor as it picked up movement, four riders on horseback, charging across the open terrain.

"Sir..."

"I see it, whatever Covey One-Four has to do to keep them, have them maintain those riders at all cost."

"Yes, Sir."

The Colonel picked up the microphone from his station and keyed up.

"Nimble Lead, Zero-One Actual, ETA."

"Overhead, two mikes."

"Steady Flight, Zero-One. I want Four-Three to land and establish blocking position, south entrance of the tunnel with troops on the ground. Four-Five, I want you blocking position north side of tunnel, we get them before they get to the border. Nimble Lead, prepare to interdict horses."

"Steady Four-Three, wilco."

"Steady Four-Five."

"Nimble Lead." The helicopter pilots acknowledged in sequence.

*   *   *

Tom kept flashing his GPS face until the Sheriff and the other three riders were hauling back on the reins, just about over top of him. Leaving everything but his carbine, which he slung hard over his back, his prize 1911 in his waistband and his Bible tucked in his BDU pocket, he took a few painful steps out of his hide. The Sheriff reached down with a gloved hand and a big smile.

The sound of helicopters swarmed behind him.

"Tom, you're gonna have to hang on tight, 'cause this is gonna get rough," he yelled as he helped Tom up. Swinging his right leg over Betsy's croup, his swollen right ankle came down hard against her right thigh. The pain had to be quickly forgotten, as soon as his arms were wrapped around the Sheriff's waist, they were off at a punishing gallop.

*   *   *

"They picked up a rider"

"That's it, that's gonna be him, get that description out," the Colonel said to the Controller.

"All stations, be advised, suspect is wearing black hat, brown coat and camouflaged BDU pants, he's riding behind the Sheriff, who is in uniform," the Controller said over the net.

"Nimble Lead, block the horse with two riders," the Colonel broke in.

"Nimble Lead, Tally-ho."

"Command, Steady Four-Five, troops out, north side."

"And ah, Steady Four Three, we got horses and vehicles maneuvering under us to deny landing... you want my gunners to lay down containment fire so we can put down here?"

"Steady Four-Three, negative, do not fire unless fired upon. Don't take any unnecessary risks to people or equipment. If you can't land, orbit overhead to give me another sensor since we're short."

"Steady Four-Three," the frustrated Blackhawk pilot acknowledged.

*   *   *

The pilot of the black Little Bird helicopter planned his flare well, and he came to a hover with the skids just inches off the ground and just meters in front of Betsy, the Sheriff and Tom. The mare came to a sudden stop, and the Sheriff and Tom squeezed with their legs and shifted hard forward against the saddle.

The sound was drowned out by the whine of the turbine and the buzz of rotors, but he saw her head shake and nostrils flare. He knew she was snorting in protest. He patted her neck reassuringly. The Sheriff looked at the riders to his left and right and gave them a nod. They broke off at a distance to give him room.

The AH-6 Little Bird helicopter, from the front, was all bubble canopy. Sprouting from the roundness of the sides of the fuselage, on the left side was a pylon with a loaded rocket pod. On the right, the pylon was occupied by a multi-barrel minigun fed with a belt of linked ammunition.

The Sheriff couldn't see the pilot's eyes, with his flight helmet's dark visor lowered, but he was close enough, he could see a slight grin, which the Sheriff returned.

This would be a man and his 20th century machine against a timeless man and his animal. Each equally determined and committed to their mission, each totally at one with their mount.

"Alright old girl, we got this," the Sheriff yelled. He hauled right on the reins and pressed gently but firmly against her with his right foot. She pivoted in place, and Tom squeezed hard to hold on as she squatted into the turn then launched up the slight hill of the open plain.

The Little Bird hovered sideways, expertly climbing just enough with the increasing grade. The Sheriff pulled her back to the right and dashed a few strides away from the whirring machine. The helicopter maintained the distance, and then the Sheriff cut down hill. Turning, he charged obliquely at the helicopter. Betsy was emboldened by the Sheriff's confident and reassuring commands. The pilot lifted at the last moment when he thought the Sheriff misjudged it, and thought he would plunge into the rotors.

This was the moment the Sheriff knew he would make it. This was more dance than pursuit, and each man relished the challenge and each knew the thrill of the hunt, but neither wanted blood here.

The Little Bird hovered back to create space, then lowered again, skids just inches above the ground, blocking Betsy's direct path, the Sheriff cut right again, up the terrain, which gave the pilot a little more to think about.

The pilot backed off more, then blocked again, each time losing more ground.

Men on the mountainside and inside the TOC each watched the exquisite ballet with equal respect for both dancers and in awe of the ultimate spectacle of whirling anachronism.

Each move and counter move brought the horse and its riders, and the helicopter and its crew, closer to the steeply rising mountainside, where the tunnel was cut.

Finally, the helicopter pilot executed a quick pedal turn to check his proximity to the dangerous terrain, then he performed another block.

The helicopter paused and so did the Sheriff, each nodding subtly to each other before the helicopter climbed out steeply, allowing the Sheriff the last hundred meters uncontested.

At full gallop, they dashed to the tunnel opening where he stopped to meet Markdale.

With the diminishing sound of the helicopter fading in the distance, the Sheriff and Tom smiled as the men positioned around them cheered.

"That was awesome, Sheriff!" Markdale yelled as he assembled the little burner flip phone and handed it up to him after hitting the power button.

"Good job gettin' everybody under that Blackhawk, Craig. But we're not done yet." The Sheriff took the phone and hit the only number in its memory then looked up at the men around him as it dialed.

"Great job everyone, but we're not done yet!" he yelled as he held the phone to his ear. When the phone picked up, he simply said. "You're up, Bob."

The Sheriff tossed the phone to his Deputy who took the battery out again and stomped it repeatedly under foot. The Sheriff walked Betsy into the darkness of the tunnel, patting her lathered neck.

*   *   *

The TOC sat a moment in quiet disbelief as they watched the Little Bird climb out on Covey's feed.

"Command, Nimble Lead, unable to continue blocking in a manner consistent with safety of my aircraft or individuals on the ground, had to terminate."

The Colonel keyed up.

"Understood, Nimble Lead, nice flying and good call."

He sat back in his chair and said aloud to no one in particular.

"Wouldn't do to have a horse and or riders decapitated, and or another helicopter down for any of this."

Steady Four-Three's sensor was now on the Team that had landed on the north of the tunnel and on Steady Four-Five's Landing Zone, where she sat idling in the middle of the rail bed. Baxter's Posse lined the rail bed, at nearly even intervals nearly all the way to the border. Unlike the men on the south entrance, they put up no effort to repel the helicopter's landing and offered no sign of resistance to the disembarking troops. In fact, they all stood at some form of 'at ease' with hands well clear of slung weapons.

"Movement out of the north tunnel entrance," the analyst announced.

All eyes shifted to the screen for Steady Four-Three's feed where they saw five men walking out, followed by the limping form of a man in a black hat, brown coat and BDU pants.

"Alright Zero-four, Zero-One Actual, you know what to do here, cover and contact."

"Zero-Four." The Ground Force Commander acknowledged.

The TOC watched as the Ground force split into two elements and Steady Four-Three hovered in close for better imagery, and better coverage with miniguns.

*   *   *

The noise of the helicopter ground idling behind them was overtaken as the second MH-60 came to a close hover nearly overhead. From the back of the advancing wedge of the contact team, Marshal Carver stole a glance over his shoulder and saw the Blackhawk crew chief diligently manning the mini-gun, sweeping back and forth looking for any sign of hostility from the posse, or the man limping out of the tunnel entrance.

As the badge for this stick, he was the official Federal representative, and when they took the fugitive down, he would be the one to put the cuffs on Tom Potter. The helicopter hovered closer, menacingly behind them. As the down wash and dust kicked up, Carver squinted and the four men in front of the fugitive parted. They offered no sign of resistance and instead covered their faces from dust and debris swirling from the MH-60s rotor. As the contact team advanced quickly the four men parted, Carver and the other three in trail held guns up making sure no one closed on them while the first two men went hands on with the fugitive. They grabbed him with great authority and took him face first to the grass and gravel of the old railbed. Levering his arms quickly behind his back, the commandos waited a moment as Carver dropped his M-4 on its sling and pulled his cuffs.

Quickly cuffing him, then double locking the cuffs, Carver patted him down for weapons and turned the fugitive over. He shook his head as he found himself looking into the slightly bloody, but smiling face of one Aubrey Harries.

"This is an old man, this is the wrong damn guy!" Carver yelled over the sound of hovering helicopter.

*   *   *

"Command, Zero-Four," the Ground Force Commander called over the net. "We have a decoy here at the Northside. We have a dry hole here."

The Colonel crossed his arms and sighed, then the net exploded.

"Command, Nimble One-Eight, we have a helicopter approaching from the West, landing south side, looks like an old French Gazelle."

Covey's feed zoomed in to show Nimble Lead making an attempt to block the old helicopter's approach. When the Gazelle seemed to show no concern about a collision, Nimble broke off, and the grey and green camouflaged helicopter flared and landed at the south tunnel mouth.

"Two men approaching the helicopter, one limping and matching suspect description."

The Colonel keyed up, skeptical now.

"Alright, Nimble flight, stay on that helicopter. Steady Four-Three, join Nimble on the Gazelle and conduct takedown where ever it lands. Steady Four-Five, maintain position and don't let anyone get to the border."

"Nimble Lead that Gazelle is airborne and eastbound, we're on him."

"Steady Four-three cresting the ridge now, we are tally with Nimble flight and ah… yeah we're eyes on the suspect helo now."

"Sir, Covey's feed…" the analyst lamented. "That's like ten guys matching suspect description coming out of the tunnel and limping toward different quads and horses…"

The Colonel leaned back in his chair with his hands behind his head watching it all unfold on the feed.

"Gentlemen, I am open to suggestions." Dozens of men were pouring out of the south entrance of all descriptions and dispersing in every imaginable direction. "I seem to have run out of sensors, assets and ideas."

A smile creased his hardened face, and he thought silently to himself;

Nicely done, Sheriff. Nicely done.

*   *   *

Tom never realized how good clean clothes could feel. And it was some quality winter wear, too. His horse was a mellow one, which was good because he wasn't a particularly experienced rider. The Sheriff had swapped out of his Stetson and uniform for a baseball cap, a heavy Carhart and jeans. He'd also discarded his AR and plate carrier and duty belt with the fresh horse, a big palomino. Now he wore an old six gun in a low-slung old school gunslinger style rig, and the saddle had a trusty old Marlin strapped in scabbard behind it.

The snow was falling harder now, and Tom looked back to see their tracks being covered as they moved.

"I appreciate everything you've done for me, Sheriff, I really do. I don't need this pack, I'll have everything I need where I'm going."

"Well, Tom, we figured you might lose a lot in the extraction. The guys all put the clothes and gear together for you. They appreciate what you've been through, and what you've done too. Just take it now as a gift. If you don't need it, maybe someday you can return it, or pass it on to someone who does."

"Fair enough, Sheriff."

"At some point here, I'm gonna be done escorting you, and I'll be on my way. There's enough in that pack to get you by even in this weather, if you don't think you're going to get to where you need to be."

"How long do you think I'll have, Sheriff?"

"Before they come after you again?"

"Yes."

"Oh, they're already after you again, Tom. This team, their commander, in the end, their heart wasn't really in it, to kill Americans. 'Cause they saw that was what it was gonna take. They'll be relieved and someone less ethically inclined will come in to take their place."

"What about Tony, Sheriff? Why did they have to kill him?"

Taylor had told him earlier in the ride what little he knew about Tony Breske's death.

"These things develop their own energy, Tom. Like the proverbial snowball rolling down a hill. People get themselves squeezed into things they don't want. You knew Tony, you know he wouldn't *want* to shoot someone. I know that too. He was a good man. Good men get squeezed into positions where they may not see another way out. Same with the helicopter crew. I have no doubt Tony would do it if he felt he had to, or that there was no other choice, and I don't blame him. Hard to blame the helicopter crew either, if Tony started shootin'."

"What will happen to you and all the guys back there?"

"That all depends on how bad it gets, Tom. Hopefully we can get some court challenges going to protect us from this new law. We'll see."

"If that doesn't work?"

"We'll do what we have to I guess, Tom. In the meantime, you'll be out here, one of the last free men in America. Don't squander it."

"I won't, Sheriff." Tom looked down at the GPS on his wrist. "I've got it from here, Sheriff."

"You're sure, Tom?" The Sheriff rode up beside him and Tom handed off the lead to him. He shook the Sheriff's hand and said nothing for a long time before dismounting with the pack.

"Yes, Sir. This is it. This is where I'm supposed to be."

"Alright, Tom. Good luck and God bless."

"God bless America, Sheriff."

"Yeah, wherever that is." The Sheriff nodded with a bit of a smile, he turned Tiger and led the borrowed horse, disappearing in the heavy snow.

Tom trudged through the deepening snow to the waypoint, fighting against the pain in his ankle. Then he marched off his hundred paces south and hundred paces west. This one didn't look so obvious under the snow and took a little digging to find.

When he did, he lifted the door, heavy with snow and dirt and propped it open, leaning his carbine inside. He just realized it was getting dark, and he turned on the headlamp that was around his neck. This cache was nearly cavernous and certainly livable. Cinder block steps descended into what could be a living area, lined with shelves that contained everything he would need to get through the winter, at least.

He sat on the steps with a strange sense of fulfillment, and his eyes welled with tears. He pulled the Bible from his pocket and started reading where he left off.

Author's Note

Students of history may recognize this story line from actual events during World War One. In the pre-dawn hours of February 10th 1918, Jeff Power, with rifle in hand, opened the door to his cabin to check on his horses, which he had assumed had been unsettled by a mountain lion. Instead, someone yelled from the darkness "Throw up your hands!". By all accounts, Jeff Power did and was mortally shot by the lawmen who had come to the cabin to take his sons John and Tom Power into custody for Draft Evasion.

The gun fight that followed left three of the lawmen dead as well and was the beginning of one of the biggest manhunts in Arizona history.

Two books that address the historical event of Powers' run are:

SHOOTOUT AT DAWN: AN ARIZONA TRAGEDY, by Tom Power and John Whitlatch

And,

ARIZONA'S DEADLIEST GUNFIGHT: DRAFT RESISTANCE AND TRAGEDY AT THE POWER CABIN,
by Heidi J. Osselaer

Made in the USA
Middletown, DE
10 September 2024

60131341R10170